997-8531

Angel Grant
Winer

DUAL DESTINY

Books by Karen Lynn

DOUBLE MASQUERADE
THE SCOTTISH MARRIAGE
DUAL DESTINY

DUAL DESTINY

KAREN LYNN

DOUBLEDAY & COMPANY, INC.
GARDEN CITY, NEW YORK
1983

All of the characters in this book
are fictitious, and any resemblance
to actual persons, living or dead,
is purely coincidental.

Library of Congress Cataloging in Publication Data

Lynn, Karen.
Dual destiny.

I. Title.
PS3562.Y4447D8 1983   813'.54
ISBN 0-385-18219-8
Library of Congress Catalog Card Number 82-45204

For
Dr. F. A. Smith
with love and appreciation
for his professional assistance

DUAL DESTINY

Although the Ehrenburg stage massacre
actually occurred some years later,
for our story purpose we have moved
it to 1863.

—Author

CHAPTER 1

Big John swung his whip and let out a roar as it cracked over the heads of his team. The horses coursed over the dusty main street of Tucson, as if the devil were after them. The stage rocked violently, much to the discomfort of its occupants. Samantha Salsbury found herself swaying wildly in her seat but she merely braced herself. This was nothing new to her.

The dust rose in clouds, causing passersby to turn away to avoid the choking particles, as the driver pulled the team to a plunging stop in front of Tully and Ochoa's merchandise store. Big John liked to make a spectacular entrance into town.

A few men stood on the porch watching the stage come in for this was the social event of the day. They gathered around to swap stories with the driver. Henry Salsbury walked over to the coach's door and assisted his sister to alight, nodding at the other male passengers.

"Good journey?" he murmured in a casual tone.

Samantha was occupied in straightening her bonnet and shaking the dust out of her skirt. She gave him a wide smile, revealing perfect white teeth, and answered as casually as he had asked. "We saw one bunch of Indians but we were far enough ahead to outrun them." She looked critically at her tall, broad-shouldered brother. "You haven't changed any."

They bore no resemblance to each other, Samantha the image of her half-Spanish mother and her brother like his father with fair hair and striking brilliant blue eyes.

He took her by the arm and drew her toward a buckboard that was tied at the hitching rail. "I can't say the same for you. You look tired and thin."

Anyone watching them would never realize they hadn't seen each other since Samantha had left for medical school in the East two years ago. When anyone questioned them about their ability to appear calm under stress they attributed it to their English blood. Their father had brought them up that way. In his book it was almost a sin to display any emotion in public. He had learned that lesson at Eton along with hundreds of other young sons of the British nobility.

A troop of Union Cavalry wearing crisp blue uniforms with shining gold buttons trotted by, reminding them the Civil War was being fought in the East in this year of 1863. The soldiers' erect posture and their precision proclaimed them a crack military unit.

Henry, called Hank by his friends, assisted Samantha into the wagon. He jumped lightly into the driver's seat and flicked the reins. Hank started with his usual vigor. The horses hit their collars and the tugs tightened with a jerk. They started forward and the buckboard lurched as it moved off. Hank took a quick glance at his sister as she sat so composed beside him, her hands folded comfortably in her lap. He couldn't call her beautiful, for her mouth was too large, but her lips were curved and generous. The line of her jaw showed she possessed determination and courage. As she became aware of his scrutiny she turned to him and flashed him her brilliant smile, allowing him to glimpse the sparkle in her huge dark brown eyes. He found himself revising his opinion and decided that when she smiled like that she was more than beautiful. She was wearing her silky dark brown hair parted in the middle and drawn back tightly into a bun and he thought it made her look too severe.

He wrenched his thoughts back to his present problem. Should he tell her the bad news on the way to their ranch or should he let her tell him of her experiences first?

She settled the issue for him. "How have you been making out? What's new at the ranch? Why didn't Father come with you?" The questions tumbled out. She had been busy gazing at the Santa Rosa mountains in the distance. The air was so clear one could see thirty miles away. She had missed them; they were like old friends. The sun beat down on Hank and Samantha but neither seemed to notice it.

Hank pressed his lips together tightly before replying, and, at his hesitation, she gave him a sharp look. Something was wrong. "I received word about a week ago that Father was killed near a little place called Wickenburg, about two hundred miles northeast of here."

Samantha drew in a deep breath and pressed her hands together until the knuckles showed white, but she said nothing.

Hank reached over and squeezed her hand, giving her a reassuring look, and when he saw she was in control he released his hold and paid attention to his driving. "It seems that someone by the name of Henry Wickenburg, one of the People's Party from California, was out prospecting when his burro stopped. He picked up a rock to throw at it to make it move and discovered that the rock he was holding was gold. This led to the discovery of a mine he called the Vulture. Men started coming in droves and other claims were being staked. When Father heard of it he decided to see for himself." He paused for a moment recalling some of his father's adventures. "You know how he was about traveling."

She heard the words and felt a sense of great loss. She had been very close to her father, for he had spent time with her and taught her along with her older brother just as if she also had been a boy. George Salsbury had believed a woman should be educated as well as a man and, with the classical education he had gained in England, he passed on his considerable knowledge to his two children.

He had always had an itchy foot. That was how he came to America in the first place. His father had let him go with his blessing because his older son, Sidney, was the apple of his eye and at that time was engaged to be married to a very eligible young lady. George Salsbury traveled extensively and had finally settled in what was now called Arizona Territory.

He had fallen in love with the desert and had started a horse ranch outside the walls of Tucson. He met and successfully wooed Señorita Margarita Santiago, the young daughter of a Spanish marquess. Margarita's mother had been an Englishwoman traveling in Spain when she fell in love with the handsome Don Felipe. Her fair complexion and flaxen hair contrasted with the marquess' swarthiness and raven wavy locks. They had migrated to the States soon after their marriage.

When Samantha was small her mother was killed in an Indian raid, leaving her father heartbroken. Soon after her death Samantha's father had started to move around again, leaving his seven-year-old son and five-year-old daughter in the care of the old Don and his fair wife. Samantha remembered her grandparents with pride. Theirs had been a storybook romance and had lasted until the day the Don died. His adoring wife followed closely behind. All this seemed to run quickly through Samantha's mind. She wet her lips and then asked, "How did he die?"

There was a note of pride in Hank's voice. "He was riding down the road to the Vulture mine, which cuts off the main road to California, when he heard shots behind him. They seemed to be coming from the main road. Knowing the danger of Indian raids, he turned his horse about and raced back to the road. When he arrived the Ehrenburg stage was under siege by a large number of Indians. Our father didn't hesitate. He rode to their aid. Unfortunately all were killed but Mollie Shepherd, who lived long enough to tell the story."

Tears welled in Samantha's eyes and rolled silently down her cheeks. Her father had died as he had lived, gaily, bravely, and thinking of others. She couldn't have asked for more.

They both sat pensively and watched the view as they passed, seeing

the never-ending expanse of sand, cacti, and mesquite. This was home to
them.

Hank kept a careful lookout for Indians for there were still occasional
bands of renegades who caused trouble. He had his rifle handy although
there hadn't been much danger around Tucson since peace had been
made with Cochise.

Several years before Lieutenant Bascomb had been sent out by Major
George Stein to pursue Apaches and rescue a child, Mickey Free. His
troop came up to a band of Apaches and, under a flag of truce, proceeded
to murder them. Some were bound while awaiting their fate. One was
able to cut himself free with a hidden knife. He proved to be Cochise and
escaped to wreak vengeance for American treachery. It had taken a tall
redheaded man by the name of Tom Jeffords to negotiate a peace with
Cochise.

Each was immersed in thought as the horses moved steadily toward the
ranch. They came to a cutoff marked by wagon tracks and the horses trotted down it. They knew they were home.

The solid adobe ranch house was nestled on a gentle rise of a low hill
above a spring, on whose flat roof two men had always kept guard, to
warn against Indians. One of the reasons the ranch didn't flourish as it
should was due to the constant depredations of the stock by the Apaches.

As Hank drew up in the yard a Mexican vaquero ran up to welcome
them and take the team. The heavy wooden door opened and a short
heavy woman, dressed in a multi-colored voluminous skirt, bustled forward and embraced Samantha.

"*Mi niña*," she cried.

Samantha laughed and hugged her for this was Guadalupe, her old
nurse. She greeted the old woman in Spanish, which was her second
tongue, but she was equally at home in French, Greek, or Latin. Her father had seen to that.

They strolled into the house arm in arm. Samantha gazed about her at
the spacious room with its huge stone fireplace, gay hand-woven Navajo
rugs, and deep comfortable chairs. The room was a mixture of Spanish
and English, combining the comforts of both. It was just the same as she
had left it.

Guadalupe scuttled off to bring a cool drink and Samantha took off her
bonnet and settled into a chair, her mind dwelling on her father and wondering about the future.

Hank came in and sank into a large chair beside her. He threw his
black flat-crown sombrero onto the floor, stretched his long legs, and
waited.

"I've missed you and the ranch. I know I haven't been much of a writer, but at first I didn't have anything to write and then, of a sudden, I was busy every waking hour. I suppose I should start back at the beginning when I went off so happily to New York."

Hank nodded. He had been glad for her to be able to utilize her talent for healing.

Old Dr. Mueller had discovered she had a way with sick people and didn't faint at the sight of blood. She had helped the doctor with gunshot wounds, scalpings, and the results of many other violent incidents. He had been mightily impressed at her dedication and skill in dealing with these injuries.

"I certainly was naïve to think that just because Dr. Mueller gave me a glowing recommendation for medical school I would be accepted easily."

Hank turned his head questioningly. "You met with trouble?"

"More than trouble. I didn't want to worry you with my problem, but in spite of my sterling reference no school would consider me as a student. I heard of a Dr. Elizabeth Blackwell, who had received the first medical diploma granted to a woman in 1849. I found she was at present in the New York Infirmary and I spoke with her regarding my problem. While I was waiting for Dr. Blackwell to see if she could influence the college board to take me, I found a professor who agreed to teach me anatomy in his spare time." She contemplated her strong aristocratic hands for a moment as she recalled those days.

"Dr. Blackwell told me of her troubles in getting admitted. A Dr. Warrington, a Quaker doctor, had advised her to go to Paris and don masculine attire to gain knowledge, but she had persisted in gaining admission as a woman. No one wanted a woman, but she had finally convinced Geneva Medical College in western New York and she had been accepted. She advised me to try there and give her name as reference along with the others I had." Samantha paused and took a sip of her drink, recalling the situation vividly. "I didn't write. I marched myself over to that school and applied in person. I agreed to an entrance exam, which consisted of questions in French, Greek, and Latin. I think they thought they'd be rid of me pronto." She smiled as she thought of the face that showed shock as she had replied to those questions.

She had equally amazed them with her knowledge of mathematics. Their last protest was that no lady could stand the sight of a cadaver and therefore would not be able to work on a naked body. Her reply that she had seen scalped naked bodies and had worked on them in the hot desert without benefit of good medical supplies had effectually stopped that line of protest.

"Well, I convinced them to enroll me but they saw to it I had a hard time. Due to our father giving us such a good education"—she swallowed hard and then continued—"I was able to pass many courses by merely taking tests. However when I completed all the courses I was refused a diploma, simply on the grounds I was a woman." Her eyes darkened with anger at the memory and her brother thought she looked striking.

"What did you do?" He took a long swallow and swirled the rest in the glass reflectively.

"There wasn't much I could do. I gained the education I wanted but through persistence finally got my diploma to show for it. I packed up and came home, eager to begin practicing."

"You've had a tough time. There are plenty of people here that will be glad of the help you can give them." He finished his drink and as he set the glass down he remembered the letter that he'd picked up in town before the stage came in. He rummaged in his pocket and brought out a somewhat crumpled envelope. He looked at it ruefully.

"I guess a little wrinkling won't hurt it any," he apologized as he opened it. He scanned the lines quickly, his expression changing from polite interest to incredulity. His eyes dilated and finally a slight smile touched his face.

Samantha watched with interest. When he finished he passed it to her without making any comment. The heading was marked Throckmorton and Throckmorton, Solicitors, London, England. He answered her unspoken question by nodding. It was a legal matter that involved them. She read on and it was all she could do to suppress a gasp. The Earl of Helmcrest and his older son and heir, Sidney, and his wife had been killed in a boating accident. Sidney had married but had no issue and therefore the title went to George Salsbury, their father. The solicitors had spent considerable time locating him and were now informed of the fact that George had two children. At this point Samantha stopped reading and gazed at her brother.

"Now that our father is gone does that mean you inherit? Are you now the earl?" There was a definite note of doubt in her voice. No one could look less like an English lord than her brother at the moment. She studied his handsome face, so darkly tanned, his light hair bleached to the color of straw from the sun, his faded plaid shirt, and his old jeans tucked into well-worn boots.

At the skepticism in her voice he laughed outright. He loved this talented sister of his. He had to agree with her that he looked nothing like an English nobleman at the moment, but he was proud of his American heritage and was satisfied that he looked the part.

"According to English law I am the next in line to the title. As our uncle Sidney had no heir, it will come to me, but I'm not sure if I want to claim it."

Samantha understood his feelings. They had been raised in this country and it was home to them. The ranch had more than sufficient income for their needs. How would they fit in English society? She dropped her eyes to the letter and continued to read. When she came to the amount the estates were worth and the number of properties involved she was staggered.

"With the size of this inheritance I don't see how you can refuse to claim it." She knew that a good portion of their income came from the horses they broke and trained. The Army was buying all the horses they could break, but that would not last forever. A fair portion of their help were old retainers from the Santiago family, and had they not been able to pay them, they wouldn't leave, but she knew Hank felt a sharp sense of responsibility for them.

"I admit it would be nice to have unlimited funds but"—he hesitated—"read on." There was an inscrutable look about him.

She found her place and continued. Suddenly she flung the letter from her. She was outraged and her large black eyes flashed like lightning across a stormy sky. She jumped to her feet and looked down at her brother so calmly sitting there.

"How dare that solicitor think I can't get a husband for myself?" She took a quick turn about the room, her skirt swishing. Her brother sat quietly, amused by her agitation.

There had been plenty of men here in the West who had made a valiant effort to engage her affection but there wasn't one she liked other than as a friend. In the East her fellow students felt she was cold, aloof, but they had been wrong. She had been determined to become a doctor and put her personal life aside.

"Settle down, Sam," her brother advised coolly.

At the sound of her pet name she flashed him a smile. "Silly, isn't it? But why would that solicitor think I'd agree to a marriage with a man I've never seen?" She continued to scan the page and the name of the Duke of Belfort jumped out at her. She hadn't known his name when she made her outburst. This put a new light on it. He had been pointed out to her one weekend at the races when she felt she must get away from her studies for a day. Memories washed over her and it was as if she were there again. He had been extremely handsome, but it was his manner that attracted her to him, so self-assured yet easygoing. He was gay and attentive to all those with him and ecstatic when his horse won.

Hank went on, "It's a customary thing in England, I'm told. For centuries they have had marriages of convenience, marrying land to land. In this case the Duke of Belfort has no money due to his father's gambling, but he has the estates. During the year he has had the title he has paid the gambling debts and cleared the excessive mortgages, but there is no money to provide for badly needed renovations of tenant cottages, outbuildings, and the like, to pay the enormous tradesman bills that his father ran up, and to provide for his old retainers. In short he needs money and the only way to get it is to marry it." He paused and gave her a keen appraisal.

"Fine, he gets my share of the money, which is considerable, but what do I get?" she demanded.

"You may get just what you have desired. You'll have a high social position as a duchess and as such can probably do no wrong. Think how you could help those people over there that either have no doctor or cannot afford one. You could have a tremendous practice and not have to charge for it. We'll have plenty of money we can use to help others less fortunate."

Samantha loved to be of service. She had knowledge and would be in a position to render service without depending on it for a living. The thought of the duke made it even more appealing. After all, some would consider her an old maid and to date she hadn't received an offer she could accept with anything more than mere liking. This one . . . well . . . this one was different. Mayhap she could earn his love. She turned her thoughts back to her brother. "But how about you? Will the life of an earl appeal to you?" She couldn't imagine her brother spending his days at a club and idling away his time.

"I figure I will find ways to keep busy. For one thing I might be able to aid the Union cause with England. I've heard the Confederates have men in England trying to interest her in aiding them."

That gave her pause for thought. "You mean you'd become an agent?"

"No, but I could at least present the other viewpoint when confronted with the Confederate cause." He was also thinking that he had not yet made up his mind to remain in England forever.

Hank reread the letter and decided this marriage might be just the thing for his sister. According to the solicitor the duke was thirty-five, very handsome and athletic. He was known to be a bruising rider and an excellent shot. Many women had fallen in love with him, but with the state of his finances no father would permit a marriage to him. Because of the duke's concern for his old servants and tenants he had expressed himself willing to accept Samantha as his duchess.

"I wonder what my lord duke will think when he finds his bride is a doctor and a western cowgirl to boot?" The thought of a disapproving look on that aristocratic face made her giggle. She would certainly be far from the usual duchess. "So you don't think I could practice as just your sister?"

He shook his head. "You know the trouble you've just been through trying to get into a medical school and then prejudice almost kept you from your diploma. I feel sure you'd have difficulty in getting anyone to allow you to give them medical help. We'll be those upstart Americans from the Wild West. However, as the Duchess of Belfort you'd be established and your talent would be accepted as an idiosyncrasy." Hank felt he had presented his case well and that this would greatly encourage her to accept the offer.

She had to admit he made it sound logical. From what she had heard of the conditions of the poor in England she knew there would be plenty to do. After all, hadn't Dr. Elizabeth Blackwell been over there? She had devoted herself to medicine and evidently had no interest in home and marriage. Samantha's eyes twinkled as she thought of the arguments Hank had advanced to get her to accept this marriage. They were all excellent, but unnecessary, for she had already made up her mind to accept—for reasons of her own.

"Suppose I agree to this marriage, but with the proviso that it is not to be consummated for six months, giving us a chance to know each other? Then if we found we didn't suit I might be able to get the marriage put aside and let him keep my marriage portion. I'm sure you'll have plenty to come to my aid if need be," she added roguishly.

That brought an appreciative grin from Hank. She sounded more like herself and was taking their father's death in stride. She had a great sense of humor and loved to pull his leg. Thinking of this trait, he wondered if the duke had any idea of what he was in for. "Then you're willing to accept this proposal?"

"Why not? I'll get considerable experience over there and then if we decide to come home I'll be better able to help here." She was a little pensive about it, but she was sure things would work themselves out after she actually met the duke. After all, she certainly wasn't a scarecrow or a plain Jane. Samantha tended to be impulsive, and conjectured that if Hank thought he could be happy in England then she was sure she could.

"Throckmorton and Throckmorton are going to be surprised when they find our father is gone and that I'm the heir." There was a trace of sadness in his voice but then he brightened. "He would have wanted us to go and claim the estate. Remember how he always talked about Helmcrest Hall and how beautiful it was?"

Samantha nodded, her mind busy with the thoughts of the marriage that was ahead of her. What was this duke like? He certainly had looked handsome and acted as if he cared about those who were close to him, but she couldn't be sure. Would he be kind to her or would he prove to be a domestic tyrant? If he accepted her proviso, all she could lose was the money and that was nothing to her. She was accustomed to managing on very little. On the other hand, she could win all; she would be his wife and would have many opportunities to engage his affection. She was confident that before the six months were up she would have things well in hand.

She picked up the letter again and read on. "I see they are sending a considerable draft to us for fare to go. That takes care of a big problem. How about the ranch?"

"That will be no trouble. Miguel is a good *segundo*. He knows the procedure and you can't beat him on horses. If he should run into financial difficulties I'll be in a position to send him funds. Isn't that a nice thought?"

Seeing the brilliant smile, Samantha felt a tug at her heart. Her brother was magnificent. He was an exceedingly handsome man with a very quick mind. Some girl somewhere was going to be very lucky. She jumped to her feet. "Seems you have thought of everything. All you need do now is to write the solicitors and apprise them of the situation here and our acceptance. I'll be glad to write for boat reservations as I know New York. As soon as they can be confirmed we can leave. I have little to do to get ready." She left him sitting there and darted down the hall to her room. What she needed now was a bath to get rid of the dust of travel and a little time to think over this unexpected event.

CHAPTER 2

The wharves were a carousel of motion. Supplies were being carried on board various clippers on the sagging shoulders of the dockmen. Some ships were being unloaded and cargoes were stacked according to shipping labels. Several men with clipboards seemed to be directing the chaotic scene. Whistles, engines for the new steamships, and crates being pushed added to the noise of the men barking orders and the passengers waving and shouting good-byes.

Samantha felt a surge of delight and excitement as Hank handed her from the carriage and she viewed the panorama before her. Their luggage had been brought aboard the elegant sleek clipper ship earlier in the morning. They strolled up the gangplank leisurely, surveying the huge masts. There were three of them, with sailors climbing up the rigging to unfurl the sails. It was evident that the ship was almost ready to embark on the fourteen-day voyage.

Several male passengers were discussing the Union victory in Mississippi. One had an opinion of why Hooker had been defeated at Chancellorsville. The conversation was lively, each listening eagerly for reports of the progress of the Northern troops.

Samantha and Hank passed by unnoticed and found a quiet place at the rail. Each was lost in thought and in saying good-bye to a land that had been kind to them. The ship lurched as the wind caught the sails and quickly moved out into the harbor. There were two of those newfangled steamships in the harbor, but both Samantha and Hank were glad they weren't booked on the ugly craft. The sleek clippers, built for speed, suited them much better.

The shoreline disappeared in the distance and New York seemed to sink into the water.

"I hope we've made a wise decision," Samantha said with a little sigh. She looked at Hank for confirmation.

He took his eyes away from the water and turned to face her. He squeezed her shoulder reassuringly. "I'm very sure of it but if we don't like it we can always come home," he stated matter-of-factly. He was looking ahead to a new adventure. In this he was very like his father. Dressed in a black suit with a white shirt he looked the aristocrat—very different from the western man. There was a suspicious bulge in the fit of his jacket and Samantha rightly guessed her brother wasn't setting out for a new land without a weapon handy.

She reflected he knew what he was doing. There was a great deal of traffic around them, people from all stations of life. Just then a group of tough-looking men went past, giving her a hard look, and she was glad for her brother's protection.

When she had lived in New York she had to be very careful. Not only was crime rampant but the sanitary conditions were unbelievable. Drinking water came from shallow wells, the streets were befouled by stables and privies, and filth seemed to hang in the air. It was the home of every variety of contagious disease, small pox, diphtheria, measles, scarlet fever, and typhoid.

A man in uniform came up to them. "Begging your pardon," he said, addressing Hank, "aren't you the Earl of Helmcrest?"

At the sound of his new title Hank threw a comical look at his sister. Then, seeing her very innocent look, he quirked an eyebrow at her. The minx! She'd made their reservations and must have decided to puff off his consequence. "Yes," he answered, giving Samantha a frown.

"I'm Mr. Hawkins, the purser," the man explained, "and the captain would like the pleasure of your company and that of Lady Samantha at his table."

Noting Samantha's wide smile and twinkling eyes, Hank accepted the invitation and when the man left he turned on her. "Why the devil did you use our new names?" He was not at all sure he wanted to travel with people toadying to him and he was afraid that was exactly what would happen.

"Well, I figured we are going to have to get used to it, so we might as well have this time to practice our new estate." She gave him such a demure look that he burst out laughing. Her eyes betrayed her. There was no doubt she had recovered from their father's death and was once again his amusing sister.

"If we are eating at the captain's table you will undoubtedly meet the ship's doctor. I shall introduce you as Dr. Salsbury and you can enjoy some professional conversation."

Samantha rose to the bait. "You mustn't! He'll think I'm a fraud." The thought agitated her and then she saw the gleam in Hank's eyes.

"Tit for tat! Just wait. I'll find a way to even the score."

He tucked her arm in his and they strolled about the deck noticing the number of passengers who looked pitifully poor. Many of them were now moving belowdecks to seek their allotted space.

"I can't imagine why there are so many going back to England. Having made such a sacrifice to get here why would they return?" She was genuinely puzzled.

"They probably couldn't find work and everything would be so strange to them. To hear foreigners talk you'd think the streets here are lined with gold."

Samantha knew he was right. She had felt sorry for so many of the immigrants she had come in contact with. She knew that in New York Hospital there had been thousands that died.

They made their way to their cabins and, examining them, Samantha wondered how others fared if these were considered the best accommodations. Her room was very small, a bunk screwed down to the floor. There was a washstand and a small cupboard for her clothes. A connecting door opened into a duplicate room, which was Hank's.

"How must those poor people be faring?" she asked her brother. "They must be crowded terribly."

"We can be grateful we were able to command the best." He looked at the cabin with some distaste. "Personally I'll be glad when the journey is over."

That evening they sat at the captain's table and were introduced to Dr. Locke, a dour-looking man with a prominent nose and large teeth. His scanty hair was snow white and his face deeply lined. He didn't appear to be in very good health. There was a pompous American couple, Mr. and Mrs. Morgan, who were evidently very wealthy and anxious to impress everyone with their worth. They were hoping to be received into British society. When they were introduced to Samantha and her brother, Mrs. Morgan gushed. She was sensible of this opportunity and determined to make the most of it. Captain Nielsen merely sat and listened. He had been hoping for a pleasant trip and had looked forward to talking to the new earl and his sister. The Morgans left him cold. He had seen plenty of social climbers.

Samantha and Hank, with their innate good breeding, fended off questions gracefully, turning the conversation to the others. At one point Mrs. Morgan tried to pin Hank down on an invitation to visit Helmcrest Hall, and as he pretended he didn't hear, Samantha winked surreptitiously at him. "Good practice," he murmured.

Mr. Morgan, a bluff red-faced individual, was at a loss. "What's that?" he asked.

Giving her brother a withering look, Samantha turned to the doctor.

"We were interested in your practice, Doctor," she smiled brightly at him.

Dr. Locke was busily engaged in seeing how much wine he could consume. At her question he paused, dabbed at his lips with his serviette, and cleared his throat. "There's little to do aboard ship," he answered.

Samantha was now interested. "Do you mean that with all the crowding there is and those poor people that there isn't any sickness?" She was incredulous.

"Oh, them," he answered. "They manage. I have nothing to do with them. I take care of our first class passengers only."

Samantha was outraged. "What about your Hippocratic Oath, Doctor?" There was an unmistakable accent on the last word.

Captain Nielsen, hearing Samantha's anger, quickly changed the subject. "We have the promise of good wealther and I am expecting a good voyage."

Brother and sister exchanged glances and at the warning in Hank's eyes, Samantha didn't push the subject. In her opinion Dr. Locke was a poor example of his profession. To be fair, she admitted to herself, she should actually see him at work.

The opportunity came sooner than she expected. They had been at sea for only three days when rumors of sickness in the steerage reached Samantha. One of the stewards inadvertently mentioned it. When Samantha tried to question him he grew evasive. As he hurried off she turned to Hank. "It sounds like there is trouble in the steerage. I think I'll hunt up Dr. Locke and see what he has to say." This might be an opportunity for her to be of some assistance.

"You can't resist a chance to practice," he teased her. Then another thought struck him. "I wonder how Diablo is? I haven't been down to see him today." He was referring to his Appaloosa stallion, which he had brought with him. He had raised the horse from a colt and couldn't bear to leave him behind. He knew there would be blooded stock at Helmcrest but there wouldn't be a horse like this one.

That caused Samantha to smile. "Of course, I will go down with you to see him and while we are there we'll see exactly what this sickness is."

Hank started to protest but looking at her determined chin he merely took her by the arm and led the way below.

Diablo heard their voices and whinnied as they came near. As he saw Hank he threw up his head and whistled, dancing in the stall. He was not a pretty horse with his cream color marred by dark spots on his hindquarters, but he was powerful, well muscled, and lean. Even in Hank's vast experience as a horse trainer, Diablo stood out as most intelligent. He was broken to gun, able to cut cows, and Hank had even taught him a few tricks like rearing, bowing, and playing dead.

They made a fuss over him and checked to see he had grain and water. Diablo loved Hank, tolerated Sam, but with anyone else, he proved worthy of his name. Hank gave him a final pat and they made their way to the quarters of the steerage passengers.

There were no cabins; it was one large space with pallets on the floor. Everywhere there was confusion. A number of people were stretched out on their makeshift beds. A man hurried up to them.

"Please, sir," he addressed Hank, "can ye help us?" He was dirty, poorly dressed, and an unprepossessing figure. At the urgency in his voice and the pleading light in his eyes, Hank turned to Samantha.

"What do you think?" he asked. She was the one qualified to give an opinion.

Not bothering to answer she addressed the man. "What seems to be the problem?" Her eyes were busy taking in the scene before her.

The man turned and led the way to where a woman lay. She was in delirium. Samantha dropped to her knees beside her. She took in the flushed face and found her pulse was fast and weak. Without asking for permission, she unbuttoned the woman's waist and examined her chest. Here she found some rose-colored spots. Samantha pursed her lips as she saw them. Quickly she bared the abdomen and noted more of these spots. Palpating the abdomen she found it rigid. She refastened the woman's clothing and pulled a thin blanket over her. Rising to her feet, she addressed the husband. "Do you have means to get clean water and soap?"

He nodded. "Tell me, mum, what do ye think it is?" He twisted his hands, feeling his helplessness.

Samantha first looked at Hank, who had been standing by, content to leave the examination in his sister's capable hands. There was a worried frown on her face as she shook her head at her brother. "Before I commit myself I'd like to examine some of these others." She turned to the waiting man. "Get me some water and soap. Clean towels too if you can." In her mind she was certain it was typhoid.

He ran to do her bidding and others crowded around her. "Please, it is necessary that I wash my hands before examining anyone else." She remembered lectures by Dr. Semmelweiss about the importance of washing hands. Many doctors refused to accept his theory, but she felt the proof lay in his success with so many women suffering from gynecological and obstetrical problems. His patient death rate was so low it was impressive when compared with others. He firmly believed that the washing of hands and instruments in a solution of chlorinated lime, to say nothing of working in clean clothes, had a good deal to do with it. Samantha had an open mind and she was willing to be guided by his judgment.

There was nothing in her training that prescribed a cure for typhoid but it was suggested a patient be given lots of fluids and sponged with cold cloths to try to reduce the fever. Samantha followed Dr. Semmelweiss's precepts. With no chlorinated lime available, she used plenty of soap and water.

After she had carefully washed her hands she made her way to the next pallet where a man was rolling and tossing about. His eyes were bloodshot and it was evident he had a fever. He held his hands to his abdomen as if trying to relieve pain.

Having made up her mind as to the cause, she bypassed other examination and opened his shirt searching for the telltale rose spots. At the sight of them she looked up at Hank.

"Would you look at some of the others, checking for spots like these?" Her lips were pressed into a firm line but her large black eyes held a compassionate look.

He nodded and started toward the next pallet. There was more here than any one person could handle. As he turned he heard a cry and spun around. A large laboring man held a club over Samantha's head. He was shouting she was to come to his wife immediately. This was no place and there was no room for fighting, so Hank smoothly palmed his pistol and in a calm voice ordered the man to drop the club. Samantha, fully cognizant of Hank's fighting ability, had paid no attention but kept on with her work. The man stopped in his tracks when he saw the businesslike gun in Hank's hand. There was a martial light in Hank's eye and his stance suggested he'd like nothing better than to make a personal fight of this.

The tough dropped the club and stood looking a little sheepish. "It's my missus. I be really worrit about her," he explained. His actions showed the depth of his affection, though perhaps not his intellect.

Hank put his gun away but all who watched now knew he was not one to try to take advantage of. Force was one thing most of these people understood and respected.

Many who were watching thought that Hank was the doctor while Samantha was a nurse. The brother and sister didn't try to disabuse them of this notion, but both of them steadily examined those who were sick and a comparison of notes made it evident to Samantha that they were in the midst of a typhoid epidemic. This must be reported to Dr. Locke and Captain Nielsen promptly. Without mentioning the dreaded word typhoid, merely calling it a fever, she urged everyone to take precautions on cleanliness and to dispose of body waste immediately and again wash their hands.

They made their way back to the deck where they sent a steward with a message for the captain and the doctor.

"While we are waiting I suggest we change our clothes and scrub ourselves. If we should come down with this, there will be little help for those poor people." She turned to enter her cabin and then paused. "Thanks, Hank, for watching over me." She accompanied the statement with a pert smile.

He returned the smile and shrugged off her thanks. For a few moments there he had enjoyed himself, although he wouldn't tell her that. He felt he was going to miss the daily excitement he had had in his ranch life. Things would probably be very staid and commonplace in England. He'd be glad to see his sister settled and his estates in good running order so he could return to the life he knew and loved. He didn't feel he was cut out to be an English nobleman with nothing more to occupy him than a day at the races or gaming in some club.

A short time later they met in the captain's quarters. His space was considerably larger, having two easy chairs, a desk, and some bookshelves. There was a window seat that looked out the aft of the ship and the captain was seated there pensively. He stood as they entered.

"I felt this was the best place to talk when I received your message." His voice was grim and there was a slight frown on his weatherbeaten face.

Dr. Locke was sitting in one of the easy chairs and stood belatedly. He cleared his throat importantly. "I believe this is a figment of your imagination." He looked down his nose at Samantha. He was reluctant to get into any situation that required hard work.

She never refused a challenge. "I don't understand, Dr. Locke. I merely sent a message that there is illness in the steerage that needs immediate attention. Surely there is no imagination involved when people are flushed with fever and in delirium." She gave him a hard look. "Perhaps I'd better tell you I am a graduate of Geneva Medical College and am fully qualified to recognize typhoid fever when I see it."

That was a double shock. Lady Samantha a doctor? Typhoid? He was used to the routine fevers and diarrhea that accompanied most steerages, but typhoid? He stared at her in stunned disbelief. He could not accept that this could happen on his ship.

Captain Nielsen's eyebrows raised and his eyes widened with the shock of hearing of the dreaded disease. He was most happy to accept the news that Lady Samantha was a doctor, but he certainly hoped her diagnosis was mistaken. "Please be seated," he said in a voice devoid of emotion. "I am pleased to hear we have another doctor on board, especially if this does prove to be typhoid."

Her eyes thanked him and she turned to address the doctor. "Well, Dr. Locke, what would you say to symptoms of malaise, headache, backache, diarrhea, rigidity of stomach muscles, and telltale rose spots on the chest and abdomen?" She managed to pose her question in an even voice but inwardly she was seething.

He was taken aback. He pursed his lips and gave the appearance of profound thinking. "It does seem to bear out your diagnosis," he condescended, with doubt in his voice.

"Very well, come with me and we'll examine some of these patients together," she flashed.

Hank, who had seated himself on the bunk, had an amused look about him. His sister was hard to beat when she had the bit in her teeth.

Dr. Locke blanched visibly. He had no desire to expose himself to typhoid. "I think I'd better check on the passengers we have up here." His eyes were evasive and couldn't face Samantha's keen stare.

She gave him a look of scorn and turned to the captain. "Did you take on water in New York?" she asked.

He had been sitting quietly, taking in the conversation and watching the exchange of expressions, but at her question nodded affirmatively. He wondered what that had to do with it?

"It is very possible that is where these people are getting the infection. There were some discussions I heard when I was in school that shallow wells catch the runoff from stables and the water is full of disease. Not everyone accepts this theory but in this case we might be wise to consider it. I would suggest we boil all drinking water. This might be effective but I don't know for sure. The other thing—do you have any chlorinated lime aboard?"

She had everyone's attention, but Dr. Locke was openly showing his contempt. He would be glad when she was proved wrong. Then he would show her how inferior her understanding was.

"Well," said the captain, "as you know, this isn't only a passenger ship. We do take cargo to help make a profit. I'll have to see the manifests before I can answer." He was courteous to her but she could see he didn't understand her request.

"This is the chemical that Dr. Semmelweiss proved to be of much worth in preventing disease. I propose, if we have any, to make up a solution for everyone to wash their hands in and to wash down the walls and the floor in the steerage." She thought for a moment. "We must see if

there are any cases up here." She sat bolt upright in her chair, every line
of her body showing her concern.

Captain Nielsen, taking in her earnest face with her enormous black
eyes, her small pointed nose, and her slender figure, found it hard to believe that such an attractive young lady could be a qualified doctor. He
was impressed with her assurance and decided to go along with her thinking. He would get Dr. Locke to check on the first class passengers. "I'll let
you know if we have what you're after, Dr. Salsbury. In the meantime,
Dr. Locke, I would like you to visit everyone topside and give me a report.
I'll see what we have in the line of extra soap and towels and I'll see it's
sent down. Say nothing of this to anyone!"

He rose to his feet, obviously dismissing them. Samantha felt she had
accomplished all she could and, with Hank escorting her, made her way to
her cabin.

CHAPTER 3

The next morning they had breakfast *à deux* as no one else at their table showed up. They discussed this in low tones, Samantha wondering if the Morgans were ill. She felt the absence of Dr. Locke and Captain Nielsen augured well. They were probably busily engaged checking on the situation.

She was finishing her second cup of coffee, reflecting as she did so that she would need to acquire the habit of drinking tea. The door to the dining compartment opened and Captain Nielsen and the doctor came in.

She gave the captain a bright smile but he merely nodded at her. His face was grim and lined as if he hadn't slept. Dr. Locke wouldn't meet her eyes and slid nervously into his chair.

It was Hank who opened the conversation. "Well, gentlemen, what conclusion have you come to?" He had faith in his sister and if she said they were in for an epidemic he knew it would prove to be.

Captain Nielsen toyed with a fork. "Dr. Locke thinks it is all a mistake. He can see no signs of typhoid." He said it without emphasis but Samantha could see he was not sure about Dr. Locke's opinion.

Dr. Locke cleared his throat pompously. "We appear to have one or two passengers with some respiratory problem but I can see no signs of typhoid." He gave Samantha a malignant stare. "It is my belief that Lady Samantha is mistaken in her judgment."

He hadn't given her the title of doctor and it caused her a momentary pang. This is what she would have to put up with. However, no one could take her hard-won skill and knowledge from her. The word respiratory grated on her. Hadn't she been taught that it was sometimes hard to distinguish beginning symptoms of the disease from respiratory infection? "Dr. Locke," she began calmly, holding her temper, "will you come with me below and examine some of these people?" She believed in a direct approach and it was all Hank could do to repress a smile. There was a little bulldog in Samantha as Dr. Locke would find out.

Captain Nielsen was very interested in the conversation and withheld any comments. He waited to see what Dr. Locke had to say.

There was a harassed look on the doctor's face as he swallowed hard. "I fail to see the necessity. After all, you haven't had the experience that I have. You have mistaken a few insect bites for rose spots. After all, these people are far from cleanly." His tone indicated that his diagnosis was final.

At this point Captain Nielsen entered the conversation. "We can hardly afford to take a chance. I suggest we take all precautions. Lady Samantha"—he spoke directly to her—"I have found we have a few bags of chlorinated lime consigned to a hospital in London. I propose we allow you to have the use of whatever you feel we need and start a preventive program."

Captain Nielsen was being cautious. He didn't feel he could afford to offend his ship's doctor much less a British peeress who also happened to be a doctor. He decided to tread a middle-of-the-road path.

Samantha was gratified with his decision and expressed her willingness to start to work. She raised an eyebrow at Hank, who nodded his agreement. She knew she could count on him. This left Dr. Locke. She was determined to pin him down but he was very experienced at sliding out of anything that resembled work. She could see there was no way she was going to get him belowdecks. Did he really believe what he said or was he afraid of catching typhoid? He knew how often the disease could be fatal. The percentage of death was high. "Dr. Locke," she tried again, "if you can't see the necessity of visiting the steerage, will you allow me to accompany you when you visit your 'respiratory' patients?" She was going to be hard to refuse.

Captain Nielsen could see a negative answer coming from the doctor and decided to take a hand. "Dr. Locke, it will please me if you allow Lady Samantha to observe your technique."

Put to him this way Dr. Locke permitted himself a superior smile and gave his consent. He intended to show up this so-called woman doctor for what she was. No female could begin to compare with a man.

Not wanting to give him the opportunity of evading her, Samantha waited patiently for the doctor to have his breakfast. Hank, having been instructed by her as to the mixing of the chemical, left them to take care of it. Captain Nielsen had promised the aid of two seamen to do the work. Hank intended to oversee the job.

Finally, the doctor could no longer put off his rounds. He threw down his serviette and rose to his feet. "Well," he grumped, "come along." He stalked ahead of her, making his way to the cabin that housed the Morgans.

Samantha followed behind, for all the world like a new probationer, and the thought brought a grin to her face. At home the local Indians would approve. She was acting like a well-behaved squaw. However, she thought, squaws were known to be more ferocious than warriors in many cases. Dr. Locke had a surprise coming. The thought put her in a more cheerful frame of mind.

They knocked on the door and entered at Mrs. Morgan's invitation. She was sitting in a chair near the bunk on which Mr. Morgan lay. She was surprised to see Samantha with the doctor but was effusive in her welcome.

"I'm sure you are right, Doctor," she said brightly. "He just seems to have a cold."

Mr. Morgan added his opinion. "I'm just not feeling all that good. I can't put my finger on it. You must be right for I keep chilling."

Dr. Locke moved over to the bunk and with a theatrical gesture picked up Mr. Morgan's wrist and checked his pulse. "Mmmmm," he murmured.

Samantha didn't hesitate. "How fast is it, Doctor?" she enquired. Seeing Mrs. Morgan's raised eyebrows, she explained for the woman's benefit before the doctor could put in a word. "I am a graduate of Geneva Medical College, ma'am, and am interested in Dr. Locke's methods."

Dr. Locke gave Samantha a hard glance but her face was devoid of any emotion. "Well, it is a trifle fast but that is to be expected. Rest and plenty of food. You'll be up and about in no time." He turned and addressed Mrs. Morgan. "Have you made arrangements for meals to be served here?" He was so ingratiating that Samantha felt ill.

"Do you need to do any further examination?" she asked innocently. The old humbug had better. She was sure he was missing the right diagnosis.

The creaking of the ship's timbers and the rocking motion caused by the waves did nothing to dispel the intensity in the cabin.

"With my background and experience I can trust my opinions, Lady Samantha." His haughty tone and hard stare were supposed to take Samantha down a peg but to his astonishment she walked around him and approached Mr. Morgan.

"If you please, Mr. Morgan, I'd like to examine your chest." She was very matter-of-fact in her request.

Mrs. Morgan uttered a faint scream and started to slump into the solitary chair at the foot of the bed. "A woman to see my husband's chest!" This was unheard of. She appealed to Dr. Locke. He came over and patted her hand in agreement, but Samantha hadn't waited for permission. She leaned forward and unbuttoned Mr. Morgan's nightshirt. There were no rose spots as yet but she saw faint pink marks that she felt might develop into some.

By this time the outraged doctor had bustled forward. "This is entirely unnecessary, Lady Samantha. You are embarrassing dear Mrs. Morgan and her husband!"

Mrs. Morgan pursed her lips primly. She didn't want to offend a British aristocrat but at the same time she didn't want to be put in such a demoralizing position. Conflict raged within her but she managed to remain quiet.

Mr. Morgan, however, lifted his head and spoke in a positive voice. "Nonsense! It's quite enjoyable to have such a pretty girl touching my chest." Then, as a strangled sound could be heard coming from his wife's throat, he colored and looked guilty. Quickly, to cover up his mistake, he added, "I must have a fever, I hardly realize what I'm saying."

This explanation mollified his wife and she rushed to his side. She straightened his nightshirt and smoothed the bedcovers.

Dr. Locke was opening his mouth to give Samantha quite a setdown when she beat him to it.

"Doctor, are you going to caution the Morgans about the possible contamination of water?" She carefully avoided the word typhoid. "I understand that drinking large amounts of fluids is beneficial also." She looked him squarely in the eye.

He averted his gaze and a muscle twitched in one cheek. "Well, yes, as a matter of fact I was going to suggest that you drink copious quantities of coffee or tea. Do not take any cold drinks for now." He managed to sound as if this was entirely his idea and Mrs. Morgan nodded her understanding. She acted as if an oracle had spoken.

Dr. Locke turned to leave and Samantha dutifully followed behind him but she was biting her lip in frustration. She was positive in her belief that they were in for an epidemic and was anxious to do all that was within her power to avoid the death devil claiming more than his share. It had been known to happen that entire ships were lost to the dreaded disease.

She excused herself quickly, not wishing to have her feelings detected, and made her way below to see how Hank was making out.

CHAPTER 4

By the third day, there was no doubt. Samantha was proven right, even Dr. Locke had to admit it. The ship was full of typhoid cases. Moaning and cries of distress could be heard throughout the ship. Nausea and rose spots were everywhere. The smells were noxious coming from below and general chaos ensued.

Samantha worked day and night without much-needed rest. Hank tried to reason with her for she was only just back from her exhausting training in medical school. He had noted how tired she had looked when he'd met the stage. He was afraid for her; although she was scrupulous about washing her hands and keeping herself clean, in her weakened state she could be a target for the disease. She just smiled at him, shaking her head. This was something she was trained to do and intended to do. Dr. Locke was proving of very little help. The burden was falling on her capable shoulders. Hank was at her side in constant attendance on the sick.

People begged her to do something about the pain in their back, arms, and legs. She could see blood in their waste and knew that these cases were severe. She worked hour upon hour with the sick and directed much sanitary activity. In spite of all she could do passengers were dying and the captain had them read over and consigned to the sea. Fear enveloped the ship like a deep fog.

Finally, she felt that they were over the worst, for there had not been any new cases for several days. When she reported this to the captain he was immensely grateful.

"I'll never forget what you have done for us, Doctor!" he said. He took her hand and pressed it warmly.

At the title, Samantha's eyes lit up. It had such a good sound and she appreciated the compliment he paid her. Their percentage of deaths had been low and she felt it was quite a victory.

The captain spoke to her at some length on the slow crossing. He usually made the trip in about fourteen days, but with this sickness aboard only a skeleton crew were available for duty and he had to be content with about half sail. With the inclement weather approaching, it could still be quite some days until they made port.

Samantha listened understandingly. As the wind started to blow she felt a chill come over her. A horrible thought struck her. It couldn't be; it was just the cold. She had been so careful and there had been no new cases. Managing to keep calm, she thanked the captain and gave an excuse to leave.

She made her way to her cabin and prepared for a siege of the illness herself. As she was considering washing down her walls with chlorinated lime, Hank knocked on the connecting door.

He took one look at her and asked sharply, "Are you coming down with it?" There was deep concern in his voice.

She looked at her tall, handsome brother, presenting a figure of health and strength. She prayed he was immune to the disease. "I feel a chill and a general malaise. It could be I've taken the sickness." She assayed a smile. "I must not practice what I preach."

"Nonsense! You've overworked yourself and have no strength left. Now, we're going to take care of you." He was positive in his statement and hearing it she knew no one was going to change his mind.

"Very well, to be on the safe side I'll get into bed. Will you see if someone can wash down our walls? If I should come down with fever, see if you can get all the hot fluids possible down me."

He left to get some buckets and the chemical while Samantha wearily changed her dress and got into a clean white linen nightgown. She had slipped between the sheets when he returned.

He came over to her and stood looking down at her exhausted face. Picking up her wrist he felt her pulse. It was faster than it should be. He was almost certain they were in for a siege. He would take care of her himself regardless of what anyone might think of the proprieties. There was no woman on board he had met that he would trust her to.

For seven days she raged with fever. It rose so high that Hank was afraid he would lose her. He was at her side constantly, coaxing hot soup, tea, and coffee down her. He had found a middle-aged woman from the steerage who had not taken ill and was not afraid to come and sit for a few hours with Samantha so he could get some sleep. All attempts to get Dr. Locke in to see her failed. Hank was ready to use force on him but decided it wasn't worth it. Mrs. Burke, a large and buxom lady, assured him that between the two of them his sister would be fine. She changed the bed linen and Samantha's nightdress with regularity. She bustled around the room making sure that everything was as it should be. They followed the instructions Samantha had given and which she had used on the other patients.

On the eighth day the fever broke and slowly came down. Samantha opened her eyes and saw Hank sitting beside her bunk. "Sorry," she whispered.

"Sorry? I have never been so glad in my life. You are going to be all right." He swallowed hard. He didn't want to show how much he cared. He took her hands in his and noted that they looked like claws. She had been thin to begin with but she now looked like a skeleton. Her skin had turned slightly yellow and was drawn over her cheekbones so tightly her face had the appearance of a mask. Then his gaze traveled to her head. What would she say when she saw that the high fever had taken her beautiful brown hair? Every time he had brushed it it had come out by handfuls. Well, it would grow back. The most important fact was that she was alive.

CHAPTER 5

She would never have believed she would be so happy to see England. To leave all the horror of the past weeks behind her was a relief. They had been quarantined for several days until the ship was pronounced clean by the port authorities. Now, as she left it, the passengers clustered around her to thank her one last time for all her help.

As Hank assisted her down the gangplank the wind caught her veil and she pulled the heavy fabric a little closer around her neck to keep it from blowing away. She had wound a silk scarf around her head and then placed the veil over it. No one was going to see she had lost her hair. At the first opportunity she must buy some sort of wig. As for her skin, a good diet was beginning to show.

However, it would take weeks—possibly months—to repair the damage and bring her back to her beautiful self. It had been a severe shock when she saw herself in the mirror but her innate sense of humor came to her rescue. What a bride she would make! Somehow she would have to put the marriage off until she had gained some weight and her hair had grown in a few inches.

Hank had succeeded in hiring a lorry to drive them to the station where they would take the train to Crestwood, the nearest station to Helmcrest. Diablo trotted contentedly behind. They were both quiet on the drive. Samantha was glad to be alive and knew she owed her life to her brother's faithful nursing. Mrs. Burke had been such a dear, but Samantha knew that the largest share of the nursing had been done at Hank's direction. She would fully recover but it would take time. What was she going to do about the Duke of Belfort? Should she cancel the wedding at this late date? It wasn't fair to him for she knew he was depending upon her money to put his estates in order. Could she postpone the event until she was more herself? She weighed the pros and cons carefully, trying to come to a logical conclusion, but somehow logic wasn't winning this debate. Hank would be surprised at her thoughts. She had never told him why she had assented to the proposed marriage. She had railed against it until she had read the name of the prospective bridegroom.

Her mind flooded with memories of Belfort at Saratoga. She had watched him with fascination as he moved about the racetrack. Just the vision of his tall, athletic figure made her pulse rise. There had been something about his handsome countenance that had appealed to her and she hadn't been able to forget the thought of being his wife had a certain attraction. He mustn't see her until she had a chance to look like herself. She admitted she wanted the opportunity to earn his regard.

Hank's thoughts turned to Diablo and he was glad that he had had the forethought to leave orders with the grooms that he himself would lead the horse from the boat. Diablo would be difficult for a stranger to handle. A comfortable box stall was reserved for him on the train.

He studied Samantha's pensive face for a moment. She had been so lovely before all this erupted about them. Now her complexion was ravaged and her body looked like something the vultures might have left. She was plucky that sister of his. She never complained; she accepted the situation and looked to the future. She had so much courage, intelligence, and such a good way of looking at life he wondered if she was going to be wasted on a British duke?

As for himself, he was anxious to see his new estates, put them in order as best he could, and return to the land he loved. He was prepared to visit England each year to check on his tenants and see that his manager was taking good care of them but he preferred to live in the beautiful and challenging Southwest. Nothing could be so magnificent as the sunset on the desert. Surely no country could be prettier than that.

There was a deal of traffic about the station, carriages and lorries moving to and fro, porters calling to various persons, baggage being wheeled to the cars at the front, and a general bustling everywhere. No one paid the least attention to the Salsburys. Even Samantha's heavy veil was totally ignored. They could see that the British were entirely different from Americans.

Hank settled Samantha in their compartment and returned to see that Diablo was safely in his stall. The man he had found at the station seemed competent, but he wanted to be sure. The horse snorted, tossed his head, and all but talked to his master. Hank rubbed his nose, gave him a slap, and told the horse to behave himself. Being assured he was in good hands, Hank made his way back to Samantha.

The countryside passed quickly by. Hank marveled at the hedgerows. He asked the conductor about them. The answer came back that it took about a hundred years to grow a good hedgerow and the shrubs in them were usually blackberry, honeysuckle, blackthorn, elderberry, and hawthorn.

The hedgerows had a wire fence in them sometimes, but they were manicured and colorful and very thick. The foliage was several shades of deep green, while the flowers were yellow, pink, and white. The base of the shrubs was very twisted, wandering, and massive. They punctuated the countryside with regularity, making a checkerboard pattern.

When the train pulled into the station Hank wondered if he would be able to hire a carriage or vehicle of some sort to convey them to Helmcrest Hall. If he had understood correctly, it was about an hour's drive from the station. They had been standing for a moment, looking for a conveyance, when a middle-aged man in livery approached them.

"Pardon, sir, are you the Earl of Helmcrest?" The man was polite but not effusive. "I am Links, a groom at Helmcrest."

Hank was surprised as he didn't expect anyone to meet them. After all, how could anyone know when they would arrive? The boat had been late due to the sickness and loss of some crew members.

Hank acknowledged his title and added that this was Lady Samantha. The man gave them a cursory look and led the way to a carriage with a crest on its panel.

Samantha noted the man's weathered face and his calloused hands. Her curiosity got the best of her. "Tell me, how did you know we'd be here at this time?"

Links answered matter-of-factly, his accent pronounced. "The train stops at Crestwood daily, and I've met it each day now for two weeks."

Hank whistled softly. This was service indeed. He was being treated with exceptional distinction. After handing Samantha into the carriage, he addressed Links.

"I have a horse I must see to. I'll tie him on the back." With this hurried explanation he hastened back to relieve the men who he knew were struggling to get the big horse down the ramp. Diablo reared and plunged, kicking out at the men.

Links retained his impassive countenance at the news that the new earl had brought a horse to England. It must be a magnificent creature if it were to compete with the thoroughbreds that were in the Helmcrest stables. Then he saw Hank leading the huge spotted horse around the corner. He involuntarily drew in a breath and the expression on his face was ludicrous. He had brought this clown to England? His training asserted itself and his expression was wiped from his face as he moved forward to offer to tie Diablo on behind.

Hank shook his head. "Thank you, but it's best that I do so." A broad smile appeared on his lean brown face, making him extremely attractive.

Diablo followed him like a lap dog and meekly permitted himself to be tied. Seeing the creature's docility, Links couldn't understand why the earl should feel it best that he take care of him. The groom then looked around for their luggage and was surprised to see only two small trunks. He had no way of knowing that where they came from they had little need of an extensive wardrobe and that they were waiting to see what the prevailing mode was before going to London to outfit themselves.

They swung through the wrought-iron embellished gates and brother and sister had their first glimpse of the hall. The way was lined with ash trees reaching eighty feet toward the sky, making a triumphal shady arch through which they would ride.

The hall sat at the end of the drive, majestic and stately with its straight tall lines. The stone was of cream color and it blended in well with the surroundings. Pinnacles and spires proclaimed its ancient history and gave the stone structure a certain elegance. Compared with the small adobe and wood buildings that Samantha and Hank were accustomed to seeing, this was a palace. It seemed to stretch out forever.

The carriage stopped in front of the grand entry. There were twelve stairs leading up to the tall pillars supporting the overhanging roof. As they ascended the steps the massive oak door swung open and a tall gray-haired man stood ready to greet them.

Hank had just time to squeeze Samantha's hand and whisper, "Father didn't do justice to it." He was impressed in spite of himself.

The man bowed majestically as Samantha and Hank entered through the oversized doors. "Welcome home, yer lordship, m'lady," he greeted them. "I am Meadows, yer lordship's butler."

Both the newcomers gaped at the magnificence of the grand entry hall. The ceiling spanned all three floors, for there could be seen two balconies, one above the other, extending around the three sides of the immense room in front of them. A beautiful curved stairway led to the balconies. This room, then, must connect the wings of the house. Many flags proclaiming the heraldry of the ancient lineages connected to the hall were hanging from the railings. Ornate giltwork adorned the vaulted ceiling and a large sparkling chandelier gave the room its finishing touch.

Meadows then motioned forward a tall angular woman past middle age with salt and peppered hair and introduced her. "This is Mrs. Clarke, your housekeeper."

Mrs. Clarke bowed and murmured a greeting. A quick glance at the American heir didn't impress her but no hint of her thoughts was visible.

"May I escort your ladyship to your bedchamber? You might like to freshen up." She took assent for granted and led the way across the room to the stairs.

As she followed Mrs. Clarke, Samantha heard Meadows ask Hank if he'd brought his valet with him. An irrepressible chuckle rose in her throat. They should see Hank roping cattle or standing off an Indian raid. Trying to picture a valet in that scene, laughter almost overcame her. She permitted herself a small smile and continued up the elaborate staircase.

Mrs. Clarke led her into a large attractive room. There were windows overlooking the park and she had an excellent view of the formal gardens with their manicured rows and paths interspersed with tree-shaded benches and a gazebo at the far end. Colors were vivid, with yellows, pinks, reds, violets, oranges, and blues splotching the green like a patchwork quilt.

Samantha surveyed the room with pride and a little wonder. The furniture was old and lovely, polished until each piece gleamed. She noted there was a sitting room adjoining her bedchamber and a dressing room on the other side. Her rooms were larger than their whole house in Arizona. She was uncertain if she could become accustomed to so much space.

Mrs. Clarke enquired, "Is there anything you need?" and then added, "If you like, I'll send Mary to you. She's a young country girl the manager has just taken on, thinking you might like some help until you can make a choice of your own."

"Thank you, I appreciate your thoughtfulness." Mrs. Clarke shut the door behind her. Samantha had never had a maid in her life and she was not sure how she would manage with one. She could hear Hank say to roll with the punches. As the phrase came into her mind she started to giggle. She would have to learn to control her unruly tongue. She would shock the countryside. She remembered how it was in medical school when she told of some of her experiences dealing with wounds from Indian raids. She could see that there was much of her life that she must keep to herself. Those professors, Americans and men at that, didn't believe her stories—and these British were much more staid than any American. She admitted to herself that she had a lot to learn about the customs of this new land of hers.

Shortly after Mrs. Clarke had left her there was a soft knock at the door. Samantha called, "Come in!" and a young apple-cheeked country girl entered timidly.

"I'm Mary," announced the tall and lanky girl. "I'm here to act as yer maid." She twisted a pair of large red hands. It was evident she had been used to hard work.

Samantha gave her a quick scrutiny. What she saw pleased her. This girl would not try to make her over. She felt they could get on extremely well together. It was sixes as to who was the most unsure—Samantha or the new maid. She wondered what the girl thought when she saw her new mistress hadn't removed her bonnet or the huge veil.

Samantha was always one who met trouble head on and she made no exception of the situation she found herself in. "I'm glad to have you, Mary. You can be of great help to me." She paused for a moment seeing the girl relax. "I have something to tell you that will be a secret between you and me."

Mary's eyes grew wide with excitement and she clasped her hands before her. "A secret, m'lady?" she breathed.

Her reaction made Samantha smile. All young girls loved anything that sounded like romance. "It's not what you might think. I have been very ill and have lost not only a deal of weight but due to the high fever I lost my hair."

"Ah," Mary sighed sympathetically.

As she finished speaking Samantha took off the silk scarf and heavy veil, and waited for Mary's reaction. It was immediate.

"Oh, m'lady!" she gasped, and shoved a large hand over her mouth. She saw the tight yellow-tinged skin making Samantha's huge black eyes look like sunken pools. Her eyes went involuntarily to Samantha's head and she saw there was a fine down of hair covering the skull.

Samantha waited patiently for her response. If it was such a shock to the maid, who had been warned in advance, how would the duke react? Well, with luck he would never know.

"M'lady," Mary said shyly, "it could be worse. Have ye noticed yer hair is agrowing in?" Then she blushed, embarrassed at her boldness.

Regardless of conventions Samantha gave the girl a quick squeeze of affection. "Thank you, Mary, that's just what I need. Now what I would like to buy is a brown wig, long straight hair—so it will look like mine did. Is there such a place in the nearest town?"

Mary stood there twisting her apron while she thought. "There is a millinery shop in Crestwood—where you came in on the train. I think they have some wigs being as so many of the fine ladies like to change their style."

"How would you like to have a groom drive you into the village and see what is available?" She paused for a moment thinking how she could best do this. "Buy the long brown one and also a medium length and a short one, if possible."

Mary was puzzled at the order of the different lengths but Samantha was thinking of making everyone believe she wanted a wardrobe of wigs, not that she had need for one. If she knew small towns, the gossip would

fly as soon as Mary had made the purchase for her and it was in her mind
to keep everyone guessing.

"Oh, m'lady, I'll be glad to go for you." She drew herself up and stuck
out her chin. "Ye can depend on me. I'll never say a word to anyone."
Her face turned rosy red in her earnestness.

"I can see you're going to be invaluable to me. I shall count on you."

Mary left importantly on her errand and Samantha turned the key in
the lock of her door. She had no intention of allowing anyone to walk in.

Hank was shown to the master's suite and found it composed of large
masculine rooms with every comfort. He nodded his approval at the huge
fireplace with its flanking brocaded easy chairs. The walls were done in
pale blue with many gilt embellishments where the walls met the ceilings.
There was a fine tapestry depicting a hunting scene on one wall and several pictures and portraits on another. He wandered across the thick blue
carpet to the windows where he could see a lake shining in the distance.
He reflected that the bedroom wing was the base of this "T"-shaped
house, while the front of the house was the crosspiece.

Meadows himself had escorted Hank and stood waiting for any orders.

Hank turned back to the elderly man. "Tell me, what happened to the
late earl's valet, my grandfather's?"

Meadows permitted himself a slight cough. "When the late earl was
lost, our estate manager, Mr. Clifford, felt we had no need for Smythe."

Hank raised his eyebrows incredulously. With all the money this estate
had, the old valet hadn't been kept on?

Meadows, seeing the expression on Hank's face, hurriedly added, "He
was pensioned off. He lives in a small cottage on the estate." He wasn't
going to have this new American earl mistaken about how Helmcrest took
care of its people.

Hank's face cleared. He was glad to hear his people were being valued.
Then a thought struck him. He was expected to have a valet and he had
no idea of how to get along with one. Smythe was the answer. "Tell me,
how can I get in touch with Smythe?"

Meadows was too well trained to show his surprise. "I can send him a
message you'd like to see him," he said austerely.

"No, I don't want to put him to that trouble. Give me his direction and
I shall look him up."

Meadows complied but he was thinking that this new earl didn't know
what was due his consequence. The old earl could have put him straight.
The servant's hall would be busy with speculation tonight.

With Hank, to think about something was to do it. He didn't believe in
putting off anything that needed to be done. He strode past the startled

Meadows and ran lightly down the stairs, remembering Meadows' instructions on the easiest way to the stables. This was a good excuse to put Diablo under a saddle and get the kinks of the voyage out of him. Besides, he would like to examine the stables and see what horses his grandfather had selected.

He strolled into the yard and one of the grooms, seeing him coming, ran to meet him. Hank smiled at the young man who was busily inspecting the American heir. The groom's first thought was that here was a man he would be proud to serve. He looked at his trim waist and powerful thighs and knew this was a horseman.

"What can I do fer ye, sir?"

"I would like to take a look at the horses and then I want to have Diablo saddled." Hank accompanied this with a charming smile, which never failed to win him obedience and a willingness to do whatever was required.

By this time the head groom was coming to meet him. He pulled his forelock in a respectful gesture. Then giving his young assistant a look that obviously meant to take himself off, he addressed his new master.

"Good day to ye, yer lordship." His tone was deferential. "That's quite a bit of 'orseflesh ye 'ave 'ere." Diablo had made quite an impression on him. He had never seen his like but he had looked him over critically and found he was an unusually well-muscled and strong horse. Diablo was feisty but he didn't hold that against him.

"Come along. I'll introduce you to him and you'll have no trouble in the future in saddling him." Hank's face seemed quite serious as he spoke.

Old Peters found this amusing but he kept his face void of emotion. He'd heard of the Americans and the jokes they liked to play. Well, he wasn't the one to be caught.

Hank made his way slowly down the long double row of stalls. He patted the noses of several, ran a hand over one's glistening coat, and generally inspected each as he went. He took in the proud bearing, excellent grooming, the smooth bones and features, and made suitable comments to Peters as they stopped at each stall. This was the first time he could say he was glad to be here. These horses were magnificent.

Peters walked with him appraisingly. Here was a man who knew horses. For that, he didn't give a farthing if he was an American. What he wanted to see was his lordship ride. That opportunity was not long in coming.

Diablo was in a loose box at the end of the stable, separated from the other horses. He heard Hank's voice and flung up his head, a shrill whistle signaling his pleasure.

Hank called to him and he stood like a statue. As Hank approached him he started talking softly to the horse and as he reached the stall door, he opened it and put a hand on Diablo's neck. The big horse lowered his head and bunted him gently, whistling softly through his wide nostrils.

"Diablo, you have a new friend," Hank addressed him, then rubbed his nose. He turned to Peters, who was standing by, viewing the proceedings with a fascinated eye. "Here, Peters, put your hand alongside mine," Hank commanded.

Peters complied, feeling he might have a few fingers taken off in the process, but he wasn't one to let an American see an Englishman had any fear. He did as he was told and the intelligent horse seemed to acknowledge the introduction. "Now, you'll have no trouble, but I wouldn't advise you to try to ride him." The earl smiled as he spoke.

The old groom was offended. He had been riding since he was a tad and he could put a leg over any horse that had ever been brought into the stable. Of course, he was getting on in years but what was that to say to anything?

With no further comment Hank opened the gate and Diablo followed him out into the courtyard as docilely as a broken-down old hack. By this time all work had stopped in the stables and most of the hands had inched forward to get a better view of the proceedings. None of them wanted to miss this. One of them came running with Diablo's gear but Hank pointed to Peters. "Will you please saddle him?" There was a hint of a smile in his deep blue eyes.

The old groom stepped forward and threw the saddle blanket over and quickly followed it with the saddle. His deftness was gained from years of experience. Peters wondered if there would be trouble so he finished the job quickly and gave the cinch a last tug and pulled the strap tight. He nodded to the earl, who flashed him a bright smile.

The horse stood completely still. The stable hands crowded forward to get a better view of this strange horse. A general buzz of conversation could be heard over the soft calls of horses in the background. Hank surveyed the group that had assembled and warned them all to step back. They would have understood an order to get back to work but this one was inexplicable until Hank put a foot in the stirrup and threw himself into the saddle.

The moment he put weight into the stirrup, Diablo went into his act. He took a few short stiff-legged jumps, whirled around, then pawed the air for a minute and finally settled down to a good bucking. Hank merely sat there and let the horse work out his spirits. He swayed gently back and forth in rhythmic motion in time to the horse's kicks.

"Coo," breathed one young stableboy as he twisted his hat in his hands. "I never seen the loikes o' that." He expressed the sentiments of everyone who had the luck to be there. "It's loike one of them Wild West shows we be ahearing about."

As soon as Diablo had worked out his kinks and saw that his rider was still master he settled down, shook his head, and let a breath out noisily. Hank gave him an affectionate pat and the horse behaved as innocently as a baby. "I'll be back in an hour or so," Hank told his appreciative audience and with a general sigh they trooped back to their work.

It was good to be on horseback again after being subjected to the rigors of the stagecoach, ship, and finally the train. As he trotted down the path through the home wood and headed for the estate cottages near the south pasture, Hank had a feeling of well-being. The air was fresh and although there were clouds in the sky the peace and serenity of the woods engulfed him. Sounds were muffled here and all that could be heard was the chirping of a nearby bird and slight rustle of the leaves on the trees.

Upon enquiry at the first cottage, he found that Smythe was at the end of the row. He jumped down and ground-hitched Diablo. A young boy playing nearby scrambled to his feet and offered to hold him.

"No, thanks, sonny," Hank replied. "This horse is dangerous. Don't get near him—he might kick you."

Seeing he was in earnest, the boy kept his distance but he found the ugly horse fascinating.

Hank rapped on the door of the modest cottage and as it opened he found himself confronting a tall, dignified, white-haired man. He had a lined face, faded blue eyes, and a hint of resignation in his old voice.

"What can I do for you, sir?" he asked.

"I'm Henry Salsbury, the new Earl of Helmcrest." Hank felt ridiculous introducing himself like that but it had to be accepted.

At that, the old man gave him a piercing look. "Come in, your lordship." He spoke eagerly, his hands visibly shaking. "I should have known you anywhere. You are the image of your dear grandfather. Ah, he was a man." The valet pulled himself together. "Will you honor me by sitting down?" he enquired.

Hank dropped into an easy chair by a small fireplace. "Please, sit with me," he said, as he saw that Smythe had no intention of sitting in his presence.

Smythe started to shake his head but at the winning smile he received sat gingerly on a chair near Hank. "You're just like the old earl. He didn't stand on ceremony. Many's the time he—" The old man stopped as he realized he was rattling on.

Hank, seeing his embarrassment, took over smoothly. "I suppose you wonder why I've sought you out. What I need to know is if you are happy with your retirement?" He raised a hand to stop Smythe as he saw he might be misunderstood. "What I mean is, how would you feel about coming back to valet for me? I need you."

These were powerful words and they invigorated Smythe. "Oh, my lord, you have been most generous with giving me this cottage and a pension to go on, but I admit, I miss the hall and all the activity. I'd be honored to serve you—if you think I'm up to it." There was a suspicion of moisture in his eyes, but already his voice sounded stronger. The opportunity was acting like a tonic.

Hank had already thought the job might prove too strenuous for Smythe, although he didn't really know what a valet's duties were composed of. "I thought you might like to select a young man you could train as your assistant. Give him all the running around," Hank suggested. After all, what good was money if you couldn't use it to help someone worthy?

Smythe was profuse in his thanks and willing to start walking over to the hall immediately.

"Nonsense! I'll send a gig over for you tomorrow. I can manage until then." He left with a good feeling. He didn't think he had any need for one valet, let alone two, but he'd had the pleasure of making someone happy.

Smythe came to the door to see him off and was startled to see the horse standing there patiently without being tied. He had never heard of the western method of ground-hitching. He had a feeling that life might prove to be interesting again.

When he arrived back at the hall, Hank handed Diablo over to Peters and the horse trotted off with an air of "see what a good boy am I" that made Hank chuckle.

He was whistling softly as he took the marble stairs two at a time. He left behind him disapproving looks that went completely unnoticed. He passed down the long paneled corridor decorated with ancient armor of days gone by and stopped at his sister's bedchamber. Knocking softly on her door, he wondered how she was faring. He called to her and at the sound of his voice she turned the key in its lock and opened the door, quickly shutting it behind him.

He stared at her. How had she done it? She had a full head of brown hair, pulled back in a bun at the base of her neck. She looked surprisingly like she used to except for her extreme thinness and the poor color of her complexion.

Seeing him stopped in his tracks staring at her as if transfixed, she burst into laughter. "See what I've accomplished." She was proud of how she had managed. "I took my new maid into my confidence and she went into the village and bought me several wigs."

Hank found his voice. "Several?" He couldn't take his eyes from her. It was good to see how her spirits had risen.

"I had to think of some way to fool the countryside. I am sure it is the same here as at home. No one can help passing on a little gossip and I was determined to make my purchase commonplace."

"Clever, Sam." He was pleased with her. "Now do you think you can go through with this marriage?"

That was the big question. She didn't want to call it off, but was it fair to the duke? She had been thinking about that for some time. "He's buying a pig in a poke but he is getting paid well. Then, too, someday in the near future I hope to give him a shock when he sees me as I really am." She picked up her skirt and danced about the room happy in the knowledge her hair was starting to grow back. She pirouetted in blissful ignorance of the prophetic nature of her words. She would soon be enlightened.

CHAPTER 6

The next morning, Hank, having given her so much confidence, found Samantha coming down for breakfast. As they selected their breakfast from the many tempting dishes on the sideboard, she wondered what Guadalupe and her Mexican help would have thought. One thing was the same—her old clothes. That was the next thing to accomplish on her program. She would ask Mrs. Clarke to recommend the best available shops until she could make a trip to London. Several returning passengers aboard the ship had been free with recommendations of the best shops to patronize and where they were to be found. There had been one in Albemarle Street and there were several in New and Old Bond streets. Her head was awhirl with visions of beautiful creations to help her regain her customary figure.

They were finishing the inevitable cup of English tea when Meadows appeared with a silver salver in his hand. He extended it to Hank, who took the card from it. He read James Throckmorton, Throckmorton and Throckmorton, Solicitors, in large block print. He passed it to Samantha.

"Our solicitor calling." It was mighty early. Well, he supposed they'd better see what was in the wind.

Meadows waited in rigid formality. "Show him into the morning room," Hank ordered as he got to his feet.

Samantha took her last swallow of tea, wishing it was good old American coffee, strong enough to float a horseshoe in, and followed Hank to the morning room.

Mr. Throckmorton was a dry stick of a man, being short and extremely thin. His luxuriant sideburns, reaching to his chin, were his only remarkable feature. The twiglike line of his mouth set the tone for his impassive countenance. He bent a stern pair of brown eyes on the earl and his sister as they entered the room.

"Won't you sit down?" invited Samantha as she made her way to an easy chair near the large window.

Mr. Throckmorton seated himself, giving the impression that his every act was carefully thought out. "Thank you." His voice was impersonal and he inclined his head slightly as he spoke. He waited until Hank had seated himself, then he opened a small leather case he had brought with him, placing piles of papers on the table beside him. Everything about him was precise. He wasted no effort in readying his materials. "I have here some important papers which need both of your signatures." Without any further explanation he handed one pile to Hank.

While Hank read the crackling documents Samantha sat looking out the window enjoying the myriads of color from the formal gardens. Flowers of yellow, pink, orange, red, blue, and many shades in between raised their heads toward the sun. The lawns and shrubs extended to the park that surrounded the hall. This was something they didn't have in Arizona. Little patches of green where there was water to irrigate could be seen after the spring rains, but mostly Arizona was various kinds of cacti, mesquite trees, paloverde, and never-ending sand. She was brought back to the present when Hank handed her the papers.

"This assures you a substantial sum in your own name. You also agree that the balance of your share of this estate is to be given to the Duke of Belfort upon your marriage. I, of course, get the bulk of the lands and most of the fortune. Is this satisfactory to you?" He gave her a questioning look. He wanted to be sure she hadn't changed her mind. Did she still think it was worth it? Did medicine mean so much to her? He didn't think it could be the social position she would attain.

Samantha gave him a reassuring smile. Sometime she would explain the truth to him, but for now she wanted to keep her thoughts to herself until she found how she would be received. It wasn't medicine that prompted her to accept this proposal. She had been a little in love with the duke for over a year. She often wondered if his winnings with his horse at Saratoga had tided him over. She scanned the documents, noting the large sum to be put into her own name. She would at least be independent of him if this didn't turn out as she envisioned it would. She took the pen Hank handed her and, taking a deep breath, signed her name boldly. It was done. A sigh escaped her lips and she sat back in her chair.

Hank signed in several places and handed the documents back to the solicitor. He exchanged them for the second set and when both copies were completed to his satisfaction he cleared his throat importantly. "His Grace asked me to inform you he will be calling upon you tomorrow at your convenience. He is anxious to meet Lady Samantha." He gave her a quick glance, wondering in his mind how His Grace would feel when he saw how plain—almost ugly—she appeared. Her hair lay limp and lifeless and her skin was a disaster. Her clothes hung on her and she looked like a skeleton. Well, one couldn't have everything. His Grace was getting a handsome fortune, one that would straighten out his estates and more than he could spend in a lifetime. He pondered the girl before him again. The information he had received referred to her as quite pretty. If that was the American version of pretty, he was sorry for it.

After the departure of Mr. Throckmorton, Samantha turned to her brother. "How can I meet him now? It is too soon! I wanted to at least get some weight on and my skin in better color," she wailed. She wrung her hands together, her face apprehensive.

Hank took her hands, his matter-of-fact manner calming her down considerably. "Now, Sam, you are looking more like yourself every day. That wig does a dandy job. If you could get a few good dresses—" His voice trailed off. He hoped he was distracting her from the things she could not change immediately.

"Just like a man! Fine birds make fine feathers. Clothes can cover a lot —including my skinny look." Visions of creations to disguise her boniness came to mind. "He has agreed that this marriage is not to be consummated for six months. By that time I will have both my figure and three or four inches of my own hair back." She had heard that shorter styles were the rage in London now. There was the possibility nagging at her that she would not find him the romantic figure she remembered. She wasn't expecting Sir Galahad. She knew every man had many facets, but she hoped that most of the duke's facets were ones she could get along with. If she found otherwise, well, there was more than enough for her needs in the amount to be placed in her name and the marriage could be annulled. She decided her best course of action was to postpone any meeting with him as long as possible. "I don't want to meet him just yet. Put him off, Hank. Let him come and meet you but give him the excuse I'm ill."

Seeing the earnest look she gave him and hearing the tone she used, he softened to her. She was his beloved sister and he would do anything to help her. "Very well. I will have a note sent over to have him call tomorrow morning. When he arrives, I shall say you are ill and cannot meet him." Then a sudden thought struck him. "When do you intend to meet him?"

"Not until the day I marry him!" she flashed.

"Oh, Sam, you can't do that to him." Hank was appalled. He was putting himself in the duke's position.

"Why not? What difference will it make? We both know it is merely a marriage of convenience." When she stuck her chin out like that Hank knew her mind was made up.

She was afraid that if the duke saw her as she looked now he might be the one to call off the marriage. Although the wig was a tremendous help it did look dull and lifeless. She had no decent dress and the ones she did own looked like flour sacks to her. No, she didn't want his first look at her to turn him off. It would be better this way. Hank could try for a later date on the marriage to give her a little more time to recover.

Accordingly, the next morning she didn't go down for breakfast. Mary was puzzled. "Be something the matter?" she asked solicitously.

"No, Mary. It's just that the Duke of Belfort is calling sometime this morning and I do not want to see him just yet."

Mary was enthralled with the scent of romance. "What a intrigue! Just like a storybook," she exclaimed, proud of her knowledge of the right word.

Samantha didn't correct her supposition. "Just remember, we have a secret. No one must know and now I don't want anyone to know anything except that I am ill this morning. Seeing the way I look, no one will think anything of it. Do you understand?"

Thus appealed to, the girl bobbed her a curtsy and her eyes sparkled with excitement. There had been no secrets or love affairs in her realm before and she was going to remember every detail so she could recall it in the years to come.

Samantha was busily trying to take in the waist of one of her dresses when she heard the sound of wheels. Peeping out the window she saw an elegant curricle drawing up to the front steps. She had picked this room on the front side of the hall this morning expressly so she could see the duke's arrival. She stood back from the window so as not to be seen and watched the lithe figure jump down from the curricle and throw the reins to a waiting groom. She recognized the duke's tall, athletic frame and gazed intently as he jauntily ascended the steps and disappeared inside. Just that quick glimpse of him brought the past rushing back to her as she remembered his many facial expressions and his manner at the race so long ago. Her heart began to thud and her face flushed. This was ridiculous. She had never even spoken to the man. How could he affect her this way? She resolutely turned back to her sewing. She set tiny stitches in her yellow muslin dress, thinking that if one of the maids saw her, the job would be taken from her. Would she ever get used to the idea of someone always waiting on her? If it left her free to spend some time healing the sick she wouldn't mind. She began to think about how she could set up a small clinic on the Belfort estates. She bit off a thread and shook out the dress. It was anything but stylish but at least it wouldn't hang on her. She hated to think of spending much money for dresses she wouldn't be able to wear in a few weeks when she regained the weight she had lost. She would manage with a few new gowns until then, when she could give herself over to planning her trousseau with verve. Hank must make the duke understand the wedding must be set at least six weeks away. That would give her plenty of time to put some color back into her cheeks as well as a deal of flesh. Since they wouldn't be sharing a bedchamber, her lost hair didn't trouble her much. She would just be careful for a while, then when the need for the wig was over she would explain everything. She had all the details worked out to her satisfaction.

Meadows outdid himself in his majestic bow to the duke. Taking his hat and gloves, he then led the way to the small salon, where Hank was leaning against the marble fireplace.

At the duke's entrance he straightened and came forward, his hand outstretched in welcome. He appraised the man before him. He must be of a size with him, just over six feet, but so well proportioned he didn't look the least bit heavy. Hank thought the duke must carry at least one hundred ninety-five pounds. He couldn't call him a handsome man, his nose being on the aquiline side and his heavy dark brows turning upward giving him a devilish appearance. His dark brown hair was carefully disordered furthering the impression. When he extended his hand to Hank and broke into a smile Hank could understand how the ladies might find him irresistible. It was charming, lighting up his dark eyes.

"Welcome to Helmcrest," Hank said warmly.

The duke took his hand and they exchanged a firm grip. Each liked the other immediately. The duke prided himself on his good judgment of men and horseflesh and his look gave unqualified approval to Hank. He reflected that if the sister was anything like the brother he would not have a bad bargain. He noted the fair hair and deep blue eyes, which had a hint of laughter in them. The tanned skin set them off to perfection.

"I'm Belfort," he announced, "and of course you're Helmcrest."

Hank found it hard to think of himself as Helmcrest. "Just call me Hank," he returned. "If we are to be brothers let's not stand on ceremony." He motioned to an easy chair and they both dropped casually into the pair facing the fireplace.

There was a moment of silence and then the duke spoke. "I want you to know how appreciative I am of your consenting to my marrying your sister and the speedy way in which the arrangements have been made." He paused momentarily and then leaned forward earnestly. "I dislike the position I find myself in." Then seeing the expression in Hank's eyes, he hurried on. "I don't mean anything against your sister. I mean I hate to be in the position of seeking money from a wife. If it weren't for all the Belfort retainers and tenants that depend on me I wouldn't have agreed to

Mr. Throckmorton's suggestion. Do you understand?" He appealed to Hank.

Hank admired the duke's forthrightness and nodded his agreement. This was no gazetted fortune hunter. He put his cards on the table. After all, he had a lot to offer a girl. Being the Duchess of Belfort would be considered quite a plum. Besides, looking the duke over carefully, Hank came to the conclusion that he was a good man and one that might suit Samantha quite well.

"Samantha is deeply interested in medicine. She has shown this tendency since she was a little girl. Our local doctor, noticing her talent, took her on his rounds and taught her a great deal. Our problems are very different than what you have. We have violent crimes, knifings, shootings, and Indian attacks with torture and scalpings. Samantha has helped on many of these cases." He paused as he saw the incredulous look on the duke's face. "It is true. I'm not exaggerating. Finally, with our doctor's help she went to New York to get into a medical school there. After many disappointments she finally was granted admission to Geneva Medical College, where she graduated. She wants to be able to help the sick, especially the poor, and when your offer came she thought it might be a means for her to have a small clinic. With your name and prestige she felt people might accept her." He dug his hands in his pockets when he finished his explanation, waiting for a reply.

The duke did not hesitate in his answer. "If Lady Samantha would like to start a clinic on the Belfort grounds I will have no objection." He was amazed, for he had not had much contact with intelligent women. The ones he usually favored with his company were interested only in the frivolous things in life and money and jewels. "All I ask is that the clinic is open only two or three days a week for a few hours, those to be decided upon. This way she will not overwork and will still be able to attend to the duties of her position. Surprisingly, there are some."

"Fair enough. I am sure Samantha will be very happy over your offer." Both men exchanged satisfied smiles, each feeling he had done well.

The duke glanced casually toward the door, feeling it was time Lady Samantha put in an appearance. He was about to question Hank when that astute young man caught the duke's enquiring look and interpreted it correctly.

"I'm sorry to have to tell you that Lady Samantha will not be down to meet you this morning." He made it a habit never to lie. It caused too much trouble. "She wished me to tell you that she has been very ill. She had typhoid on the ship coming over. It was probably brought on by her working night and day for the many others who had caught the disease.

She is still not herself and today is not a good day for her. Will you please excuse her and we will arrange another meeting?" He skirted about the truth but failed to commit himself about her actual health.

The duke quirked an eyebrow at this piece of news but politely held his tongue. The marriage arrangements needed to be made and he decided to come directly to the point. "Will it suit your sister and you if we have the wedding Tuesday week?"

Hank knew this was much sooner than Samantha would like. This was Monday and that gave her only eight days. "This is so soon," he suggested. "There is so much to do to get ready. Would it be all right with you if we made it in about a month?"

The duke sat up straighter in his chair. He needed this wedding to take place as soon as possible. His creditors were pressing and had only agreed to hold off for another week. They had expressed their fears that Lady Samantha, upon encountering the more rigid social conventions of English society, might change her mind. They wanted no slip. "I am embarrassed to say that I need the wedding to take place as quickly as possible. Seeing that we will each have our own apartments—connecting suites— and the fact that I am willing to accede to her conditions, I can see no reason why we cannot proceed." With that he rose to his feet and put a hand to his brow, as if wiping away some imaginary sweat, and started to pace to and fro.

Hank stood up, moving over to where the duke was pacing, and reached out to touch his arm. He could see that the duke was disconcerted. "Whoa!" he commanded. "Don't get bucked off. We'll manage."

At the unusual words the duke smiled. These Americans didn't even speak the English language but he knew by the tone that Hank meant well.

"You mean Lady Samantha can manage this Tuesday date?" he asked, now doubtful.

"We'll manage," Hank agreed recklessly. "Where do you want the wedding to take place?"

"Unless Lady Samantha prefers St. George's, Hanover Square, I would like to have it in my chapel and performed by my chaplain. All the dukes for the past three hundred years have been married here." It was a simple statement but one couldn't miss the note of pride.

"Well, Samantha wouldn't want to break your tradition. I'll explain it to her." He thought he would have to do some tall talking over this date.

"One other thing, do you think Lady Samantha will mind wearing the wedding gown and veil we've used for the past few duchesses? It is in excellent shape, having been worn only for a few hours at each wedding and then carefully stored away."

This was another Belfort tradition and the duke would like to have Samantha follow it even though this was only a marriage of convenience. Hank didn't hesitate in accepting for Samantha; he knew she would agree on this. She wanted as quiet a wedding as possible and there would be no time to obtain a suitable wedding dress. In fact, she would have her work cut out for her to get even a few gowns made.

"Now the only thing that remains is for me to meet Lady Samantha. Will you send me word as soon as she feels up to it?"

Hank felt a deal of compassion for the man. The duke was being extremely decent and here Hank was tied down by a promise to his sister. "Yes, of course," he answered, and left it at that, hoping that Samantha might change her mind, but knowing that determined young lady, he seriously doubted it.

She needed a strong hand but she had always turned her brother around her little finger. Well, Hank thought, it might prove different with the duke. The man seemed to be cut from a strong piece of cloth. There was a glint in Hank's eye as he thought that this marriage might prove to be very interesting.

Thoughtfully, he made his way upstairs to the yellow sitting room where he knew Samantha to be. She was seated near the window watching the curricle bowl down the drive between the rows of ash trees. She turned as she heard him.

"Tell me, what did he say?" she asked anxiously.

"Well, I think he's a good man and you know I very seldom make a mistake in judgment. You'll have a man's man, and I believe he'll be very considerate of you." He was delaying telling her about the wedding date.

"Fine, I am betting my future on that." The look she gave him was thoughtful. "Tell me, did you set a date for the wedding?"

"You are not going to like it, but there was nothing else to be done. He feels it necessary to have the marriage not later than Tuesday week." His tone was apologetic.

"Oh, Hank! I'll look awful!" She threw herself into her brother's arms and cried on his shoulder. She had so wanted to be looking like herself and give this marriage a promising start.

Hank patted the dull hair. It was anything but becoming but it was better than none. "Now, now," he murmured. He felt inadequate to deal with the problem. Then he had an inspiration. "You'll need new gowns, something to tide you over until you gain some weight. Why don't you send to the village and have the local modiste call? Remember," he said with a twinkle in his eye, "money is no problem, and you can have more stylish gowns made up when you can get down to London."

Samantha gave her brother a kiss, pulled his hair as she used to do when she was little, and gave a watery chuckle.

"Nothing like clothes to take a woman's mind off her troubles." He gave her a hug and left her to plan her interim wardrobe.

She had to agree. The die was cast and her only alternative was to try to call the whole thing off, but those signatures seemed very legal and perhaps it was even too late for that. Besides, even the glimpse she had of the duke had reinforced those feelings he had aroused in her when she saw him in New York. This was her man and she was going to try to win him.

She had practiced economy for so long it had become habit. It was good of Hank to remind her that she needn't spare expenses. She was sure she could come up with some tolerable if not stylish gowns.

CHAPTER 7

The following days found the hall in the midst of more activity than it had seen in some time. Mr. Smythe had arrived and the swarm of haberdashers involved in renovating Hank's wardrobe almost rivaled the flow of modistes to and from Samantha's rooms.

Smythe had taken his old room again and started to put things to rights. When a disparaging remark was made about the American, he stopped it with a raise of an eyebrow. The earl's valet had an important position in the servant's hall. He was more aristocratic than the duke himself. He put every servant in his place and let it be known that their master might be an American but he was the earl. This recognition from Smythe had made the other servants realize that there was more to the American than they had thought and consequently gained respect for the earl.

Smythe viewed Hank's wardrobe and set about ordering articles he knew to be needed. So far he had found no one he felt was equal to training as his assistant but that didn't bother him. Hank had won his heart and soul and he was extremely happy to be back at his job.

Samantha had sent for the best modiste the village had to offer. She contemplated how many gowns she would need for the few weeks until she had gained back her weight, and which styles would best disguise her thinness. Waists were certainly in style, a deep point in the front, emphasizing the trim figures of the day. Samantha noticed on the many pattern cards brought for her inspection that there were yards and yards of material in the skirts and several rows of ruffling were standard. Many sleeves clung closely at the shoulder and widened to immense size before being caught at the wrist. She selected bright colors, mindful of her sallow complexion. A fancy bright pink crepe for informal evenings, several shades of green and blue printed muslins for mornings and afternoons, and, because it was expected of her, several *robes de nuit*.

The modiste insisted that she also have one of the new "artificial crinolines," or cage petticoats, which consisted of a dome-shaped steel wire instead of the numerous petticoats usually worn with the cane hoop. Samantha wondered if she would be able to manage such a thing, for it looked as if it would swing up over her head if pushed in by someone standing too close. Madame showed her the style and skill that moving through doorways and standing and sitting required. She assured Samantha that everyone wore them and she would accustom herself to it in no time. The large hoop skirt was not suitable for ranch life or in her chosen profession, so she'd had no experience with one. Samantha remained skeptical but ordered it just the same.

Several days later the wedding dress arrived, with a short note requesting Samantha to make any adjustments that were needed. She opened the box and found herself looking at a white gown of handmade Brussels lace, as delicate as a spider web. There were rows of ruffles and a sweeping train in the back. A long matching lace veil accompanied it. Samantha fingered it gently. This was an heirloom beyond price. The modiste was in raptures over it and suggested that she try it on.

Carefully the gown was lowered over Samantha's head and buttoned up the back. Madame shook out the train, revealing the flowing lines down the back. Madame was all smiles. This dress had been the height of fashion a century before and like court dress had stayed in vogue. She surveyed Samantha critically with her well-trained eye, noting where small tucks were needed. The cascading train would conceal these admirably, making extensive renovations unnecessary.

While the dressmaker was pinning the adjustments, Samantha had time to think ahead to her wedding day. She worried about her appearance but, after noting the improvement brought about by this enchanting dress, decided that with a heavy veil she would do. By doubling the lace on the veil instead of having it flow back with the train she could camouflage her ravaged countenance. She began to gather her self-confidence and gave the necessary instructions to the modiste. Her thoughts dwelt for some time on the handsome figure of the duke.

A note arrived from Belfort. He regretted that he had to make a quick trip to London. He was working on a committee, with Lord Palmerston at its head, in regard to the Confederate contracts for ironclad steamers to be built in England. There was important business to be decided as the American minister in London, Charles Francis Adams, demanded the British government seize the vessels. The duke would return as quickly as possible but it probably wouldn't be until the day before the wedding. This meant that he would meet his bride at the wedding. He sent his profound apologies.

Samantha took the news with a lift in her heart. It seemed that everything was working for her. She stood for the rest of her fittings with new energy and oversaw the many details of getting ready for her wedding.

The day of the ceremony was clear and bright. Hank handed her into the glass carriage with tenderness. He squeezed her hand while the maid was busy fussing with the train of her dress, settling it just so, for no hint of a wrinkle must be seen.

Peters was on the box and Links climbed up beside him, both looking very important in the earl's blue and silver livery. With a flick of the reins the coach was off. The clattering of horses' hooves announced the advance of the vehicle as it swept down the drive.

A baggage coach followed with Mary and Smythe. Several outriders rode alongside. The horses were tasseled and the silver trimmings glistened in the sun. It was an impressive entourage.

Samantha noticed how splendid Hank looked in his deep blue tailed coat and immaculate white starched shirt with high points. A tall beaver top hat sat on the seat beside him completing this striking outfit.

Samantha asked her brother, "How do I look? No quick answer—I want the truth."

Hank gave her a critical eye. It was surprising how much better she looked in clothes that fit. The wedding dress was becoming on her even if she didn't have her customary enticing figure, but her face was still abnormally thin. Her cheekbones stood out, making her eyes look like sunken pools, but there was a sparkle in them and he could see she would soon be herself again. He picked his words cautiously. "Your dress emphasizes your tiny waist and is quite eye-catching, but you still have a way to go to be your charming self."

"In fact, I've come at least one step up from the grave!" she joked.

Hank's laugh rang out naturally. That sounded like his sister. She was going to be all right. He only hoped the duke would not be too disappointed when he saw her. It was his only concern.

Their first glimpse of Belfort Castle was breathtaking. Samantha had read about old English castles but had never imagined one could look as magnificent as this. It stood at the top of a rise and was surrounded by trees. The pale gray stone gleamed as the rays of sun bounced from its surface. There were turrets at each corner and a tall gateway with double oaken doors. Guards stood at each side, the doors thrown wide open, and respectfully bowed as they passed.

Red and gold liveried stable hands ran forward to take the horses' heads.

Discreetly concealed heads peeked through the front windows of the main structure in order to obtain a view of the bride and new mistress of the castle. The maids giggled as they waited expectantly for her to descend.

Hank handed Samantha from the carriage, her veil already in place. Mary bustled forward to fluff out the train of her gown, making sure each fold was in the proper place. Hank squeezed her hand as he took her arm in his and led her up the crimson carpet to the front door.

The butler, also in red and gold, augustly ushered them into the grand entry, where an elderly lady greeted them warmly. Her carriage was erect and her patrician air announced her nobility. She was a tiny thing, her hands and feet small and delicate. Her snow-white hair was piled high on her head and a pair of deep blue eyes pierced the newcomers.

At their entrance she waved away the butler, who bowed respectfully before retiring. "Of course, you are the new Earl of Helmcrest and this is Lady Samantha." She tipped her head to one side in an unconscious gesture that was common to her. "I am Belfort's only relative, his aunt, the Countess d'Avigny. I told him it was unlucky to see his bride on his wedding day before the ceremony and so I am doing the honors." The countess wondered at the veil already covering Samantha's face but forbore comment.

They expressed their happiness at meeting her but Samantha thought the old lady looked formidable. She was relieved she needn't see the duke until the actual ceremony. They exchanged a few commonplaces and the countess rang a bell on a side table next to her.

"There is just time to refresh yourself and see your room before the candlelight service. We will have dinner following, but due to the circumstances, there will be no guests other than myself. Belfort has explained to his friends that you have been ill and as yet are not up to entertaining." She paused, giving Samantha a sharp look. "I was to ask if this suits you?"

"Yes, thank you," she managed to say demurely, but inwardly she was elated. She had postponed the moment again.

The housekeeper must have been waiting for the summons, as she appeared promptly. She was a short, plump woman with a kind face. They followed her up the long marble staircase with its portraits of former members of the household staring down at them. She opened one door and indicated it was Hank's and led Samantha farther down the hall.

"This is the bride's room, where all the duchesses have slept," she announced with pride. She was looking covertly at Samantha as she spoke. She couldn't believe His Grace would have chosen a bride who was as quiet and mysterious as this girl. Well, the servant's hall knew the difficulties that beset him and could sympathize with his troubles. Nevertheless, she was determined to be pleasant to the new duchess for the poor girl had come from foreign parts to rescue His Grace.

Samantha stood and gazed about the huge room. She had thought that her room at Helmcrest was impressive but it was nothing to this one. The fireplace was the focal point of the room and was made of white and cream swirled Italian marble. A fire was laid all ready to be lit.

The room was adorned in ivory and gold. Large comfortable chairs covered in ivory silk with gold legs flanked the fireplace with small tables and a lamp on each one. The bed seemed large enough for a whole family, she thought, and could picture some of the Mexican families she knew making it a community property. She almost giggled as she pictured it. The silken canopy was hand-embroidered with gold threads running through it and fell around the bed from beneath a gold corolla suspended above the middle of the bed. There were thousands of tiny stitches in the canopy forming the ducal coat of arms. It was a treasure.

"Your trunks are coming up now," said Mrs. Thompson. "I can hear them on the back steps. Your maid will be with them. Simmons, our butler, will tell her the procedure in our hall. If there is anything you need, have her tell me and I'll see to it." She paused. "May I wish you every happiness, my lady." She glanced at her watch and reminded Samantha it wanted fifteen minutes until five and was gone on the word.

Almost immediately there was a knock on the door and Mary entered. Her cheeks were rosy with excitement. She had never thought she would get to see the castle. When Mr. Clifford selected her as a maid for Lady Samantha she was told it would be temporary as her mistress would want a more experienced maid, yet here she was and her ladyship seemed to be pleased with her. She ordered the flunky to put the trunks in the dressing room and started opening one. She smoothed out the first gown and opened the armoire to hang it up.

Samantha wandered through the private hall that led to a luxurious sitting room, passing the doors to the dressing room and bath closet. A door on the other side of the hall led to the main hall. The sitting room was done in shades of yellow and seemed to radiate a pleasant feeling. She knew time was getting close and so made her way back to the bedchamber. As she entered she noticed a door in the paneling on the opposite wall, which held the fireplace. She tried the handle and found it locked on her side. Curious, she unlocked it and opened the door. A swift look showed her that this was the master bedchamber. Everything in it was masculine in appearance. She could imagine the duke in it and with the thought she hastily shut the door, relocking it.

Mary brought in a bottle of perfume now unpacked and delicately dabbed some around Samantha's throat. She adjusted the lace veil and was inspecting the train as an authoritative knock was heard at the door.

It was just before five o'clock and Hank stood in the doorway, a smile beckoning her to him. "You'll do," he said somewhat gruffly. He was feeling her fears. He offered his arm to her and escorted her down the broad staircase where Simmons himself waited to lead them to the chapel. He bowed and gestured for them to follow him.

As they moved through the many corridors footmen and maids respectfully bowed and curtsied as they passed. It seemed to Samantha that they walked forever. She wondered how the countess managed it but rightly guessed that a couple of footmen probably put her in a chair and carried her where she wanted to go.

They passed through the long hall, gazing at the original works of art by the old masters. Several statues stood in silent vigil. They walked on across the covered portico and could hear organ music coming from the chapel.

The tall double doors stood open and Simmons paused and bowed, allowing Hank and Samantha to precede him. He closed the doors behind them and the music seemed to swell and fill the entire chapel. Samantha stood in awe for a moment admiring the magnificence. Lovely stained glass windows with pointed arches allowed sunlight to dance in a myriad of colors throughout the room. The scent of white roses with baby's breath permeated the air. They were arranged everywhere, surrounded by luscious greenery.

A middle-aged man in a white surplice stood waiting at the altar and in front and to his right stood the duke. His face was set in stern lines and he was evidently holding himself in rigid control. To Samantha he was the most handsome man she'd ever seen and her heart swelled to think that she was to be his wife. She promised herself to do her very best to make him happy and, please God, he would learn to love her. She started down the aisle on Hank's arm, noticing that the diminutive countess was seated in a front pew. She walked slowly in time to the strange music. It was not a piece she knew, Mozart possibly or Haydn. As she drew alongside, the duke took her from Hank, who stepped back and sat beside the countess.

Belfort closely scanned his bride but could discover very little about her, the veil covering her face completely. He could see she was drastically thin but her illness accounted for that and he didn't worry. His solicitor had been lavish in her praise, assuring him that he would have nothing to complain about in her countenance. Besides, her brother was a fine-looking man.

The ceremony was simple and moving. When the chaplain told Belfort to kiss his bride, Samantha inwardly shuddered. Timidly she raised her veil just above her mouth and felt him lightly brush her lips. His touch alone sent a delicious vibration through her.

Belfort was puzzled why she didn't completely raise the veil but made no issue of it. He gently led her up the aisle and they made their way to the main part of the castle. The countess was being carried in her chair and Hank walked alongside.

"You must excuse an old lady," she said to Hank, dabbing at her eyes. "I am a little touched at a wedding. I don't believe I can make the dinner. I feel a trifle indisposed. Will you present my excuses to Their Graces?"

Hank assented and thought that since the bridal party would be small, he'd really be in the way. Consequently, he made up his mind to present his excuses so that Samantha and Belfort could be alone.

Samantha stole a look at the duke as they walked down the long hall. His attitude was one of great courtesy but he showed no warmth. She knew he was waiting to see what she looked like.

Belfort was thinking he had been assured by Throckmorton that the American solicitor he had engaged confirmed Lady Samantha was a most attractive young lady but when Throckmorton had come back from his recent interview he had said nothing. Belfort was uneasy. He had a distinct feeling that something was wrong.

"If you please, Your Grace," Samantha began in a low voice, "I must stop in my bedchamber for a moment." Her head was itching so badly she couldn't stand it. Partly it was nerves but also she had been so keyed up her head had started to perspire under the wig.

"Certainly, my dear," he answered, "but don't you think it's time you called me Brooke?"

Samantha was flustered. She hadn't even remembered his first name! "I'll try," she promised.

He opened her door and said, "I'll wait for you in my room," and went down the hall to enter his bedchamber from the hall. As he did so he found Hank just behind him.

"Your aunt sent her regrets. She can't make dinner and that makes three of us. I decided that's a crowd so I'll have something sent up to me and you and Samantha can be alone."

Belfort saw the engaging grin on his brother-in-law's face and it brought an answering smile. "Under the circumstances, you are probably right. We will have a lot to say to one another."

As Hank took himself off, Belfort, with his hand still on the handle of his door, was struck by an idea. Instead of having dinner in the huge formal dining room, perhaps it would be more comfortable to have it in Samantha's sitting room. They could have a more relaxed atmosphere and get to know one another without the prying eyes of servants.

As he went back down the hall to Samantha's room he intercepted Mary, Samantha's maid, telling her of his plans and asking if she would relay the message to cook. She hesitated, not sure whether to answer her mistress' bell, or do His Grace's bidding. Under his piercing gaze and raised eyebrow she returned down the hall, hurrying so as not to be long gone because her mistress would still need her.

Samantha sank into a chair before her dressing table in the large bed-chamber and carefully lifted the fragile veil. Then she seized the offending wig and pulled it from her head, throwing it on the table. One look in the mirror revealed to her how repulsive she looked but closer examination showed her that her hair was indeed growing in. It looked surprisingly dark and seemed to have a tendency to turn on the ends. She started to rub her head vigorously, making the damp tufts stand out like a scare-crow's. She heard a knock at the door, and mistakenly, thinking it was Mary in answer to her summons, called, "Come in." She was at the far end of the room and as yet had not learned to distinguish a knock on her bedchamber door from one in her own hall, which Mary would have used. She caught a glimpse of a tall, masculine figure in her mirror and she turned in horror, a grotesque look on her already hideous counte-nance.

Belford stood there as if transfixed. Time seemed to stand still. He took in the scrawny figure before him, sparse hair standing on end, sallow skin drawn over prominent bones in her face, and an expression that defied de-scription. Why she was almost bald! A look of repugnance spread over his features. This was too much! He couldn't take this! A groan involuntarily burst from him. "Oh, my God!" and he wheeled and left the room.

Samantha sat frozen at the table. She couldn't move. Her face grew pale and she started to shake. This couldn't be happening to her. What could she do? Slowly large tears rolled down her cheeks and she began to sob in earnest. Never had she felt so alone. No one could ever have been in her position before—a rejected bride.

Belfort closed the door and felt he was closing off a part of his life. He was willing to keep his bargain but he wouldn't have his solicitor taking advantage of him and making a fool out of him. The man had made much of her beauty. True the word had come from solicitors in America, but the man's sources had never been wrong before.

His temper was up and without pausing to think or try to straighten things out he called his valet and started to pack. He knew there would be a great deal of gossip in the servant's hall so he told Smythe he'd have to return immediately to London on Admiralty business. Everyone knew of his importance and no one would question that even though it came at an inopportune time. He needed to get away.

His thoughts kept returning to the repugnant figure of his bald bride and the haunted look in her sunken eyes. He must deal with this crisis but he couldn't face it now.

Possibly her appearance would improve with time, but he had never seen anyone look nearer to death.

CHAPTER 8

Samantha was riding a spirited black mare, its playfulness reminding her of her horses at home. The day was bright. The sun shone down, bringing a welcome warmth. Flowers were in full bloom and the green countryside was a delight to her eyes. In fact, she was as happy as she'd been for a long while. She let her mind wander and it meandered back to what she had termed "that awful night."

A maid had brought the wedding supper and gave her a pitying stare. She had forced herself to take a bite but it almost choked her. She toyed with the food so it would look as if it had been eaten. The look the maid had given her convinced her that the servants knew everything, and it had taken all the fortitude she had been able to muster to face the duke's household the morning after the wedding. Mary corrected her mistaken supposition in the morning, but it had been a very sleepless night.

She met the countess at breakfast and under those sharp eyes and quick intelligence she was unable to keep her secret. In the privacy of her room she unburdened herself to the old lady. Surprisingly, she was most understanding. The countess, the older sister of the former duke, had refused all advantageous offers and had married a Frenchman, Count Armand d'Avigny, against her brother's wishes but had never regretted it. For years she had lived in France but at the count's death she had returned home to England and lived luxuriously in London. She knew her nephew, how strong and determined he could be, and that great pride of his. She had consoled Samantha to wait and see if he returned and to face him with her problem. Failing that, she advised Samantha to wait until she was herself again and go to London after him. The countess would be glad to have Samantha as her guest. A smile lit Samantha's face as she thought of the domineering old lady. She had an air of resolution about her that was difficult to gainsay.

Her thoughts traveled on to Mr. Maitland, the Belfort estate manager, who had presented himself to her and told her the duke wanted a clinic built on the estate, near the tenant's cottages, and she was to ask for what she needed. She was now riding there to see what had been accomplished as she was anxious to get started.

Her thoughts completed their circle and she again found herself thinking about the duke and wondering what he was doing. Six weeks had gone by and still there was no word from him. Thinking of him brought on a deep depression and so she wrenched her thoughts in another direction.

She had put on weight already and her hair was growing faster than she'd have believed possible. The most surprising part of that was that it was coming in black and showed signs of being more than just wavy, almost tightly curled.

Hank had left the morning after the wedding to go back to Helmcrest and luckily didn't know that there was trouble. She had managed a smile and said all that was proper. Thank goodness her brother was an early riser and was anxious to return to his estates.

Hank had returned to Helmcrest in great good humor. The wedding was over and he approved of Belfort. He was sure this marriage was going to work. Samantha would have what she always wanted, a chance to heal the sick and a good husband. This left him free to go about his own affairs.

Finally, everything seemed to be running like clockwork at Helmcrest. Hank had taken weeks to familiarize himself with his estates and how they were run. Clifford, the manager, was doing an excellent job and there seemed to be little for Hank to do at present.

He decided that he would like to explore the countryside and he didn't mean to do it by train. He would saddle Diablo, put on his old saddlebags to carry a few necessities, and take off.

When he told Smythe what he needed the old man was distressed. "Please, m'lord, it's not fitting your consequence to ride about the countryside this way. What will the gentry think?" he pleaded. He knew what was due the Earl of Helmcrest.

Hank placed an affectionate hand on the old man's arm. "No one knows me and I don't intend to announce my title everywhere I go. I'll just be plain Hank Salsbury."

Smythe shook his head and grumbled softly to himself. He was going to have a bigger job than he'd planned to teach the earl his position, but he started selecting apparel he felt was necessary.

Hank, seeing the pile of clothing that was accumulating, said gently, "Hold it. I won't need all that. In fact there will not be enough room."

Smythe was astounded. "But m'lord, I've only put out absolute necessities!"

Hank laughed. "You should see how I travel about on our ranch at home. This is real luxury."

He proceeded to select a few items, which he stuffed into the saddlebags he had brought up to his room. He changed his clothing, putting on a comfortable pair of buckskins and a jacket.

Looking at the earl, the elderly valet shook his head but had to admit that even the old clothes couldn't disguise his erect carriage and aristocratic air. Thinking of the old earl, the valet thought how proud he would have been of this grandson.

Hank felt in his pocket to make sure he had a few bank notes and some change. With that he raced down the stairs like a schoolboy just let out for recess and whistled his way to the stables. England might not be so bad after all.

Peters had been successful in saddling Diablo but disapproved of this western saddle, the likes of which he had never seen before.

Hank assured the groom that this was the only one the horse would tolerate and so the man had to be satisfied. He swung himself into the saddle quickly and Diablo went into his morning routine and from the smile on Hank's face Peters could tell he enjoyed every minute of it.

Hank trotted down the path with the intention of acquainting himself with the terrain. He wound his way through narrow paths and lanes. He had a feeling of peace and contentment as he passed through the open fields and meadows. It was like shaking off his responsibilities for a while and becoming just plain Hank again.

It was about noon on the third day when he saw he was coming into a village. There was no sign of a train station and so he realized it must be a very small place. He walked Diablo down the dusty road and seeing an inn pulled up before it. He had just swung down when his attention was caught by a soft cry.

A young girl had evidently come out of a shop ahead and a heavy-set man was barring her way. As Hank watched, the man attempted to take the girl in his arms and she repulsed him with all her might. That was enough for Hank. In a few quick steps he reached the assailant and caught him by the shoulder. With an iron grip he spun him around. He caught a glimpse of a startled look on the man's face before Hank's doubled fist caught him flush on the chin.

The man stretched his length in the road. Hank stood over him waiting for him to get up. He scrutinized the figure before him, the long aristocratic face, the thin nostrils, the elegant clothes, and found that he didn't like a thing about the man.

Hank watched the girl pick up a basket she had dropped in the struggle and then run to a pony cart that was tied at the hitching post. He returned his attention to the man he'd knocked down.

That young sprig of nobility got slowly to his feet, his eyes glinting through narrow slits, and his rage out of control. "How dare you!" he sputtered as he put a hand gingerly to his chin. He looked Hank over, and seeing the old clothes and noting the horse a few feet away, came to the erroneous conclusion he was dealing with a raw country bumpkin. "I'll have you horsewhipped," he cried. "Do you realize who I am? I am Lord Entwhistle and I own most of the land about here." He paused to get his breath. "If you were only a gentleman, I'd challenge you to a duel."

Hank took this all in with amusement. "Duel?" he asked politely. "I thought the queen had outlawed those little games. However, if you must bandy names about I believe I am a trifle higher than you. I am the Earl of Helmcrest!" He stood erectly, a hand on each hip, waiting to see how this news was taken.

It stopped Entwhistle cold in his tracks, then his ferretlike eyes showed a gleam of disbelief. "Now you are impersonating your betters," he cried. "Well, this isn't the end of this—I will see to it!" He staggered away to a showy chestnut and slowly mounted, shaking a fist at Hank, who stood there with a satisfied grin on his face.

He had enjoyed himself more than he had since he had come to England. If this man was a sample of English nobility he was sorry for it. Then the humor of it struck him. He'd said he was going to travel incognito and the first thing he did was to announce his consequence. He shook his head. Then he thought of the girl who had been the cause of it all. She had not looked back but kept her attention focused on the road ahead. He didn't blame her for running away. She might have been afraid that she was being thrown from the frying pan to the fire. His impression was that of a young girl, not very tall and exceedingly graceful. He would like to have made her acquaintance and assured her that she had nothing to fear from him and, if she wished, he would take up the matter further with Lord Entwhistle.

Accordingly, he entered the building she had just left and found it to be a chemist's shop. An elderly man stood behind the counter, a small linen apron at his waist. A long drooping mustache twitched as he spoke. "What may I do for you?"

"Well, for first things, why didn't you go to that young lady's rescue?" Hank eyed the man intently.

The chemist didn't seem the least bit discomfited. "Seeing as how you took care of it mighty handily I didn't feel as I was needed," he answered calmly. "Besides, it doesn't pay to get on the wrong side of Lord Entwhistle. He can be a bad enemy."

"You'd let a lady be molested?" Hank felt his temper rising.

"Nay, he was only funning. No harm in it."

"We have different views in Arizona Territory. We respect women there," he retorted. "However, what I want is the young lady's name and where she lives. I'd like to present my apologies if I frightened her."

The chemist looked him up and down. He hadn't heard the conversation outside, for the door was closed, but he had seen the action that had taken place and he too thought this was a countryman. He seemed to give careful thought to the situation before speaking. Then, as if he'd come to a decision, he said, "That was Miss Douglas. Her pa is the local doctor. Take the first lane to the left and you'll see a white cottage with a fence around it. His sign is on the gate."

Thanking the man, Hank went back to his horse and slowly trotted down the main street until he came to the described lane.

He swung down and looped a rein over the fence. He noticed the yard was neat and the house in good order. After knocking lightly on the door, he waited with anticipation. The door swung open, held back by the young girl he had seen at the chemist's.

When she saw who stood there her eyes grew large and she caught her lip between her teeth. Her chestnut hair framed a piquant face. She stood studying the handsome figure before her. It took her only a moment to remember her manners.

"Did you come to see the doctor?" she asked. They very seldom had visitors but this broad-shouldered young man certainly didn't look as if he were in need of medical assistance. It had been startling to watch him knock Entwhistle down. She thought he must be the strongest man anywhere.

Hank fingered his hat while an engaging smile lit his features. He watched her intently, thinking her a very special young lady. Her smile would light a darkened room. "I didn't mean to bother you, miss. I just stopped by to see if you were all right. I must apologize if I frightened you but I couldn't let that bully get by with such behavior."

This explanation brought a slight inclination of her head. "Won't you come in?" she invited. She was tingling with excitement. No one of such strong character or charm had come her way before. The doctor's office was often busy even into the night, but this man was different. He looked to her as if he had come out of a fairy story. She pushed such thoughts aside and gestured toward a chair in the living room.

He stepped over the doorstep into the modest parlor, which was scrupulously clean. He noticed that it was a comfortable room, the furniture old but sturdy.

Dr. Douglas must have heard the knock for he came hurrying into the room. When he saw Hank he sighed. He didn't like to miss a patient. They were not too plentiful, at least the paying ones.

"Good morning, sir," he said. "I see Marianne is helping you." He looked Hank over carefully and liked what he saw but was afraid this wasn't a patient.

Marianne turned to her father. "He is calling to see if I got home safely. This is the man I told you about." Marianne's eyes lit up as she spoke to her father.

"My dear fellow," exclaimed the doctor as he came forward to shake Hank's hand, "I can't tell you how happy I am to be able to thank you for your service to my daughter." He paused for a second. "I don't believe I caught your name." He waited expectantly.

"I'm Hank Salsbury, sir. Glad to be of service." As Hank gripped the old doctor's hand he noticed how frail he was. He must have had Marianne late in life or his physical condition made him appear older than he was. It seemed an effort for him to get around. The color of his skin had almost a bluish cast and his breathing was labored. Hank wondered what Samantha would say if she saw him.

He took the chair that was offered him and prepared to make himself agreeable. He liked what he saw in Marianne. He had never met a girl who had interested him before but this girl stirred a mixture of emotions in him. Clearly, she and her father had catalogued him as a provincial gentleman, from foreign parts. He wasn't about to proclaim his title but wondered if they had already heard about the Americans at Helmcrest Hall. Then he remembered there was no train stopping here and it must be a full twenty miles to Crestwood. So perhaps they hadn't heard. Then, too, he might be mistaken for an American groom who came over with the new earl! He chuckled to himself. He would like to interest this girl in plain Hank Salsbury and with that thought in mind he made himself comfortable and tried tactfully to gain some background on her while telling her of his adventures in Arizona.

There was a knock on the door and Marianne went to answer. She brought in a young man whose appearance proclaimed him a farmer. He was holding his right side and sweat was pouring down his face. He was evidently in great pain.

"Please, Dr. Douglas, can ye do sumthung fer me?" he gasped.

Dr. Douglas jumped up, took the boy by the arm, and led him into his office, which adjoined the parlor.

Marianne's eyes followed her father and the boy as they left the room. Hank could see that she was worried.

"Is your father ill?" he enquired.

That brought a startled reaction. "How did you know? Does it show so plainly?" She was so sweet in her anxiety and her long, curling lashes lay so beautifully on her cheeks as she closed her eyes in her distress that he wanted to pick her up and hug her. He realized he was smitten badly.

"No," he answered her gently. "I happen to have a sister who is a doctor and some of it has rubbed off on me." His gaze caressed her tenderly.

Marianne became eager, clasping her hands before her. "Is your sister with you?"

"Not exactly, but we live not too far apart," he answered cautiously. He wasn't sure what was in her mind.

Marianne looked around as if to be sure her father hadn't come back into the room and lowered her voice. "You see, for some time now my papa hasn't been well. He went up to London to see a specialist and he wouldn't tell me what he was told. All I know is he's been very worried since then and he seems to go at a slower pace than usual. What he desperately needs is someone to help him with some of his difficult cases." Her big brown eyes were like softest velvet.

This was more than Hank was bargaining for. He couldn't answer for Samantha. "I'll be glad to tell my sister about your father's predicament and see what she has to say." He felt as if he were letting her down.

At that moment, the young man came out of the office and Marianne let him out. He was clutching a small bottle of medicine in one hand.

Dr. Douglas followed shortly and joined Hank and his daughter. He shook his head. There was a line of wrinkles showing on his forehead and his step dragged as he sought a large easy chair. Hank, watching him closely, saw a fine bead of perspiration around his receding hairline. It was clear to Hank the man was in pain.

"Is there something I can get you?" asked Hank solicitously.

Marianne gave him a grateful look but almost imperceptibly shook her head. There was nothing anyone could do. She was worried about her father and tried to push back thoughts of how she could possibly manage if something happened to him.

Dr. Douglas gave Hank a tired smile. "Thank you, my boy, I appreciate your offer but this is something I must live with." He placed a hand over his heart for a moment as if to stop the pain and then with effort said, "That poor boy will probably die if he can't find someone else to help him. He's beyond my ability." A little groan escaped him. "I don't usually talk about my patients, but you'll never see him again, so I can tell you I think it's a case of typhlitis."

Hank sat up alertly. He had heard Sam talk about that. "Isn't that a condition that responds only to surgical removal?"

The fine old eyes rested on him. "You're an intelligent young man. Where did you hear of typhlitis?" He was more than curious. He hadn't heard Hank tell Marianne his sister was a doctor.

"My sister, who is a doctor, has sometimes discussed new things in medicine with me. We live on a horse ranch in Arizona Territory and it is often a case of life or death to have basic medical knowledge."

Dr. Douglas took this in, never questioning the astounding fact that a woman was a doctor. All that interested him was what she knew about typhlitis. "Is there a possibility that she has seen the surgery?" He grew excited at the thought. "I'm unable to go to her. Do you think she could make the trip over here to me?" He realized he was asking what might be embarrassing to them. Perhaps they didn't have the means to make the trip. Judging from the way his visitor looked and the glimpse of the horse he saw at his gate, he wasn't too well endowed with worldly goods.

Hank, with acute perception, guessed what was in the old doctor's mind. "We can manage without any hardship to us," he replied. "First, I must see if she is home and how soon I can get her." He paused as a thought struck him. "How long do you think your patient can wait?"

The doctor shook his head. "I've no idea. All I could give him was laudanum for pain and suggest he not eat anything for twenty-four hours —merely take sips of water." He rubbed one hand over his head. "I don't know what else to do."

Hank stood up. "It sounds to me as if time is important so if you'll excuse me I'll start back. In any case if you'll permit, I shall return here tomorrow." He gave Marianne a warm look that said as plainly as words that he found her extremely attractive.

It brought a faint blush to her cheeks and a curve to her enticing lips. This was a new experience for her. "I'm sure you will be welcome," she said demurely. Her heart seemed to be having some trouble. It had started to pound. She took a deep breath and hoped no one noticed. She had much to ponder as she closed the door. A slight sigh escaped her and she wondered what the morrow would bring.

Hank left the cottage in a daze. He was conscious that the grass looked greener than when he came and the birds were singing a sweeter song. He had heard tell of love at first sight but he never thought it would happen to him. He knew almost nothing about Marianne except that she was the girl for him and he intended to win her.

CHAPTER 9

Diablo had been wanting a good run ever since he had left Arizona and he finally got his wish. Hank let him go and he bolted across the fields, hardly seeming to touch the ground. He sailed over fences with room to spare and was hugely enjoying himself. In that, he wasn't alone, for Hank had missed a good ride and this was an excellent excuse.

Hank loved this horse for his amazing stamina. This was the type of animal the American government wanted to buy. He had chosen Diablo for his own, knowing the distance his mount could travel and his courageous unbroken spirit. It was this that carried him home in near record time, just under two hours. Villages and cottages went by unnoticed as Hank pushed his mount onward.

Peters, having been called by a stableboy as the earl approached, came out to meet him, his face showing surprise at the speed at which his master had ridden into the yard.

Hank threw him the reins and demanded another horse be saddled at once. That did it. Peters couldn't stand it.

"If ye please, yer lordship, be summat tha matter?"

"Everything's fine! The day was wonderful. I'm feeling better than I ever did, but I need that horse right now." He finished on a stern note.

Peters disappeared, flinging orders as he went, and stable hands scattered, obeying. Within a surprisingly short time a powerful gray was brought out to the earl.

Hank eyed the flat saddle and it brought a grin. He might as well ride bareback but he supposed, seeing he'd no need to rope from it, it should serve.

It was late in the day when he arrived at Belfort Castle. A groom came running to take the gray. As Hank swung down he gave him a pat. This was a good horse and he had relished the ride.

"Tell me, can you direct me to the duchess?" he asked.

The groom looked at him, noting the dusty clothes that had a country look, and was about to snub him when Hank forestalled him.

"I'm her brother, the Earl of Helmcrest," he announced, seeing the disparaging look the groom was giving him.

That put an entirely different expression on the groom's face. He was a snob, like so many of his fellow countrymen. The nobility had their peculiarities and who was he to say anything? "She be in tha rose garden, m'lord," he answered with servility.

Hank sauntered off in what he hoped was the direction of the gardens and, as he wasn't stopped, he concluded he'd made the right choice.

Behind the castle and extending around to the east side stretched a huge green lawn that had been freshly scythed. Hank walked on around to the west side where there were many gardeners tending the very formal rows of flowers. They were laid out carefully, executing a precise pattern, and the colors came in waves. All shades of yellows, pinks, oranges, reds, blues, greens, and violets dazzled the eye as they stood in stately array. Hedges surrounded this special place and a small fountain and statue were the focal point at the far end of the garden. He passed this delightful spot and moved on to where he could see roses, still blooming at the end of the season. As he came to the lovely curved beds wreathed in a rainbow of roses, he recognized his sister bending down cutting them and placing them in a basket she carried over her arm. From this distance she looked lovely. Her figure was graceful, but there was a line of strength in her. Regardless of custom he called to her.

Recognizing his voice, she dropped the basket and ran to meet him. There was a definite spring in her step as she hurried toward him. Her face was radiant as she flung herself into his arms and placed her head against his shoulder. "Oh, Hank," she cried, "I've missed you so."

Hank patted her gently. He was sure there was nothing wrong with her now. He should have been over sooner but had felt it was better to let the newlyweds have time together without guests. "I thought it was better if you were alone for the first while," he explained.

That brought on a sob, and Hank, hearing it, held her at arm's length to see what was troubling her. She had looked so happy to see him and now there were big tears that slowly rolled down her cheeks. Even with those unaccustomed tears, she was looking like herself. Her face had filled out, the texture of her skin was as smooth and soft as a magnolia petal, and her eyes were large and lustrous. All she needed was to get rid of that awful wig.

"What's the trouble, Sam?" he enquired.

At the sound of her pet name she sniffed and managed a watery smile. She controlled her breathing and gulped. "It's Belfort. He left me directly after the marriage. He opened the door to my bedchamber and caught me without my wig. I thought it was Mary, my maid." Here the tears started again. "He was so repulsed by my appearance he just packed and left." Her shoulders were still shaking but she spoke more calmly now. "He told the staff he'd been called to London on state affairs in connection with the war in the United States. Everyone seemed to feel it came before his marriage, so nothing was thought of it."

"Poor Sam! You've had bad luck. But now you are looking like yourself." He was afraid to ask about her hair.

That brought a smile and it made her look enchanting. His obvious efforts to keep his eyes from her hair brought a small chuckle. "You want to know how my hair is growing. I am no longer a Little Eva. I have become Topsy! My hair is black and curly. In another month's time it should be long enough to dispense with the wig but you won't know me." She sparkled at the thought.

"Belfort is in for a surprise when he comes home." He thought he could understand the other man's feelings but resented the treatment given his sister. Well, there were exciting times ahead. Sam wouldn't take this sitting down and as soon as she dispensed with that awful wig he could count on things becoming lively. "How about your clinic? Was anything done?" He had reason to be interested in her medical career, now more than ever.

"Belfort kept his word on that. Our estate manager, Mr. Maitland, has had a small building erected for me and I'm in the midst of ordering furniture and medical supplies for it." There was a happy note in her voice. "I will be able to open it soon and see what I can do for the people hereabouts."

"Well, I know of a medical problem concerning a young man not too far away that needs immediate attention and I've come to ask your advice."

Samantha was interested immediately. "What's the problem? How did you happen to come across it?" Her fears and troubles were cast aside for the moment and she listened intently.

"I was riding around the country when I happened to meet a young girl whose father is the local doctor. He mentioned he had a patient he could do nothing for. He said he thought the man had typhlitis."

Samantha grasped the few details of the brief explanation that was so typical of her brother. The word typhlitis caught her attention. "This doctor you met—he's not a surgeon?" she asked.

"I don't know. He could be, but he has a problem of his own. His skin has a bluish color and he has difficulty in breathing. He walks very slowly and it seems to be quite an effort for him. I suspect that on occasion he has severe pain as I saw him having a spell." He watched Samantha closely for her reaction.

Samantha's eyes narrowed thoughtfully. "I would need to examine him to make sure but it sounds like a heart condition. If what you say is correct, he is in no condition to take on any surgery."

Hank nodded. "That's what I thought." He tipped his head back while he thought this over. "How soon can you be ready to go to Whistlehurst?" he asked abruptly.

"Me?" She was a little shocked. She hadn't even heard of it so it must be some distance away. "I can't just go and burst in on a doctor. Besides, it's customary to be asked." Even while she was saying this she was wishing she could go. This was a great opportunity to show what she could do. From the sound of it the patient could die without surgery and the old doctor was not capable of performing it. She sighed regretfully.

Hank, watching her, knew exactly what was going through her mind. "Well, pack your bags. We're on our way! Dr. Douglas asked particularly for you."

Samantha flung her arms around her brother and hugged him fiercely. "You're the best brother in the world." Grabbing his hand, she led him through the flowered paths to a side door to the castle. She was flushed and excited as they flew up the stairs.

Unfortunately, by this time it was too late in the day to be able to get ready and go to Whistlehurst. Already the sun was starting to wane. They both agreed it would be best to leave early in the morning. Then the question of their method of travel entered the conversation. Hank wanted to ride but felt that Samantha should go in a carriage. She refused to listen to the suggestion. Many a time they had ridden much farther than he was proposing and under very different circumstances. The thought of riding a horse again for that distance was exciting to her. They could manage with Hank's saddlebags and her doctor's bag could be tied on behind that western saddle. They would need to take a packhorse as far as Helmcrest, for they knew that none of this English-bred stock would tolerate such use. Diablo would manage that more than easily. The two of them would look like gypsies but what fun! More than she'd had in a long time.

The next morning Samantha met Hank in the small breakfast room dressed in one of her Arizona divided skirts. She had found them very useful. The skirt came to just above her ankles and was so full no one could tell what it was until she mounted.

Hank, looking up from his selection of a large variety of dishes, nodded his approval. To him, this meant she was planning to ride astride. Very few ladies had accepted this idea, thinking it far too daring, but it was practical. He looked her over very critically and seeing the lovely color in her cheeks, the sparkle in her dark eyes, and the roguish smile on her lips, felt he had his sister back. If only she could dispense with that wig!

"Good morning, Hank." A lilt in her voice proclaimed she was anticipating a great day. There was an air of vitality about her that was singularly alluring. She helped herself to a hearty breakfast, making short work of it. Her mind was already on the medical issue awaiting her.

"Have you left word where you are going?" asked Hank.

An impish grin lit her features. "Not exactly. I've said I'll be gone for a day or two and that we are going to Helmcrest and as I'm in my brother's company no one need worry." She had told the truth, just not all of it.

Hank was thinking about the possible return of the duke but he could see she didn't think of that. Or if she did she thought it a good idea for him to have to wait. That sounded like her. He foresaw interesting times ahead. The duke would get more than he bargained for. That thought brought a smile to his face that gave him a raffish look.

Samantha, looking at him, wondered how any girl could help falling in love with him. The trouble was that so far he hadn't found a girl who in any way interested him. Perhaps this English girl he mentioned . . .

At the stables they found their horses saddled and waiting for them. Hank decided that the duke was very well served. He walked around Samantha's horse, noticing the nice long-legged look of the mare. She was well muscled and would probably prove she had an ample amount of stamina. She wasn't like their horses at home but she appeared to be one that could go the distance.

Samantha put her toe into the stirrup and swung herself easily into the saddle, leaving the groom and stableboy standing there in astonishment. Her request for a man's saddle had caused much talk in the stable but when they saw her mount they knew this was nothing new to her. She walked her horse up and down while Hank roped their baggage on an old mare that had been selected by the Belfort groom, Jenkins, as the one most likely to permit it.

At last they were ready, Hank leading the mare. The groom was puzzled by the rejection of the carriage to take the luggage to Helmcrest but knew better than to question the duchess. The duke had given specific orders that what Her Grace wanted she was to get. He shook his head as if to wipe these unheard of proceedings from his mind and then ordered the rest of the hands back to work.

It was a beautiful day for a ride. Fall was upon them, but the day was still warm, the fields green, and flowers still blooming riotously. There was a slight breeze that rustled the leaves on the trees. They rode in silence, each enjoying being out. It was only a few miles to Helmcrest and they seemed to pass very quickly. When they saw the hall ahead it seemed to be like a jewel in the sun, the panes of the windows winking with light.

"We do have a beautiful place," Samantha remarked. Then she thought, It isn't mine anymore. It belongs to Hank.

Hank looked down at her as their horses trotted toward the great gates and seemed to read her thoughts. "Remember, this is your home too if you ever find you need it."

She gave him a grateful smile. But if she couldn't work out her marriage with Belfort she would return to Arizona. England had too many painful memories. She imagined him everywhere. When she had been so despondent after he left all she seemed to be able to do was to think about how he would look here and there and just everywhere. There was a tightening in her stomach as she felt her loss. She had never really had him, except for that fleeting moment during the ceremony. How she wished she could go back to that terrible day and change everything. She couldn't; what was done was done and there could be no going back, but she had a plan. She had been turning it around in her mind for some time now.

If this didn't work out the way she intended it to—well, she would think about it later. Somehow the way Hank spoke now, it seemed he wasn't thinking of returning anymore. He had changed his mind. Giving it some thought, she came to the conclusion that Dr. Douglas' daughter must have considerable charm.

They turned into the drive that led to the stables. Here Hank gave quick orders for Diablo to be saddled and set about getting his saddlebags, which he had carried up to his room along with Samantha's things. Between the two of them they sorted out what they wanted and filled the saddlebags, deciding to rope her medical bag on behind. They now had two sets of grooms and stable hands talking about those odd Americans but it didn't bother them one bit.

They alternately cantered, trotted, and walked their horses, taking care they didn't overtax them. To Samantha this was like a little bit of heaven. She hadn't realized how much she had missed a good ride.

When the little village of Whistlehurst came into view Samantha was enthralled. She liked its size. Somehow it reminded her of home, although this place was a lush green with huge old trees. There was just one main street here too. As they rode down the street Hank pointed out the chemist's and the local greengrocer. There was only a handful of small shops but enough to take care of the needs of the few residents.

They made the turn to the Douglas house and Hank anxiously scanned it, hoping for a view of Marianne. There was an old wagon with a horse that had seen better days tied up at the gate.

"Dr. Douglas must have a patient," said Hank as he dismounted. Samantha swung down easily and tied her mount to the white fence beside the gate. Before she could knock, the door was opened. Samantha saw a young girl, a young lady she corrected herself, wearing a sprigged muslin dress that set off her trim figure. Samantha could tell the dress was not new, but the attitude of the young lady wearing it was to be admired. She was shy, but poised and welcoming. She liked her on sight, knowing she was just right for Hank. Her brown eyes seemed to sparkle even more as she saw Hank stride up the walk.

Hank was loaded down with their things and his face broke into a charming smile as he saw Marianne. His eyes almost caressed her.

At the light in his eyes Samantha knew she was right and that he was caught. He had never looked like this before.

Marianne had welcomed them and shyly ushered them in when there came a cry of pain from the next room. They all stopped to listen.

"It's Mr. Dobbs," Marianne explained. "He couldn't stand the pain any longer and managed to drive himself here. Papa is with him in the examining room." Her eyes were all for Hank and the two of them seemed to be oblivious to Samantha's presence.

Hank finally rescued his head from the clouds and presented his sister as Samantha Salsbury Benham. She refused to be known by her title. When she was accepted by the duke then she'd accept her title. The girls sized each other up quickly, each liking what she saw.

"Would you like to join Papa?" Marianne asked in a warm soft voice.

Ever since the first cry Samantha had restrained herself from rushing in to help. "Thank you, I'd be very happy to," she said with a deceptive air of calmness, and lost no time in following Marianne, carrying her little black bag with her.

At their entrance the old doctor rose to his feet. Samantha, giving him a professional eye, made a snap judgment that Hank was probably right. All signs pointed to a possible heart problem.

Dr. Douglas was genuinely pleased to welcome Samantha and she liked the old doctor immediately. This was a very likable family. "Can I be of any assistance?" she asked him.

"Is it true you have seen an operation for typhlitis?" he countered eagerly.

Samantha smiled warmly. He was touching in his anxiety. "I have not

only seen the operation I have assisted at two and performed one myself."
It was a statement of fact. She was not boasting.

She took in the man groaning on the small iron bed. His face was
flushed and his eyes were filled with pain. His head rolled from side to
side in an effort to rid himself of the agony.

"May I?" she asked, and without waiting pulled down the covers and
exposed his abdomen. Her long sensitive fingers lightly examined his right
lower quadrant and found it extremely tender, the area close to the right
hipbone being rigid. She checked his pulse and then after pulling her
stethoscope from her bag, listened to his heart. Dr. Douglas stood by
watching her intently, patiently waiting until she was finished.

Two pairs of eyes met above the patient and Samantha nodded. She felt
Dr. Douglas was right in his diagnosis.

"Will you operate, Doctor?" Dr. Douglas asked Samantha. At the title
she flushed with pleasure. This man of medicine accepted her.

"How about the responsibility?" she asked. "After all, I'm not licensed
in England."

"If you won't object, suppose we list the operating doctor as myself and
you as my assistant? There could be no trouble over that." He sounded a
little apologetic. He didn't want the glory of the surgery but he didn't
mind taking the responsibility if it failed. His object was to protect her.

Samantha was interested only in the patient before them. If necessary,
she'd face the responsibility herself. Dr. Douglas reminded her of their
doctor at home, a real man, down to earth.

"Have you a table we can use?" Her mind had already gone ahead to
the equipment she would need.

"I have a small surgery next door to this room," he said with simple
pride and opened the door to show her. She saw a long wooden table,
looking well scrubbed, an old white metal cabinet with a glass door and
shelves with various instruments on them. The room was immaculate.

"This is fine. You must have done many surgeries here." There was a
questioning note in her voice.

Dr. Douglas smiled sadly at her. "Up to a couple of years ago I was
kept quite busy but I've had to turn down everything but simple setting of
bones or suturing up a few cuts."

Samantha nodded her understanding but said nothing. This wasn't the
time to go into his medical problems. She picked up her bag and started to
take her instruments from it. They were old favorites and she felt comfortable using them. She pulled out her needles and suture and then picked
up her bottle of chloroform. It was almost empty. She had forgotten to
have it refilled.

"Doctor, do you have a supply of chloroform on hand?" she asked anxiously.

He pursed his lips for a moment and then nodded. It was a long time since he had used any. He went to another cabinet, which contained various bottles, and after searching for a moment pulled out one that was empty. "I'm afraid I haven't refilled mine either," he apologized. "However, the village chemist usually keeps some on hand for me. I could run up and get some."

Samantha wouldn't hear of that. "You'll have plenty to do to get the patient ready." She glanced quickly about the room. "Do you have a couple of large pans that can be filled with water? I like to boil my instruments and soak my bandages in boiling water."

Dr. Douglas was interested. Most of the medical men didn't go to that trouble. They didn't feel it was necessary. In fact, some felt it a mark of their profession to be splattered with the patient's blood, the more the better.

"We have a daily maid that comes in and does our cleaning and washing. I'll get her to put the water on the stove." He had an open mind and was willing to have her show him any new ideas.

As he turned to leave she called after him. "Hank will carry the patient out here and put him on the table for us. He can also undress and bathe him."

That stopped Dr. Douglas. "Bathe him?" he questioned.

Samantha smiled happily. "This is one of the things I learned from the great Dr. Semmelweiss. I think it works."

Dr. Douglas was agreeable and continued to the kitchen where she could hear him calling the maid.

Suddenly Samantha realized that she couldn't hear Hank and Marianne. She entered the small parlor and found them sitting close together, evidently in deep conversation. They were so engrossed neither looked up as she walked over to them. This amused her. She had never seen her brother so smitten. "Hank," she said, and grinned at his startled look. "I need you to carry our patient to the operating table and to bathe him for us. I have to go to the chemist's and see if I can get some chloroform."

Marianne was blushing very becomingly but was ready to come to her aid. "I'll be glad to run up and get some for you," she offered.

"Thank you, but I'd like to check it and also see what else he might have that we can use." She started toward the door when an idea hit her. "Hank, would you mind if I rode Diablo to the chemist's? It's not far but I want to go as quickly as possible. Besides, I haven't ridden him for a long time. Do you think he'll still know me?" She tipped her head mischievously at him. Diablo was supposed to be a one-man horse, but she had made friends with him and had on occasion ridden him. He tolerated her but it was Hank he loved.

"If you think you can ride him I have no objection. I'll walk out with you and remind him of his manners." He rose from the chair and gave Marianne a hand to assist her. As his hand touched hers he felt a shock run through him. Still holding her hand, he led her outside to Diablo, Samantha following them.

Marianne was trying, with very little determination, to pull her hand free but Hank ignored the little pull, merely grasping her firmly. Judging from the light in Marianne's eyes she really wasn't upset about the fact that a man, almost a stranger, was holding her hand.

Both horses were standing patiently by the fence but at Hank's approach Diablo lifted his head and softly whinnied.

Hank pulled his ear and stroked his nose. Then he introduced Marianne to him and that intelligent animal nodded his head as if in acknowledgment of it.

Samantha went up and talked softly to him, patting him, then adjusted the stirrups to fit her.

"Stand back," Samantha commanded as she put a toe into the stirrup and swung up gracefully into the saddle. She was prepared for some objections but Diablo either had had his exercise for the day or he was being a gentleman. He moved off as sedately as an old plow horse.

"The clown!" cried Hank delightedly. His horse amused him no end. Taking Marianne's arm in his he returned to the house, where he regretfully released her. He had work to do.

Samantha lightly kicked Diablo into a canter. He had such an easy gait, it was like sitting in a rocking chair. A light breeze ruffled her wig, making her feel good. Things were beginning to look up for her. She pulled Diablo in as she neared the chemist's and, swinging down, dropped the reins.

She found the chemist friendly and anxious to help. When he heard she needed chloroform for Dr. Douglas he was very interested. "Is he well enough to operate again?" he asked.

This was a question she disliked to answer. "There is another doctor to help him," she evaded.

The chemist's eyes brightened. "Do you mean to say we've a new man I haven't heard about?"

"Not exactly. It's kind of like a wolf in sheep's clothing." Then she almost laughed aloud at the ludicrous expression on the poor man's face.

He was completely at sea. He cleared his throat a few times and then viewed her over his spectacles. "You must be an American."

He had apparently placed her accent. "As a matter of fact, I was raised in the States." This was all she meant to volunteer.

She picked up the bottle he offered her, reading the label. This would do nicely. She looked over his stock of bandages and herbs. She noticed he had laudanum on hand and added that to her purchase. She left the shop quite happily, looking forward to the surgery, her mind busy with the details of the operation ahead. She had almost reached Diablo when she became aware of a shadow falling over her. Startled, she looked up into the face of Lord Entwhistle. There was a lustful look in his ferretlike eyes as he flamboyantly introduced himself. He clapped his hands together as he looked her up and down. "Well, well," he exclaimed, "a new girl in town. No one told me. Where are you working, m'dear?" he asked, as he licked his lips.

Samantha's first reaction was of anger. How dare he accost her! Then it dawned on her that he thought she was of the lower classes and as such was subject to such treatment. That brought a martial light to her eye and she became icily calm. Becoming aware she was clutching two bottles, one in each hand, she pushed them into the capacious pockets of her divided skirt.

She took a deep breath and then announced with dignity, "I'll thank you to keep your distance." Her chin came up as he continued to appraise her.

Finally Entwhistle laughed, a raucous sound. Why the chit had spirit, which was more than the other village maidens had. He liked it. It would make the sport more interesting.

While he was busy wiping his eyes of the tears caused by his laughter with a delicate dab of his handkerchief, she quickly scanned the dusty street. There was no one in sight. She would need to use her ingenuity to help her out of this tangle. Her mind was working like lightning. If she could cross the several steps to Diablo, she knew she could get away.

Entwhistle put his handkerchief away and reached out a hand to grasp her. She hit him as hard as she could in the face. It was no mean blow, for she had well-developed muscles from helping in horse roundups and cattle drives.

Entwhistle was shocked and staggered under the blow, a red light appearing in his eyes. "Why you—you'll pay for that," he cried, as he lunged toward her.

Samantha hadn't waited to see the outcome. It was the chance she needed to close the distance to Diablo. She had only one foot in the stirrup as he lunged at her. She jerked the reins, causing Diablo to turn swiftly, knocking Entwhistle off his feet. She whistled him on and they tore down the street, Samantha bent low over Diablo's neck, making quite a spectacular exit from town.

From his position on the ground Entwhistle watched her complete her flying mount, with Diablo at a dead run. Never had he seen anything like it. No woman could mount a horse like that. He stood up and watched her disappear down the lane. Then it dawned on him that he had seen that odd horse with its atrocious saddle yesterday, right here. Country bumpkins, the lot of them. He knew what was due his consequence and he would see that he got even. Well, he'd think on it. No one was going to get away with such treatment as he'd received this day. He would send out enquiries. He didn't believe, for one minute, the title the man had used. His hand went to his cheek and he found it tender. How could a woman have that much strength? Well, she'd pay. Whoever the dolt was who had ridden the horse yesterday would be attended to so that he gave no trouble to anyone in the future. Then Entwhistle would be free to turn his attentions to this delectable morsel. Her spirit would make the breaking of her all the more enjoyable. His lips curled in satisfaction at the prospect.

Samantha pulled up in front of Dr. Douglas' and, seeing no sign of her horse, decided that Hank had put her in the stable, so she took Diablo around. She expertly pulled the saddle off to make him more comfortable, for she had no idea how long she would be. The animal seemed to give her a grateful glance. She patted him and told him how great he was. In fact, she was thinking, if it hadn't been for him, what would that dressed-up fop have done?

When she entered the house Hank met her, intending to tell her that the patient was ready when she was, but one look at those stormy features told him she had encountered trouble along the line.

"You had better sit down for a moment and tell me what has happened to upset you like this," he said quietly. She wasn't one to be disturbed easily so he knew there was something very much wrong.

"It's really nothing. Some dressed-up dude calling himself Lord Entwhistle accosted me in the street and tried to put his hands on me. He thought to dangle his title in my face." As she remembered the scene her eyes flashed and she looked magnificent.

Marianne had come into the room and had heard. Her eyes went to Hank. "He does this quite often," she murmured apologetically.

"Is there no man in this town that can put him in his place?" asked Hank angrily. "Is no young girl safe in this town?"

It was Marianne who answered him. "Unfortunately, this is really his town and all the land hereabouts. No one dares to cross him. We could all be turned out of our homes. The young girls make it a point to keep out of his way. There have been some that haven't . . ." Her voice trailed away. A spot of pink appeared in each cheek and she couldn't bring herself to mention their desperate situation.

Hank couldn't stand to see her look so sad. "Well, I shall serve notice on him, if necessary, that if he so much as looks at either one of you I'll take him to task."

Marianne's eyes had a light of adoration in them. Hank appeared to her like a knight in newly polished armor.

Samantha was more practical-minded. She knew Hank meant what he said and as far as he was concerned Lord Entwhistle would have his last piece of land, six feet long and six feet deep. No one in Arizona fooled around with women and lived to tell it. Her mind came back to the matter at hand. "Well, we've no time for that now. Let me wash my hands, get a clean apron on, and we'll see what we can do about Mr. Dobbs's typhlitis."

CHAPTER 10

When Samantha entered the small surgery she noted that everything was in place. The patient was moaning on the table; her instruments had been placed on a clean sheet on a little table that had been brought into the room. Her eyes checked the instruments over, making sure that her needles and suture were there.

"We're ready to start the anesthesia," Dr. Douglas addressed her. "Whom do you want to administer it?"

Samantha knew exactly what she wanted. Without hesitation she answered, "Doctor, it would please me if you would put him under. Then you could be free to assist me. If he starts to waken, Marianne can hold a sponge under his nose for a moment or two." Then she thought that perhaps this might be too much to ask of Marianne. Before she could ask her, Marianne, her face pale but determined, assured her she had assisted her father on many occasions and she need have no fear for her.

Hank looked at Samantha quizzically. "What do you have in mind for me?" he asked.

"When a patient goes into the first stages of anesthesia he's apt to thrash about. I'll need you to hold him steady until he's completely under." She looked at Hank's muscular frame and knew he could handle whatever came.

"Well, if it's a matter of muscle I guess I can do it." He grinned boyishly and lifted his shoulders as he looked from one face to the other.

Marianne felt her heart jump as she received a wink when he turned in her direction.

Samantha gave him a reproving glance for she knew on how many occasions he had performed rough surgery on some of their cowhands. "Doctor, if you please."

Dr. Douglas moved to the head of the table and began to drip the chloroform slowly onto a handful of lint he held under Mr. Dobbs's nose. He felt for the patient's pulse often to make sure the chloroform didn't weaken or stop the heartbeat.

Mr. Dobbs began to buck a little but Hank held him down firmly. In a few seconds he relaxed completely and Dr. Douglas stopped the chloroform. Pulling up a chair for Marianne, he instructed her to sit at the patient's head and, at a motion from Samantha, to give him a little more anesthetic. Then he took his place opposite Samantha, the small table at his right containing the instruments. He picked up a scalpel and passed it carefully to Samantha.

Feeling for a landmark, she pressed down firmly with the scalpel and a small red line appeared. She made an incision about three inches long. She nodded at Dr. Douglas and he pressed a pledget of linen against the opening and checked for bleeders. Finding one, he clamped it off, and then passed some suture to Samantha. She tied it expertly and held up the ends of the catgut suture for Dr. Douglas to cut.

"On the knot, please," she murmured, and as he cut she felt some embarrassment. Of course, he knew how to do it.

They found two others and tied them off. Then Samantha picked up her scalpel and delicately cut a little deeper. When she could see the peritoneum shining she stopped and again tied off bleeders. Picking up a curved scissors she cut through it. Dr. Douglas was watching intently. Now would tell the story. He placed a small retractor in the wound and widened the incision.

Slowly she placed a finger in the wound and felt about. Her face was grim with determination. A little sigh escaped her as she carefully pulled a loop of intestine from the incision. Attached to it was the vermiform appendix, bloated, purulent, and almost black in color. Quickly she asked for a clamp and upon receiving it clamped and ligated the appendiceal artery Then she asked for two more clamps, which she applied near the base of the appendix about a quarter of an inch apart. She tied close to the proximal end. She picked up her scalpel and cut between the clamps, the appendix with one clamp on it falling loose. Dr. Douglas caught the clamp and held up the offensive appendage.

Samantha gave it a serious scrutiny. "We were right, Doctor. This is undoubtedly the cause of his trouble. It looks as if it is ready to perforate at any moment."

Dr. Douglas agreed with her and dropped it into a waiting pan. He wanted to see how she intended to close.

"Under the circumstances, we should cauterize the appendiceal stump. Do you have a small iron heating by any chance?"

Dr. Douglas smiled. This had been one of his ideas while Samantha had gone for the chloroform. He had one on the stove and left immediately for it.

Samantha lightly touched the hot iron to the end where she had cut, and as she did so, the patient started to moan. She nodded to Marianne, who dropped a little chloroform onto the lint and placed it under his nose while Hank again held the patient firmly.

Samantha started working her way out of the wound. Using her needle with great expertise, she sutured layer after layer. When she finished she wrung out one of her hot cloth bandages, placed it over the wound, and then bound it with dry linen.

"Hopefully, he'll be all right if infection doesn't set in. Can you keep him here in bed for a few days and keep checking it?"

Dr. Douglas' eyes were shining. He had enjoyed every minute of the surgery. He had never gone into a peritoneum and to him this had been very exciting. His diagnosis was correct—it had been typhlitis and with luck the man would live.

Hank easily lifted Mr. Dobbs and took him back into the little bedroom that served as a ward. Marianne followed him and helped pull the covers over him. She volunteered to sit by him for a while to be sure he was all right.

Hank grasped her shoulder lightly with affection. This was the girl for him. He knew it without a doubt but it was too soon to speak to her father. They had known each other such a short time he would probably be refused. Besides, both Marianne and her father must believe he had nothing to offer her. Somehow, he didn't want to tell them of his title. He wanted to win her by just being himself, plain Hank Salsbury.

Samantha and Dr. Douglas set about cleaning up. Samantha put all her instruments into the pan of hot water and took them to the kitchen where she added soap. She thoroughly washed not only them but her hands and arms. Then she stripped her apron from around her chest and rolled it into a ball. That would also see the hot soap and water. She was remembering all of Dr. Semmelweiss' lectures. She hoped she had performed this operation correctly and with luck Mr. Dobbs would live. It was certain he wouldn't have if he hadn't had the surgery.

Dr. Douglas was looking frail and tired. Seeing him, Samantha suggested he rest for a while. He smiled gratefully at her. He was exhausted but he was also happy. This young girl was a doctor. She had real talent and it was a shame the way women were treated.

After Hank made sure there was nothing more he could do he went back to the little ward and, pulling up a chair, sat beside Marianne. He could hardly bear to have her out of his sight. As he looked at her innocent face he had to ride roughshod over his emotions to hold them in check, otherwise he would have swept her into his arms right there and damned the consequences. He clenched and unclenched his fists as he thought of the time he must wait before he could make her his own.

Samantha walked back into the small parlor after a last inspection to see that everything was clean and back in place. Dr. Douglas was stretched out on a sofa. She went over to him and picked up his wrist. Feeling the irregular pulse she raised an eyebrow at him. He smiled weakly back.

"You're a good doctor, Samantha," he said. "Now I suppose you can guess what my problem is."

"Do you have a fluttering sensation in your chest?" she asked. At his affirmative nod she continued, "You appear to have some kind of a heart condition." She was being cautious. She felt that it was a serious condition, one that might take him on short notice.

"I've had Sir Hector Hartpool himself look me over. He has told me there is nothing he can do and it's a matter of time." He stated it matter-of-factly. He was not looking for sympathy.

With her keen perception Samantha knew the core of his worry. "How about Marianne? Do you have some relative she can turn to?" She pulled up a chair and sat beside the old doctor, her eyes resting on his kind face.

"I have an old sister living in Scotland that might take her. My older brother, who inherited the family estates, is a clutch-fisted man and I'd not send her to him, even if he would have her. It worries me."

Samantha reached out and patted his hand affectionately. "You need not worry. Marianne can have a home with me for as long as she wants." She was thinking it wouldn't be too long before Hank carried her off and married her, but it was up to him to plead his own cause.

"Thank you, m'dear. That's most generous of you. However, if you don't have a practice, can you afford to take her in?"

Samantha felt a little ashamed of deceiving this fine old man but it wasn't her secret alone. She had Hank to consider. "I have enough to live on. Hank and I have a small place in Arizona that is ours and we have a little income from it." She was telling the truth as far as it went but just neglecting to tell him of their change in fortune. Then she had another thought. She had forgotten Hank had introduced her as Mrs. Benham, the family name of the duke. "My husband has a place just outside of Belfort village. We have ample room and I know he'd be happy to have Marianne."

At this news the doctor's eyes brightened. This was a good possibility. He liked and admired this girl and her brother seemed to be a man of principle. If Samantha's husband agreed and he was also a good man the doctor would be happy and feel his precious daughter was in good hands.

He felt as if part of his burden had been taken from his shoulders and closed his eyes as relief flooded his consciousness.

Seeing him relax, Samantha quietly got up and left him to rest. She tiptoed into the surgery to retrieve her black bag, her thoughts in a whirl.

The taste of surgery had sent Samantha's thoughts flying. She had agreed to this fiasco of a marriage for two reasons, the first of which she seemed to have failed at so far. The second was to be able to set up a private practice under the protection of the duke, but he wasn't here to lend her his cloak of respectability. True he'd had the little clinic built for her but it wouldn't be of much use if she couldn't get the patients. Metaphorically speaking, all roads seemed to lead to Rome, or in this case back to the duke. The two reasons she had gone along with the marriage were still the two things uppermost in her mind. It seemed that she must admit to herself that she was head over heals in love with her husband, even seeing him for so short a time. Anything worth having was worth fighting for and she made up her mind to fight for him. If he couldn't come to her, then she would go to him. The plan that had nebulously swirled around in her mind started to coagulate. She smiled to herself and nodded her head up and down. Yes, it just might work.

CHAPTER 11

Samantha sat before her mirror and pulled off her offending wig. Christmas had long since come and gone. She had kept up a brave front throughout the holiday season, feeling that she couldn't accept pity from the servants. She had organized the events as if she had been supervising large dinners for some time. The special dinner she had ordered for the servants' Christmas party had been a great success. She missed Hank, knowing he had spent the time with Marianne. He was making a regular path between Helmcrest and the village of Whistlehurst.

Most of all she missed Belfort. She had a constant ache in her heart, wanting so desperately to be able to put the past behind her. Now that spring was approaching she could put her plan into action.

Gazing intently at the face that stared back at her in the mirror, she found that she was looking at an entirely different person from the sickly creature who married the duke. Her eyes and skin had regained their beauty but her hair was now a deep black and was riotously curly. True, it was only about three inches long, but with it brushed up the curl would give it body and make it look like some of the styles she had seen in the fashion plates. She was ready to try. "Mary?" she called.

The young maid came to stand behind her. "Yes, Your Grace," she responded, waiting to see what her mistress had in mind.

"I want you to help me wash my hair and let's see how we can dress it." Her eyes were sparkling in anticipation.

Mary was only too eager to do her bidding and ran out of the room to order water and collect the soap and towels.

Samantha sat there thinking back to her visit to Whistlehurst. Hank had insisted on going back, ostensibly to make sure her patient was doing well. Dear Hank! The excuse had been flimsy, for although he might have concern about Mr. Dobbs, she knew his primary reason was to spend more time near Marianne. It had been gratifying to know Mr. Dobbs recovered. She sighed. That one trip had started a series of many more. It was surely a case of true love between them and she wondered how soon Hank would approach Dr. Douglas and offer for Marianne. It would be wonderful for him if she accepted him without knowing how well situated he was. She bit her lip thoughtfully. Hank had been spending every minute possible with Marianne, seeming to have his affairs in hand, and while he worked out his romance she would go to London and see what she could do. At the thought of confronting the duke as she was now, she laughed aloud.

She knew how poorly she had appeared when they were married what seemed an eternity ago and she could easily forgive him for reacting the way he had. Now she hoped to push the past aside and concentrate on the present and the future.

As she again saw her reflection in the mirror she tingled with anticipation. She would take that young man a step or two and enjoy every minute of it.

When the two of them finished, Mary stood back and admired their work. Samantha's hair was like a halo around her head, the color so deep a black it looked like midnight, while the highlights were like the stars twinkling in the sky. A thin fringe of bangs lay becomingly on her forehead and a wisp of hair curled about her ears, the balance being brushed up and away from her face, accenting her enormous eyes and her creamy skin. She had never looked better.

"Oh, Mary, you've worked a miracle!" Samantha's smile was infectious and they both grinned at the figures in the mirror. "Take my wigs and see that they are burned." She threw the one that had lately adorned her head into the air.

Mary caught it, giggling as she did so. As she turned to retrieve the others Samantha stopped her.

"Just a moment. I want you to know something of what I am planning."

Mary obediently stood still, her eyes concentrating on Samantha. She felt flattered that she was a confidante of Her Grace's.

Samantha came to stand in front of Mary, letting her hand rest on the girl's arm, smiling at her. "Mary, I find I must go to Helmcrest for a time. I have some unfinished business there I must take care of. I will not be able to have you with me." She stopped as she saw the long face Mary pulled. She put an arm around the girl and gave her a hug. "It's not that I don't want you, but circumstances are such that there will not be room for you. You needn't worry about your position for I shall talk to Mr. Maitland and explain that your wages go on as if I were here. You may have a little holiday. All I expect is that you keep my things in order and get rid of my wigs."

Mary gave a deep sigh of relief and her face relaxed into a broad smile.

She didn't understand why she couldn't accompany Her Grace. Helmcrest was a very large establishment, but it wasn't her place to question the strange ways of her mistress. She would do as she was bid, for she loved Samantha. "Yes, Your Grace, I'll take care of everything for you."

"Thank you. We must pack a trunk now with the things I need to take with me. Then I shall make arrangements for Somers to drive me over." Her mind was leaping ahead. She must get to the station without being suspected. This would take some careful thought.

Mary was all smiles now. She went off singing under her breath as she fetched the trunk.

Samantha would stay at Claridge's, a hotel of fine repute and nicely situated, the first night, while she hired a Spanish maid, and then with her in tow, would arrive on the countess' doorstep. She didn't want the servants to know her whereabouts in case it might get back to the duke and spoil everything.

The following day found Samantha ready for her journey. Her bonnet was perched on top of her new coiffure, making it look like an enticing confection. It gave her a welcome confidence. She was bubbling inside and could hardly wait to arrive in London.

Mr. Maitland, the manager, looked askance at her as she stepped gaily into his office.

"Mr. Maitland, I would like a very large sum of money. I am going to spend some time with my brother at Helmcrest and he has offered to take me shopping in Crestwood and stop in at an estate sale," she manufactured on the spur of the moment. It was not as easy as she thought it was going to be to ask for money and give no reason. Mr. Maitland's upraised eyebrows had almost shattered her composure.

"Ah," said Mr. Maitland, "you must mean the old Clark estate. There will be some fine things there, but I didn't think it was until the end of next month."

Samantha almost sighed with relief as she found out there actually was an estate sale. "Hank has told me that if we go over they might consider taking some early bids."

Mr. Maitland went to the desk and unlocked it, apparently satisfied with her explanation. He counted out bills, then added a few gold coins for good measure, and handed her the lot. He knew that when dealing with some agents they preferred only cash.

Samantha thanked him kindly and regally swept from the small office.

Mr. Maitland watched her go with a sense of foreboding. He shook it off, realizing that this new American duchess was very different from the typical English one. She had a mind of her own and didn't seem to take kindly to advice. He hoped she didn't come home with something His Grace would banish to the attics.

Samantha was very pleased with herself. She had a considerable amount of money to defray the expense of the trip and the new clothes she intended to buy. She knew from the start that she wouldn't be able to charge anything to the Belfort estate or Mr. Maitland would relay that information to the duke. She thought that the purchase of some things from an estate sale would not warrant a special communication. After all, she brought this money to the estate and she ought to be able to spend it as she pleased. Evidently the duke thought so too, for she hadn't had any trouble getting it from Mr. Maitland.

Somers drove her over to Helmcrest, where she had her things deposited in the front hall. She ran up to her old room, gathering some of the small pieces of jewelry from the Helmcrest collection. She didn't dare take anything large or valuable for she was sure that it would be recognized.

Meadows was very puzzled when a very few minutes later Samantha asked him to have a carriage brought around and left a note for Hank. She told him that she was having some dresses altered at the dress shop in Crestwood. Meadows knew better than to question Samantha and went to do her bidding. There was some mystery here, the old butler decided, but it wasn't his place to solve it.

Once at the dress shop she sent the carriage home. In getting a hackney carriage to take her to the train station at the end of the village she left no trace. She found no difficulty in getting a ticket and boarding the train. It arrived in London on time at Victoria Station, where she hired a carriage to take her to the well-known Claridge's.

As she signed the guest register she saw the clerk looking about for her maid, but glancing down at the signature, Marquesa de Cienfuegos, he bowed respectfully. Samantha drew herself up and gave him a condescending glance.

"My maid has been taken ill," she explained. "I would like you to have the manager of your best domestic agency call on me here, *por favor*." She used a Spanish accent to her words and decided to intersperse a few Spanish expressions. She knew she could fool anybody for she could speak the language like a native. She wanted all of the *ton* to know that a Spanish aristocrat had arrived in London. This was the beginning.

She was escorted to her room, which she found to her satisfaction. A porter brought up her trunk and she gave him a gold piece, causing him to blink incredulously. She intended also to start the rumor that she was enormously wealthy.

She took off her bonnet and shawl and tossed them on the bed. She seated herself in a large comfortable chair as she waited for someone from the domestic agency to call. It was a relatively short time. Her assumed title and the way she threw gold around assured her of prompt service.

There was a soft knock at the door and she called permission to enter. A middle-aged woman dressed in gray silk entered. She had hawklike features and a small tight mouth. She stood ramrod stiff awaiting Samantha's pleasure.

Samantha invited her to sit down and introduced herself. "I am Margarita Santiago, the Marquesa de Cienfuegos," she announced, using her mother's name and grandmother's title. "I have need of a lady's maid that can speak Spanish."

"I am Mrs. Raxton, head of the London Domestic Agency. We handle only those with the best of references." She sat perched on the edge of her chair as if she felt it was not her place to sit in the presence of nobility. She delicately moistened her thin lips. "What you are asking for is not in the common way. I have several competent maids but they do not speak Spanish."

As Samantha began to shake her head, Mrs. Raxton mentally ran down her list of maids. Then she remembered the Spanish maid who had come into the agency speaking very little English. Mrs. Raxton had given her almost no chance of being placed. "I do have a Spanish maid who came here with her mistress. Unfortunately her mistress died in a railway accident and her maid was left here. I understand she is an excellent servant but she speaks only a few words of English and so it is hard to place her. Would you care to interview her?" She was thinking that if indeed she could place the woman she would be very glad to be rid of her. Foreigners! But then, this lady before her seemed to be of the highest class.

"Thank you. She sounds just like the person I need." She rose to her feet as she spoke. "How soon may I expect her?"

Mrs. Raxton hastily rose. "I'll see she is here directly. Her name is Felicia Ramirez. If you find she is not capable of serving you as you are accustomed, please send me word and I'll look about for someone else." Her manner remained cold and aloof.

Samantha hoped the servants she placed were not in any way like her. As Mrs. Raxton closed the door quietly behind her, Samantha sank gratefully into a chair. It would be interesting to see exactly what kind of servant was being sent her. Somehow she had very little faith in the head of the London Domestic Agency. However, the fact that Felicia Ramirez didn't have wholehearted approval from Mrs. Raxton might just be a good sign.

She ordered the usual tea for herself to fortify her until she could order her dinner and was in the act of pouring a cup when she heard a knock at the door. Guessing that this time it must be the new maid, she called, "*Con permiso*," and the door opened.

A middle-aged woman with dark eyes and black hair entered timidly. She was small but stood erectly, awaiting Samantha's orders. She had the appearance of one who had been on short rations for some time.

Samantha addressed her in Spanish and, at the sound, the woman's face lit with pleasure. She curtsied deeply and then, upon rising, Spanish poured from her. She expressed her gratitude in having the opportunity to serve such a gracious lady and assured her she would be most obedient and helpful. Finally, Samantha raised a hand in protest, laughing as she did so. The familiar language made her feel quite at home and she felt this woman would serve her purpose.

Felicia bent down before Samantha and gently slipped her shoes from her feet, one after the other. At this Samantha knew she had found the perfect maid. Felicia understood exactly what her needs were before she even asked. She let out a sigh of relief. It had been a tiring journey and her new shoes were not proving to be the most comfortable. She would visit New Bond Street to have some made.

As she sat there savoring her cup of tea Felicia busied herself about the room. Watching her, Samantha was deeply satisfied. This maid behind her would add to the image she wanted to give. She was sure that the duke would not recognize her when he saw her and she could begin their relationship anew.

"Felicia, please come here for a moment. I have some instructions for you." She set her cup down and looked directly at her.

Felicia left what she was doing and came to stand in front of her. She bobbed a curtsy and stood deferentially, waiting for her pleasure.

"There will be a great deal of curiosity about me," she began. "If anyone asks about my background feel free to tell them I come from near Madrid, a large hacienda called Cienfuegos. I was married for only a short time when my husband was killed accidentally." At this point Felicia murmured consoling words and devoutly crossed herself, thus reminding Samantha she was supposed to be Catholic, not Church of England. She quickly copied Felicia's gesture. "He was a much older man and we did not suit. If anyone offers to bribe you to tell them what you know, please feel free to take their money." She grinned mischievously as she saw the shocked look on her maid's face. "I want people to know just this much about me, including that I'm an extremely wealthy widow."

Felicia was clearly at a loss. She didn't understand why her mistress would countenance talk about her, but if this was what she wanted she was only too glad to comply with her wishes. After all, it was very evident that she was a great Spanish lady. She was entitled to be eccentric if she wished. *"Sí, señora,"* she answered.

"Now I'll need a carriage to take me to a friend's house. Do you have enough English to do that?"

Felicia shook her head and looked worried but Samantha patted her hand. *"De nada,"* she smiled. "We will have your first English lesson. Now repeat after me, a carriage for my lady."

Felicia was intelligent and besides, she wanted to please her new mistress. Her first attempts were not understandable but after several attempts, during which they both subsided into a fit of giggles, Samantha decided she should try it and sent her out to see the manager.

In a few minutes Felicia was back, her face wreathed in a broad smile. She felt sure her message had been understood as she had added a little pantomime to her request.

Samantha put her to work packing the few things she had taken out and by the time they were ready there was a knock at the door.

"Your carriage is ready, my lady," called a voice.

Samantha gave Felicia an approving nod. *"Gracias, señor,"* she called back. Felicia had accomplished the task. Now they were ready to brave English society.

When she had spoken to the countess after the wedding, the grand old lady told her she was prepared for a few bumps and potholes in this marriage. She had extended the invitation to join her when Samantha felt up to it. The countess had understood when she had related the story of her wedding night and she was positive that the old lady had a few ideas up her sleeve. There was no doubt in her mind that the countess would be home, for she had specifically told Samantha that she rarely went anywhere, except during the hot summer months. It was now coming on toward spring and the season would soon be starting.

Carriage wheels could be heard on the cobbled streets as well as vendors shouting their wares from many bright-colored stalls. A coal seller could be heard calling from his horse and wagon. "Iron Billy," the famous horse-bus driver, was trotting his horses down the street. His conductor called out the stops as they went. Billy wore a tall, crowned beaver hat and a long driving coat; a whip was held securely in one hand. He was the envy of many of his profession. The noise was very marked and Samantha could only be glad when the carriage reached the quieter residential area around Grosvenor Square where the countess resided.

The maid stepped out of the carriage first in order to assist Samantha, who was holding her polite smile with difficulty. She felt she was much more able to assist the maid and chuckled inwardly. She stood regally while Felicia rang the bell.

In a moment the door was opened by a liveried footman, who, taking in Samantha's appearance, bowed austerely. "Good day to you, madame."

"I am the Marquesa de Cienfuegos," she announced in her haughtiest voice. She held her head high and stared directly at the man.

The footman nodded his head and stepped aside, allowing them to enter into a small but elite entrance hall. A marble-topped table and two chairs adorned the room and above the table was an ornate gilt-framed mirror flanked by two elaborate candle sconces.

Samantha could hear the countess' voice as she gave some orders in French to someone in an adjacent room and a moment later she stepped into view. She carried an embellished gold-handled cane, but it didn't detract from her stately appearance.

"The Marquesa de Cienfuegos," stated the footman, giving the countess a slight bow as he did so.

The countess' eyes were merry with mischief as she recognized Samantha. She embraced her in true Gallic fashion while she expressed her pleasure in Samantha's arrival. She flung a few orders at her footman regarding Samantha's luggage and he motioned to Felicia to follow him.

At this point Samantha felt it necessary to explain her maid had practically no English and so there would be a communication problem. Any message for the maid would need to be relayed through her.

The countess raised an eyebrow at that and pursed her lips. "You are being extremely clever, my dear," she mused. "You have a bee in your bonnet, it's plain to see." She eyed Samantha speculatively while that young lady presented a very innocent expression. "Come into the Blue Salon where we can have a comfortable coze. I want to hear what you are up to. From the naughty look in your magnificent eyes I'm sure to enjoy myself. Why, I hardly knew you when you arrived. You have changed so much. If you hadn't written and warned me, I never would have recognized you. But," she added thoughtfully, "that's what you want, *n'est-ce pas?*"

Samantha sank into a blue velvet chair and luxuriated. Her eyes were twinkling as she regarded her hostess. "You don't know what you have gotten yourself into," she chuckled. "I'm going to make things mighty interesting for one Duke of Belfort."

"*Le pauvre homme!*" exclaimed the countess. "I can see what you are planning and I'm going to savor every moment. It's time someone stirred up his liver! Although," she added cautiously, "I've heard he has changed somewhat since he came to London. There are rumors he has been entertaining a lady or two." She tipped her head questioningly at Samantha to see how she'd take this news.

"I'm not too surprised," she answered coolly. "That's one of the reasons why I'm here. I'd like to see if I can interest him in me—as I am now. I'm going to give him an entirely different picture, one that will pique his fancy."

"This is going to be as good as going to a play. I shall have a front-row seat for the performance. Tell me, what do you want me to do?"

"Just present me to your friends, the cream of society, with the explanation that I'm a wealthy widow from Spain. I'll take care of the rest. My maid has been instructed as to what she may say but if the enquirer doesn't speak Spanish he'll get no information at all." That brought a smile to her face as she contemplated the attempts to secure information about her.

"That will be no trouble. I've already planned a small dinner to introduce you to a few special friends. But first, *ma chérie*, we should visit my *couturière* and have an entire new wardrobe made for you. You will be the talk of the town and my doorbell will never be silent. I can see very amusing times ahead."

CHAPTER 12

The next morning found them entering Madame Bienville's exclusive establishment. The countess' carriage had driven away after depositing them. The driver had been instructed to walk the horses up and down.

Presently one of the clerks recognized the countess and she rushed to get the famous *couturière*. Samantha and the countess seated themselves in two of the French gilt chairs, patiently awaiting her arrival. Samantha noted the expensive furnishings and the tasteful decorations. Exquisite French figurines were perched on ornate shelves and gold mirrors of varying sizes and several rich oil paintings adorned the walls between. There was no doubt this was a lucrative business.

Madame Bienville swept importantly into the room, spotted the countess, and made her way to her. "You honor my establishment." Her voice was of fine quality and one got the impression she was from one of the old French aristocratic families.

Samantha regarded her closely. The woman was past middle age, her hair, once very dark, now had interesting streaks of gray in it. She was tall and extremely thin but was gowned to perfection. She stood very straight as she ostensibly focused her attention on the countess. While Samantha was taking Madame's measure, that astute woman was returning the scrutiny out of the corner of one eye.

"Margarita, I would like to present Madame Bienville," the countess addressed Samantha. "Madame, this is my friend, the Marquesa de Cienfuegos. She has come from foreign parts to give me her company."

As both ladies acknowledged the introduction, Samantha almost giggled. Foreign parts! Evidently the countess didn't like to tamper with the truth and she supposed America was no more foreign than Spain. Samantha caught the countess' eye and gazed intently, while the old lady shrugged her shoulders almost imperceptibly.

The *couturière* murmured all the appropriate things and then settled down to business. "How may I serve you?" She managed to include both of them in the enquiry.

Samantha spoke up. "I find myself in need of a complete wardrobe.

Please spare no expense in securing for me the finest quality of everything." She smiled inwardly as she watched Madame Bienville's eyes widen, although her expression didn't change.

These words must have played a whole symphony to Madame. Here was an outstanding beauty, one who would be a pleasure to dress, and she calmly announced that money didn't need to be considered. Ah! Her bosom swelled at the thought of the ravishing outfits she could make for the marquesa. She would be a credit to the establishment and would certainly bring others to her, but most of all she could hear the river of gold pouring its way into her pocket. She allowed herself to be enthusiastic.

"If you will follow me to a fitting room I'll personally see to your measurements and bring some samples of exquisite silk that have just come over from France."

As Samantha started to follow her she stopped and looked enquiringly at the countess. "Would you like to come back with me?"

The countess shook her head. "It's much too close back there. I'd rather wait out here. When you find something you like bring it out here." She was relaxed and comfortable where she was and thought it wouldn't do Samantha any harm to make several trips to the front. The countess felt she had things well in hand and could keep a finger on the proceedings from this delightful vantage point.

Samantha understood as she felt that the fittings were sure to be a bore, but a very necessary one in her campaign to ensnare her husband. She also thought that her sponsor might like the conversation that went on out front.

She had no sooner disappeared through a doorway that was draped in pale yellow silk when the door opened and a tall, broad-shouldered young man strode in. One of the little seamstresses who was hovering in the background hurried forward. She recognized him immediately. "Good day to you, Your Grace," she greeted him, her eyes full of admiration at the handsome figure he made. "The *robe de nuit* you ordered is ready," she added.

The countess, seated at the far side of the room, raised her lorgnette at the sound of his voice. There was nothing wrong with her hearing. "Well, Belfort, what's this about your needing a nightgown?" She tossed him the question casually.

At the sound of the familiar voice he turned abruptly and saw his aunt sitting very primly on an elaborate gilt chair. He smiled at her and she inclined her head.

The seamstress, realizing she had made a *faux pas*, seized the opportunity to leave the room.

Belfort was a man of considerable address and without a pause he crossed over to his aunt. "I'm happy to see you out. Are you feeling quite well?" He ignored her question but thought that she was a redoubtable old girl. She never missed a trick. She'd have all the information out of him before the cat could lick its ear, if he didn't watch his step. Seeing she was gathering her forces for an attack, he hurriedly asked, "Are you in need of some new gowns?"

She eyed him severely but there was a ghost of a smile lurking at the corners of her mouth. She had always admired a man with a little spice in him. Madame Bienville parted the drape at just that moment, making a reply unnecessary.

Samantha nodded to her and she passed through into the room. She was wearing a cloth of gold gown that had been ordered for a young lady who had unfortunately been unable to pay the bill. With a few small changes it was ravishing on Samantha. Her eyes seemed larger than ever, her lashes curled upward, and the dark cloud of curly hair made the duke feel that he would like to run his hands through it.

Belfort audibly caught his breath. For a few seconds he stood transfixed. He had never seen a woman like this before. He must find out who she was. Seeing his aunt give this vision an approving smile, he threw his aunt a demanding stare.

The countess pretended she didn't know what he wanted. She started a flow of small talk to give Samantha time to assess the situation.

Samantha, seeing Belfort talking to his aunt, felt fear sweep over her. This was sooner than she had planned. Would she get away with it? Well, she was committed, so she resolutely moved forward. As both Belfort and his aunt were silent at this point, she swept a regal curtsy at the countess and enquired in a voice heavily laden with a Spanish accent, "Do you like this gown?"

"C'est parfait." The old lady was vastly entertained. This was a good beginning. The duke was more than anxious to make her acquaintance and the countess was postponing the introduction as long as possible.

Belfort couldn't understand why his aunt was taking so much time to introduce him. Hearing Samantha's accent and rightly placing it as Spanish, which he spoke like a native, he decided that she didn't speak French or she would have used that tongue in speaking with his aunt. "Introduce me at once," he muttered in French to his aunt.

Samantha, who spoke French equally well, was incapable of keeping her face straight. She had won the first engagement. Her smile was like a ray of sunshine as she watched him.

The countess had a smug expression on her face as she finally complied with his order. This was the first time she had ever seen him at a loss for words. This was going to work out after all. Some good management was needed and she was just the person to undertake it.

"Margarita," she began, "may I present the Duke of Belfort? Brooke, this is Margarita Santiago, the Marquesa de Cienfuegos." Her eyes went from one to another, enjoying introducing husband to wife. She could see a situation that could be full of pitfalls and she was going to relish it. Belfort was due for a good setdown and from the way Samantha had planned it, Belfort had met his match. She'd help the girl along.

"Belfort, my dear, I'm having a small dinner party this Friday. Would you and your wife care to join us?" There was a roguish look in her old eyes.

Belfort gave her a startled glance. This was an attack. What had he done to deserve this? However, he wasn't a successful diplomat for nothing. "I'm sorry to say that the duchess is gravely ill at Belfort. I'm not expecting her to live. If it weren't that the queen demands my presence in London I would certainly be there." He had handled that quite well, he thought, and the queen had actually recently asked for his attendance.

It was Samantha's turn to be stunned. She gave him a scorching look. Did he really believe she was dying? If so, why wasn't he there, the devil take the queen? Then she remembered her role and commented with only an infinitesimal pause, "How sad."

The tone earned her another searching look from Belfort, which she intercepted with one of bland innocence. This woman had a great appeal but there was something about her that puzzled him. In some way she reminded him of someone but he had no idea who. She was most certainly a lady of quality but her manner and eyes seemed to hint that she might be available. It whetted his appetite. He found himself leaving the salon without picking up the wisp of a nightgown he had ordered for his current *chère amie*.

After he left, Samantha felt herself unwind and then dissolved into gales of laughter, the countess joining in. The sound brought Madame hurriedly into the room. She wondered if the gown was so bad that they were laughing at it.

Samantha reassured her and returned to the fitting room. She selected materials and patterns, which Madame promised to have made up immediately; she would send a note around to let her know when to come in for a fitting. Samantha had splurged and bought exquisite materials and waved the cost away. She was going to have a very extensive wardrobe, one that was sure to catch attention. She settled her bonnet on her electrifying hair, pulled on her gloves, and announced she was ready to go to the milliner's and the bootmaker's.

The countess readily agreed but her thoughts were far away. She was still relishing the expression on Belfort's face. She didn't know when she had had so much amusement. What a romance!

It was only two doors to the milliner's and they elected to walk the short distance. They moved slowly in deference to the countess' age, Samantha being unusually quiet. A quick look told the countess that Samantha must have something on her mind. There was one way to find out. "Tell me, *chérie*, did the fittings not suit you?" She was well aware that this couldn't be the reason for that look of concentration and the firm, set lips.

That brought Samantha to herself. She laughed and tucked her arm in the old lady's. "I don't like to bother you with my problems but when you invited Belfort to dinner, his manner and reply set me to thinking. If he is entertaining several young ladies, some perhaps not classified as ladies, I wonder if my money is paying for these creatures!" There was a strong note of indignation in her voice.

At that explanation the countess squeezed her hand tightly. "There is nothing here about which you need to concern yourself. Perhaps I am remiss. I should have told you. While Belfort was so hard-pressed he didn't spend a groat on himself or entertainment of any kind. I have it on good authority that when he received the money from your estates he spent it only on his retainers, servants, and on the estate itself. He denied himself anything from you." She paused to see how Samantha was taking this.

It came as a complete surprise to that young lady. Her husband had a good deal of pride and she was happy to hear it. But then where did all this money come from that he was flinging about? She was just about to voice her question when the countess interrupted her.

"He has been very lucky. A very wealthy American visited Belfort's stables and two of his mares found instant favor with him. He offered Belfort an unbelievable sum for them and Belfort sold them. Then he had some banking friend recommend an investment. Belfort played a hunch and invested all the money he'd made on his mares into it. Within a short period he had made a huge sum, so, on advice, he sold out and banked his gains. Finally, he went to White's one evening and did something he never does. He gambled for high stakes and again he won. If this could have happened before, there would have been no need for him to marry—oh, I'm sorry. I didn't mean to hurt you. For myself, I'm most gratified he has married you and when you get all this straightened out I'm sure you will be very happy."

They entered the milliner's shop and Samantha wore a very thoughtful look on her lovely face. Her husband was now financially independent. He didn't need her money. What would happen now?

Afterward, she had no idea of what she had purchased. All she remembered was the countess exclaiming over first one confection and then another and herself agreeing. Well, she wasn't going to give up now. For she had already made up her mind that she wanted him.

The next few days passed quickly. Boxes and packages were arriving constantly and Felicia was kept busy hanging gowns and putting away all the bonnets, shoes, and accessories Samantha had purchased. She was now well fortified to take London society by storm.

The countess had spent considerable time on preparations for her dinner. She had kept her guest list to a mere twenty, preferring quality instead of quantity. She wanted the cream of society, plus a few high government officials so as to give Samantha entrée into both sets. An invitation from the countess was highly prized, as she was well known for her incomparable dinners plus unusual entertainment, so no one refused her invitation.

Not wanting it to look peculiar by having Belfort the only unaccompanied male, she invited a young American aristocrat who came from the South, one Carleton Randolph. He had been to all the *ton* parties, and was sponsored by the American ambassador himself. His manners were impeccable and his gracious ways made him very popular. The countess paired him with Samantha and her eyes sparkled wickedly when she thought of the reaction she'd get from Belfort on this. She invited Lord and Lady Leicester—Lord Leicester was a member of Parliament—and their daughter, Elizabeth. The latter was a charming young girl who had recently made her debut and was very sought after. The countess planned to pair her with Belfort. For herself the countess invited her old friend General Sir Alexander Somerhays and for leavening she invited Waldo and Amanda Farnsworth. He was always good for a laugh and she could be counted on to give all the latest *on dits*. Her propensity for picking up gossip was uncanny.

The evening of the dinner arrived and the countess and Samantha had outdone themselves. The countess wore a silvery silk lamé gown with rows of ruffles showing beneath the scalloped skirt. Her jewelry consisted of a large diamond necklace and long matching eardrops. A glittering diamond tiara completed the set.

Samantha looked at herself one last time in the mirror. She must be perfect for tonight's dinner. Her daffodil gown with many rows of ruffles circling the hem of her skirt seemed to give her confidence. It was gathered in at the waist, showing her admirable figure. The puffed sleeves gave a finished look to this flowing creation. She wore only a magnificent rope of pearls and pearl clip in her hair, which she had brought with her from the Helmcrest estate. Hank had told her that they were at her disposal whenever she felt the need. She thought that because the pearls were simply set they would not be recognized as the famous Helmcrest rubies would be.

They received at the top of the stairs on the first floor, the countess introducing Samantha to the guests as they arrived and then passing them on to the Blue Salon to meet until dinner was announced. Belfort was the last guest to arrive and he held Samantha's hand a trifle longer than fashion demanded, giving her a look that seemed to penetrate her. She managed to smile formally and gently pulled her hand loose.

"Everyone's here so shall we join our guests?" asked the countess. It was a mere formality on her part and she waved Samantha and Belfort to precede her.

Conversation was general for a few moments until dinner was announced. The countess called Mr. Randolph to her side and asked him to escort Samantha. His face showed his pleasure and Samantha, looking up at him, found him attractive. He was tall with dark curly hair and had interesting green eyes. She couldn't help stealing a look at Belfort to see what his reaction was when he found he was partnered with Lady Elizabeth but that astute gentleman covered his feelings skillfully.

The countess' chef had outdone himself. She had given him quite a challenge as her guests were used to the very best. Course followed course, each one surpassing the last.

Samantha found the Earl of Edgeworth on her left, Randolph on her right. The earl was a great horseman and horses were his favorite topic.

"Do you ride?" he asked Samantha.

She flashed him a brilliant smile that made him blink. "Yes," she answered modestly. She knew herself to be an incomparable horsewoman. In fact, Hank had often said she rode better than most men.

"I'd be happy to mount you for your stay in London," he said. He was thinking his wife had two well-mannered mares that could be counted to carry a lady without distressing her. They could loan her one.

"How very nice of you! I dislike bothering my friends and prefer, if possible, to have my own." She softened her refusal with her tone and sweet smile. "Isn't there some place in London where horses are sold?"

"Yes, of course. I always go to Tattersall's but I doubt if they will have a good lady's horse. Tomorrow I am going to a private sale at Ingrams' after lunch. I have heard that there is to be a very unusual black stallion sold—an Arabian, I believe, noted for its endurance. I intend to put in a bid. If you like, I'll look around for you."

There was no mistaking his effort to be helpful but Samantha wanted no part of anyone else selecting a horse for her—unless it was her brother. "Perhaps I shall go and see for myself." The mention of the black horse stirred her curiosity. He might be just the horse she was looking for.

The earl was horrified. "But, Marquesa, that is impossible. Only men go to horse sales." He dropped his voice as he explained.

"Thank you," she murmured, but there was a light in her eye that Hank would have recognized. Telling her that something was impossible was tantamount to a real challenge to her.

The earl found her charming and her little accent was fascinating. He was gratified that he had been able to instruct her.

Mr. Randolph claimed her attention and she enjoyed herself parrying his questions. He was extremely polite but there was a hint of insistence in his queries. Well, she had prepared her story and was sure that no one could refute it. Even Felicia knew only what Samantha wanted her to tell.

Glancing across the table she met the duke's eyes as she found him regarding her. Her heart gave a little jump. She only hoped she wasn't making a mistake but the more she saw of him the more she was drawn to him. Resolutely, she turned her attention back to Randolph.

"How does it happen that you are in London? Are you in the ambassador's party?" she enquired. After all, he was an American and most were doing their best to help their country. She wasn't prepared for the tiny flash she saw in his green eyes. Had she said something wrong?

He made a fast recovery and smiled at her. "I'm not exactly in the Diplomatic Corps but I am here trying to promote British neutrality."

There was something in his tone that didn't quite sit with her even though his answer made sense. She had come face to face with life, both in the West and with patients during her training as a doctor, and she had become very perceptive about people who were untruthful. Randolph didn't ring true. It was possible that her imagination was overworking due to the strain of this dinner but somehow she couldn't shrug it off. It was all the fault of the duke, she told herself crossly. Why shouldn't the United States have men here to try to influence England to keep out of the war? She knew Belfort was working to keep England from supplying the Confederacy with ironclads and was meeting some opposition.

The countess rose to her feet as the signal to the ladies to withdraw to the salon and leave the gentlemen to their wine. She had the tea tray brought in and served the ladies a nice dish of tea from the silver service. They sipped enjoyably as they chatted and waited for the gentlemen.

Lady Wembly, an imposing figure in violet silk, carried a fan, which she wielded with a flourish. She was considered one of the leaders of society and if she put her seal of approval on a young lady, that damsel was made. She sat beside the countess and confided to her that she found her protégée charming, a striking young woman with excellent manners. Of course the fact that the marquesa was reputed to be fabulously wealthy and that Lady Wembly had an older unmarried son, who so far had been unable to find a suitable bride, had nothing to do with it.

Lady Elizabeth was a well-brought-up young lady and with her father in the Diplomatic Corps was well used to parties of this sort. She found the duke entertaining but couldn't help wondering what the situation was in regard to his sick wife. Randolph's polished manner and his soft way of speaking intrigued her, and so between the two she passed the evening tolerably.

The teacups had no sooner been cleared away when the gentlemen joined them. They were still laughing at some jest and Samantha had the pleasure of seeing the duke at his best. She avoided his gaze, for she decided that he must do the hunting. She was not going to fall into his arms at his first overture.

When the guests had found chairs to their liking the countess held up her hand and everyone was silent. "I have been able to secure the services of Miss Lilli Lehmann. She is a very talented young woman and will go far in the operatic world. She accepts very few engagements yet, preferring to keep refining her already beautiful voice. She has consented to sing three songs for us."

There was a general murmur as the guests remarked on the countess' ability to persuade this rising young star to perform for them. She was only fifteen, yet she was already gaining acclaim in polite circles.

General Sir Alexander Somerhays was an old friend of the countess' and gave her a look of approval. She never failed her guests in providing them with unusual entertainment. If she said that this young woman would go far in opera, he would stake his last groat on it. He settled back in his comfortable wing chair to listen to the performance.

Miss Lehmann stood in the doorway for an instant, taking in the assembled company; she inclined her head slightly and made her way to the piano. Her accompanist stood a few paces behind her, a tall gaunt man who looked as if he never had enough to eat. When Miss Lehmann moved to the front of the piano, he took his place on the bench.

Running his hands up and down the keys with a few trial arpeggios, he found no fault with the pitch. He stretched his arms to let his sleeves fall back and then started the music in earnest.

Miss Lehmann was composed awaiting her entrance. At the first sound a hush filled the room, for each guest was completely absorbed in this melodious coloratura soprano voice. Her voice had a special quality and she used it well. At the conclusion of her songs, there was absolute silence for a few seconds, an accolade in itself, before the guests clapped enthusiastically. No amount of applause caused her to sing an encore. The lovely German young lady inclined her head and swept from the room, her accompanist trailing silently behind her.

After she left there was a general buzz of conversation, all those present feeling they had received a high treat. The guests got up and moved about. Seeing Lady Elizabeth in conversation with Randolph, Belfort made his way to Samantha, who had been engaged by Lady Wembly. He was in time to hear her probing Samantha about the size of her estates in Spain. That astute young lady shrugged her shoulders and murmured, *"Creo que se,"* and Lady Wembly, hearing only the "si," took that to mean the marquesa was agreeing that her holdings were vast. Belfort, rightly interpreting the remark as "I think so," gave the marquesa a sharp look. Surely she knew if her estates were large. Could it be that she didn't understand the question asked by Lady Wembly? Somehow he didn't think so. It put a small question in his mind. Evidently the marquesa thought that there was no one else here who spoke Spanish. She had a surprise in store.

He stood there for a moment, chatting casually, and then adroitly managed to take Samantha to one side. "Tell me," he said, "do you ride?"

Samantha had to smile. This was the second man who had asked that question tonight. She was not any more expressive than she was before. "Yes," she answered.

"Would you care to ride in the park with me tomorrow?"

She was very conscious of his eyes on hers. She felt a weakening in her knees and a general flutter inside. She was not sure if she could maintain the deception without showing her love for this man. "Thank you, but I won't be able to ride until the following day." Her mind jumped ahead to the sale and the black horse that she hoped to buy that Lord Edgeworth had mentioned.

"Very well, I shall plan on the day after tomorrow. Will ten o'clock suit you?"

She smiled her agreement but before she could say anything the countess was calling for their attention.

"Now for the big surprise of the evening. I present to you for your entertainment Griselda, a Romany gypsy, who is said to have great powers."

This brought a few chuckles from the gentlemen but the ladies were intrigued. A fortune-teller! Each found a chair and waited expectantly for the gypsy to enter.

The butler escorted her into the room and then left her standing there. There was no trace of embarrassment on her face. She wore a multi-colored blouse with a black skirt and vest, a red silk kerchief on her head. Her hair was raven black and streamed down her back. She surveyed the room carefully, intensifying the charged silence.

"I will tell each of you something that is true. You may not like to hear it or you may be happy with what I say. I will not answer any questions. Now, if that is understood, I will start. One more thing, if anyone objects to hearing what I have to say, tell me when it comes your turn."

She moved over to where Lady Elizabeth was sitting. "Give me your right hand," she demanded.

Lady Elizabeth was a little flustered but laid her hand in the gypsy's. She held her breath with anticipation and bit her lip.

"You are to be congratulated. I see a wedding in the near future that will be a brilliant match. It is someone you have never thought was interested in you."

Lady Elizabeth let her breath go and opened her mouth as if to say, "Oh," but nothing came out. Her eyes sparkled as she thought of how exciting that was. Of course, there wasn't a word of truth in it but, just the same, she mentally scanned all her acquaintances for the brilliant match that awaited her.

Griselda moved on. She stopped in front of Lord Edgeworth. Once again she requested a hand placed in hers. "I see a major disappointment for you. You have your heart set on a great black horse. Someone else will outbid you."

He showed his astonishment. How could she know about the horse he was interested in? Besides, he'd made up his mind to have it and he'd bid high enough to discourage anyone else.

Then she moved to Belfort. There was an amused look in his eye but he unhesitatingly placed his right hand in hers. She gazed at it for a long minute. Her eyes closed and she seemed to sway back and forth. She spoke in a singsong voice.

> "Money you wanted, money you got.
> A wife you wed and have her not.
> Bury the first and seek anew—
> A glorious life is waiting for you."

There was shocked silence as she finished. Everyone knew Belfort's wife was very ill, but to tell him to bury her— The electrifying silence prevailed.

Belfort himself was taken aback. He wondered where she got her information. If his wife was actually that ill he would see the queen and ask for leave to go to Belfort. It was odd that he had had no word from his manager as to the state of affairs.

There was some whispering as Griselda made her way to Samantha. She was tempted to refuse, not being sure that she liked what the gypsy said to Belfort. Bury her? Did she foresee an accident? Her hand grew damp with perspiration. She was afraid what the gypsy might say that would give her away to Belfort but reasoned it was probably all made up in advance so she placed her hand in Griselda's after wiping it with her handkerchief. Here again the gypsy swayed and finally she chanted.

> "You have lost your husband. I see the tears.
> Now is the time to part with fears.
> The love of your life is drawing near,
> But I can see no marriage here."

These words were a shock to Samantha. Did the woman mean that she would never gain Belfort as her husband? Fear caught at the pit of her stomach.

Belfort heard the rhyme with great satisfaction. He sat up straighter. It looked like a very pleasant flirtation was in the offing. He had already launched his first assault.

Samantha was busy with her thoughts and didn't hear any more of what Griselda had to say to the others. She had her eyes lowered and she peeped at Belfort from between her long curling lashes. She thought he looked like a tomcat licking his whiskers he seemed so pleased with himself. Well, if he thought he was going to add her to his list of mistresses he had another think coming. She wanted to gain his interest but this was going too far and too fast. She tried to analyze her feelings toward the duke. She hated and loved him at the same time. She was waging a war inside herself and she was not sure that she was winning. The time had simply disappeared as she sat there thinking.

Belfort bowed over her hand and murmured he would be looking forward to meeting her in the park for their morning ride. She gave a noncommittal answer as she said good night.

CHAPTER 13

Hank jogged easily on his way to visit Marianne. He was whistling softly between his teeth, feeling pleased with himself and at peace with the world. The lush green of England in early April appealed to him more than he had thought possible. He enjoyed the beautiful flowers, the countryside, and the people. Perhaps there was something in heredity after all, for he felt at home here. He admitted to himself that his feeling for Marianne colored his every thought.

Diablo whinnied, bobbing his head up and down. He liked to get out and have a run across the fields and was anticipating this pleasure. He carried his head high and his tail flipped up. In spite of his piebald coloring he looked like the great horse he was. Hank's reata was looped to the saddle and made that intelligent horse feel that he was in for some sport.

In describing life in Arizona to Marianne, Hank had told her of his use of the reata and she had expressed a desire to see one and have him demonstrate how it worked. Consequently, he had added it to his equipment today and had unconsciously picked up his pistol and had stuck it in his waistband. Thinking of it, he reached down and touched it briefly. He must be a creature of habit, he mused. When he had need of his reata he very often had need of his pistol. He smiled ruefully. He wondered what Marianne would think when she saw it.

Somewhere he had heard that there was the ultimate woman for every man and he was in agreement with the thought for, from the moment of setting eyes on her, he knew she was his woman. It was early yet to ask her father for her but he found his impatience rising. He wanted her now and somehow he must find the words to convince Dr. Douglas that he was the man for her. Was it fair to the old doctor not to tell him of his title and vast possessions? It would ease that poor man's concern but Hank would like to think he could win her on his own merits. As far as his intentions were concerned the whole village of Whistlehurst must know he had more than a passing interest in Marianne. Each visit he made, he stayed at the local inn and had received some very knowing looks. No one ventured a word, at least within his hearing, but there was no doubt everyone was aware of his business.

His mind turned to his sister and her problems. He had had a note from her saying that she was in London for a time but didn't want anyone to know she was there. Supposedly, she had come to Helmcrest to visit him. Now how did she think she could get away with that? Belfort would be sure to hear she was in town. He could well imagine the scene if he happened on her. Was that what she wanted? Somehow he thought not. Knowing Sam as he did he was positive that she had something more up her sleeve than that. He would plan a trip to London soon if she didn't return and see just what she was doing. She never had been one to sit by and do nothing about a problem. She enjoyed a challenge and his sympathy went out to Belfort. If he could tell by past performances, she would make life interesting, to say the least.

Marianne drove her pony cart slowly up the dusty street. She had need of provisions and she enjoyed doing her own shopping. She was conscious of a feeling of exhilaration as she remembered that today Hank would be here. Just thinking of him made her heart beat a little faster and when she pictured his manliness a little tingle went through her. This must be what it is to be in love, she thought. She was determined to show him what a good housewife she was. She had planned an excellent dinner and intended to supervise their maid to be sure it was perfect.

She stopped in front of the greengrocer's and tied her pony to the hitching post. Picking up her basket, she entered the small store. Mr. Tomlin, the store owner, was ringing up a sale on the cash register and nodding a good day to a customer. As the lady turned, Marianne recognized Mrs. Warner, the wife of the local blacksmith.

Mrs. Warner stopped to speak with Marianne for a minute. "I understand you have a fine young man calling on you," she stated coyly. She was known as the town gossip and was aware of everything that went on in the village. She never passed by an opportunity to add to her stock.

A slight blush rose in Marianne's cheeks, accentuating her loveliness. She was not used to such plain speaking and had not learned the gentle art of dissembling. "He's just a friend," she protested, "a friend of my father's."

Mrs. Warner gave her an arch look and would have continued to pry but Marianne forestalled it by turning to the grocer and asking if he had any lettuce. Mrs. Warner reluctantly left the store, her lips pursed in thought.

Mr. Tomlin was short and stocky, a friendly smile always in abundance. He had a florid complexion and only a rim of gray hair circling his head. He was not known for his force of opinion for he could be swayed by any and all. He instantly agreed with any opinion set forth. He believed it was good for his business. He was also interested in the young man who was calling so often at Dr. Douglas' and had waited to hear Marianne's answer to the question set forth by Mrs. Warner.

Marianne was all business and so failed to appease the grocer's curiosity. She let her thoughts wander to Hank as she left the store carrying her full basket on her arm.

Mr. Tomlin looked after her. She was a very attractive young lady of quality and Dr. Douglas should be making a push to find her a suitable husband. Well, it was nothing to him. He shrugged his shoulders and went back to checking his supplies.

Marianne unhitched the pony, set the heavy basket in the pony cart, and was about to climb in when she felt a strong grip on her arm. Startled, she swung around and found Lord Entwhistle at her side. He was smiling down at her in a way that made her shiver. She tried to pull herself free but he merely tightened his hold until his fingers bit deeply into her flesh and she couldn't help a little cry of pain.

"Let me go! What is the meaning of this?" Her temper was up and she hit at him with her free arm. She remembered her last encounter with him and that Hank had come to her rescue. He wasn't due for some time yet and she knew fate would not be that kind to her twice. The lurid stories she had heard of him kept coming to mind, giving her stomach a queasy feeling. The only visible sign of her fear was the slight trembling of her knees.

"Now, now, my pretty. There's no need to be upset. I have just had my new curricle delivered from London and I want to take you for a ride." He loosened his grip a little but still retained a firm hold on her arm. He nodded his head toward the elegant equipage that stood beside her cart.

"Thank you for your invitation," she answered, a note of contempt in her tone. "I have no time." She made another attempt to pull herself loose. She glanced quickly about the street. Only a few minutes ago Mrs. Warner was here. Anyone would deter Lord Entwhistle, for he couldn't afford to have his behavior observed. Unfortunately, there was no one in sight. She wondered if she screamed, if anyone—Mr. Tomlin for instance —would hear and come to her rescue. Then remembering the grocer's weak character, she knew he wouldn't. She felt herself being forcibly pulled toward Entwhistle's curricle. He thrust her in and jumped in after her, picking up his reins and starting his horses off at a trot. As he swung his team around and trotted back down the dusty road Marianne was terrified.

"Where are you taking me?" she cried.

With a sound that resembled a snort Entwhistle merely turned down a lane that led through the forest. His shoulders shook as if he were laughing at a private joke.

As they drove past the few cottages and on toward the forest Marianne knew where he was taking her. He had a hunting lodge several miles into the forest. The lane had become a track, rutted and tending to muddy the wheels. She had heard of what went on there and of village girls who were never seen again. Anything was better than that and she decided to jump even if she was killed. It was preferable to what she guessed was in store for her.

As if he knew what was in her mind he turned to her, a wolfish grin on his face. "If you jump, I'll merely stop my horses and run you down. There is no way you can escape me."

The truth of his words hit her with considerable weight. Unless she killed herself, she would still be in his clutches and much less able to repulse an attack. She would bide her time and hope the opportunity arose to make her escape. Her strength wouldn't prevail against his but perhaps she could outwit him.

Hank trotted slowly down the main street. He noticed the pony cart standing in front of the greengrocer's and felt a great lift of spirit for he recognized it as Marianne's. He would meet her and escort her home. As he drew alongside the cart he noticed the full basket set there. She must be in one of the other shops. He swung down and left Diablo next to the pony while he made his way to the chemist's. That gentleman disclaimed all knowledge of her saying he hadn't seen her this morning. Turning on his heel, Hank made his way to the greengrocer's. It was evident she had been there. The grocer should be able to tell him where he might find her. He strode into the shop and at his appearance Mr. Tomlin promptly found himself something to do. His hands were shaking slightly, which made Hank sure something was wrong.

"Have you seen Miss Douglas this morning?" It was a courteous question, the answer to which Hank knew. This was just for openers.

"Uh, uh, yes." Mr. Tomlin was reluctant even to admit she had been in the store.

"Do you know where I might find her?" Mr. Tomlin couldn't fail to hear the demanding tone in Hank's voice.

He kept his eyes lowered. He couldn't meet Hank's insistent look. "Well," he hesitated again, "no."

Hank, listening to him and observing his actions, was certain that he knew but wasn't telling. As far as he was concerned this was no time for his earl's manners. He stretched a long arm across the counter, grasped the front of Mr. Tomlin's shirt with one large hand, and lifted him easily off his feet, bringing the greengrocer's face close to his own. Arizona had its own methods of getting results.

Mr. Tomlin turned white and sputtered, "Put me down!"

Hank merely held him there. "Tell me, now, what do you know? Where is Marianne?"

Mr. Tomlin was terrified. He had heard stories of these wild Americans and was afraid for his life. He knew that Lord Entwhistle would be furious if he interfered with his dallying, but his anger couldn't match that of this wild barbarian. "I . . . saw her get into Lord Entwhistle's curricle," he gasped.

Hank released his grasp and Mr. Tomlin fell against the counter, breathing deeply. He was glad to have escaped with his life.

"Which direction did they take?" Hank's eyes were hard and cold and his tone left no doubt in Mr. Tomlin's mind that an answer had better be forthcoming.

"It looked like he was heading for the lane through the woods." He could barely squeak the words.

"What is in that direction?" Hank rapped out the question.

Mr. Tomlin was afraid to answer but was more terrified not to. "His lordship's hunting lodge."

At these words Hank spun on his heel and ran out of the shop, leaving a much relieved grocer behind. Running alongside Diablo, he picked up his reins and slipped his left toe into the stirrup. He flicked the reins and whistled Diablo forward, while he swung his other leg over the saddle. He flashed down the dusty street and turned down the lane leading into the woods.

This was the second time, thought the chemist as he watched from his window, that someone had made a flying exit from town. The last one was a woman, another of those wild Americans. He was glad that he didn't live in such an uncivilized place.

Diablo was in his stride and stretched low to the ground. Hank's face was set, his lips pulled together in a tight straight line. Mud flew everywhere as he reached the rutted track in the woods. He hoped that this mud had slowed Entwhistle down, but he pushed Diablo on just the same. If Entwhistle harmed one hair of Marianne's head he would answer with his life. To Hank, this type of behavior was unheard of. In the West all women were respected and it was as much as a man's life was worth to annoy a good woman. Well, Arizona ways were coming to England. He would take care of this problem in his own way. The carriage tracks were

so fresh that he knew that Entwhistle couldn't be too far ahead. If he
could overtake them before they got to the lodge it would be easy. If they
had already gotten inside, well, that made it a trifle more difficult, but he
would still handle it.

Diablo was at full gallop and Hank had to narrow his eyes to mere slits
to see because the wind was tearing so hard at him. Then he saw the curricle ahead. It was threading its way through the bog holes. He could
vaguely make out two figures in it. In the distance he could see the lodge
and knew he didn't have time to try to get in front of the curricle. How
best could he stop them without Marianne's suffering an injury? His mind
flashed to his pistol but he didn't dare shoot for fear of the horses running
wild. Then he thought of his reata. He mentally thanked his Spanish
grandfather for seeing that he was well versed in the art. The American
lariat was a much shorter and heavier rope. What he needed right now
was all his old skill.

Looping his reins around the pommel and guiding Diablo with his
knees as he'd done many a time, he reached for his reata. It was eighty
feet long, smooth as silk, and made of rawhide. He swung it easily about
his head, building a loop until it was about the right size twirling around
his head, and then dextrously threw it through the air. It seemed as if it
were alive as it stood straight up and then sailed out and settled over the
horses' heads. He dallied around the saddle horn and pulled both horses
and carriage to a stop. As Hank jumped from his horse, Diablo, well
versed in calf roping, kept the line taut by backing up. He maintained a
pull on the rope and caused the curricle to start backward.

As the loop settled over his horses' heads Entwhistle was stunned. He
half turned in his seat and saw Hank running toward him. With a snarl
he reached into a pocket of his curricle and pulled out a pistol.

Hank's eyes were alert as Entwhistle took the pistol out and the look on
his face told Hank that he meant to kill him. Hank's hand streaked to his
pistol, expertly palmed it, and without seeming to aim, pulled the trigger.

Entwhistle gave a cry and fell backward from his curricle landing with
a thud in the soft mud.

Marianne, who had sat frozen through the proceedings, at last found
her voice. "Hank, oh, Hank," she cried in heartfelt tones. Her hands were
still clasped tightly together, white at the knuckles from the pressure. Her
eyes were large with fright and her breathing was labored and rapid.

Hank whistled to Diablo, who at once moved forward, releasing the
rope. "Just a moment, my love," he said to Marianne as he moved to the
horses' heads and removed the reata.

Marianne thought he meant to examine Lord Entwhistle but she was wrong. Hank knew when he fired that his aim had been accurate and Entwhistle would never kidnap or harass another woman. She sat there afraid to move, her mind dwelling on the still figure on the ground.

Hank quickly recoiled his rope and placed it on his saddle. Then he reached both arms to Marianne, grasping her securely around her waist, easily lifting her from the curricle. One look at the tears welling in her beautiful eyes and he gathered her close, putting her head down on his shoulder.

She wasn't the least bit upset at his bold behavior, merely snuggling a little closer to him. When she raised her head to look at him and he saw a pair of entrancing lips so close to his, he found the temptation too much to resist. He bent and lightly brushed them with his own. He felt her response as she tightened her arms around his neck and he threw prudence to the winds as he enfolded her tightly in his arms and kissed her ardently until he possessed her mouth completely. Reluctantly he set her on her feet. There was much to be done. His lovemaking would have to wait.

Marianne was dizzy with happiness. Her senses were disordered, her feet were tingly, her heart was pounding, and she was bereft of words, a shining aura emanating from her.

"My darling, I have much to say to you and a question to ask but this is not the time. Will you trust me?" He let his hands slide down her arms until he held her hands.

She had held her breath waiting for him to declare himself, but as he finished she sighed a little. Of course, he was right. This wasn't the place or the time. She took several deep breaths to try to restore her composure, but found that it was not possible. Her heart would always flutter when he was near and she knew that she would follow him to the ends of the earth.

"Wait here for a moment. I can't afford to have you involved in this. I would gladly report my killing of Entwhistle to the authorities but I wouldn't be able to keep your name out of it." He released her hands and walked around the curricle's horses.

Marianne could see the sense in what he said, but she didn't understand what he was going to do. There was no question in her mind that he knew what he was doing. She had every confidence in him. She stood next to Diablo and hesitantly patted his nose. Diablo shook his head and then bunted her gently, asking for more.

"Oh, you fraud!" she cried. "You're like a faithful dog." It was impossible to believe this was a dangerous horse. He certainly showed no signs of it to her.

Hank, hearing her make friends with Diablo, smiled to himself. If he hadn't made sure that Diablo knew she was a friend, she would never have been able to get near him. It pleased him to know she had taken to his horse.

He saw Entwhistle spread out on the grass. The pistol had dropped from his hand and lay nearby. Blood stained his shirt front. He was as unattractive in death as he had been in life. Hank didn't need to examine him. He had seen death too many times and in many forms. The man was dead but now the question was how to make it look like the work of foot-pads.

He pulled Entwhistle's pockets inside out, removing a few gold coins and a small roll of bills. He stripped the dead man's finger of a large gold signet ring and took his watch. He looked the scene over carefully and decided that unless England had trackers like they had in the West no one could tell what happened other than a robbery, which the victim resisted, firing off a shot. Taking out a handkerchief, he wrapped up the loot to keep it safe until he could dispose of it easily. Now he must tell Marianne what he had done.

She had stayed beside his horse patiently waiting for him. What an unusual girl she was! She never questioned him as to his intentions but was content to wait for him to tell her.

"We must get out of here quickly. Someone might come out from the lodge and see us or happen to drive down the lane if they heard the shot. I have made it look as if he had been robbed. I think it is the only way to handle this in order to keep your name out of it. I won't have you suffering even a breath of scandal. I am sure if I reported I'd killed him, and the circumstances, I would have all charges dismissed against me, but I wouldn't be able to keep you from having to testify." He paused to see how she accepted this.

Marianne looked at him worshipfully. She had never known such a man. He was everything she had ever dreamed of. "Lord Entwhistle deserved to die. He has been the cause of several girls dying and bringing grief to their parents. I am not sorry he is dead." She was very positive as she spoke and the way she tilted her head was so endearing he had to restrain himself.

"But how do you feel about me killing him? Does it give you a disgust of me?" He watched her anxiously. This had been quite an experience for a gently brought-up young lady to go through. He knew when he killed Entwhistle she might suffer a reaction and possibly could not bear to consider marriage with a killer.

There was a soft light in her eyes as she replied. "You could never do anything wrong in my eyes."

This time he couldn't help himself. He gathered her in his arms and crushed her against him. "Is there a way other than going back through town to get home?"

She was reluctant to come back to reality. With Hank's arms around her she felt that nothing could harm her. He had become her whole life. It had never occurred to her that love could be so enthralling. "There is a path through the woods that winds its way to the lane next to the one where I live."

That suited Hank. He would like to go on holding her but he knew time was of the essence. Placing his large strong hands around her waist, he lifted her to the saddle and swung up behind her. Diablo didn't seem to mind the extra weight. Hank held Marianne close, his arms wrapped around her, and suggested that she place her arms around him for support. He let Diablo make his way along the path at a good steady trot.

Marianne was glad to have an excuse to cuddle against him. She lay her head against the muscular chest and could hear the strong beat of Hank's heart. Closing her eyes, she dreamed about the future. A smile lit her features as thoughts of Hank flashed through her mind. She knew he was going to ask her to marry him and that she would say yes. It didn't matter if they lived in a hut, only that he was there to share it with her.

When they came to a small stream, Hank stopped his horse. The leaves on the trees rustled and the stream babbled happily, meandering down the countryside. It was very peaceful, just the two of them watching the water splash and bubble as it jumped over rocks, gathering strength for its journey to the sea. Hank pulled out his handkerchief and let the contents fall into the deepest pool. Now all the evidence was gone. All they needed to do was to get safely home to Dr. Douglas so no one would know where she had been. He'd seen to it that the greengrocer kept his tongue between his teeth.

Hank pulled Diablo up in front of the house, quickly dismounted, and reached up for Marianne. She gave him such a loving look his heart seemed to turn over. He set her gently on her feet and admonished her to report to her father while he stabled Diablo.

As he led his horse back to the stables, he saw the pony cart pulled into a stall. The grocery basket was intact. The old pony, having grown tired of waiting, must have made his way home. Hank took care of Diablo, unhitched the pony, then picked up the basket and made his way to the house.

Marianne had left the door open for him and he saw her kneeling beside the old doctor, who was ensconced in his favorite rocking chair. She seemed to be busily relating the incident, gesturing as she did so.

Dr. Douglas was patting his daughter's hair and as Hank entered he raised his head and welcomed him. "I understand I'm deeply in your debt. Marianne tells me you saved her honor and her life." Emotion was choking him and it was hard for him to speak. The pains in his chest were more severe now and lasting longer each day.

Hank flashed him a smile. "Marianne makes too much of a trifling service." What a charming picture Marianne made with her head on her father's knee. She quickened his breath as he watched her. There were some things that must be settled immediately. "Marianne, I find myself in need of a drink. Would you be so kind as to get me one?"

She rose gracefully to her feet. "Oh, how remiss of me! I am very thirsty myself. I'll see what we have." She hurried toward the kitchen, glancing backward over her shoulder for a quick look at the two men she loved. Her father was so dear to her and Hank, well, she tingled at the thought. She bit her lip as she reached in the kitchen cupboard for some glasses. She hoped that Hank would speak to her father. That must be why he hadn't spoken to her yet. She sang a lively melody as she flitted about the kitchen.

As soon as she left the room Hank drew near the doctor and at his motion pulled up a chair. "Dr. Douglas, I have something very important to tell you and I had rather Marianne didn't hear it just yet."

The old doctor had a twinkle in his eye. He could guess what Hank was about to tell him. The signals were flying high that his daughter and this young man from the western parts of the United States were very much in love with each other. He had no objection to Hank, he seemed to be quite a man, but he wondered how he planned to support her. He had wanted only the best for his beloved girl but with the recurring pain he had been having, he doubted if he would be here long enough to find the man he always dreamed of her marrying. "I can make a pretty accurate diagnosis of your trouble, Hank," he replied, and a smile lurked at the corner of his mouth.

Hank grinned. The old man was mighty sharp and he would be proud to call him father. He missed his own sorely and the thought of having a close relationship with Marianne's father was good. "I am very much in love with Marianne and I want to marry her as soon as possible."

At these words Dr. Douglas raised his eyebrows. "Is there need for such a hurry?" There was frost in his voice.

That made Hank laugh out loud and Marianne, hearing him, found herself smiling as she filled glasses of ale for Hank and her father and a lemonade for herself.

"You don't think anything of the kind, knowing your daughter the way you do. It's just that I can't bear to part from her every day. I want to take her home with me." His voice was deeply sincere. "What I wanted to tell you is that I'm not just a poor ranch owner but I have inherited some large English estates. Through a series of accidents I have become the Earl of Helmcrest."

Dr. Douglas drew a deep breath and let it out slowly. This couldn't be true. He had hoped that Marianne would marry a member of society, but he would have been happy to have her with a younger son. It never occurred to him in his wildest dreams that his little Marianne could be a countess. "You're not funning an old man?" he asked suspiciously. There was a pathetic note in his voice.

"I would never do that!" Hank's voice was sharp. He was in dead earnest and the doctor should be able to see it.

Dr. Douglas had planned to ask his sister in Scotland if she and her husband would consider coming to London for a season to chaperon Marianne, but somehow his sister's letters gave him the impression she was not well enough to attempt it. He was sure that his redoubtable sister could have brought a younger son or even a minor lord to scratch, but this was all unnecessary now.

"The thing is, Dr. Douglas, I want to win Marianne for myself, not for what I have. I want to see if she loves me enough to take me as I am."

The doctor voiced his thoughts. "The Earl of Helmcrest! My little Marianne will be a countess. I can't tell you what a burden has been lifted from my shoulders. Yes, of course, you have my consent and best wishes. I have known you for a fine man from the first time I saw you and I couldn't ask for more for my dear daughter." There was some suspicious moisture in his eyes. "My dear boy, you really don't know my daughter very well yet. Would you please let me ask her how she feels about a marriage to you?"

"I'm in your hands. Do what you think best." Hank wondered what was in the old doctor's mind but was sure he had Hank's interest at heart.

Marianne entered the room carrying a tray that held two glasses of ale and one of lemonade. She noticed her father and Hank in deep conversation and her heart beat a little faster. She was sure now that Hank was asking for her hand. She placed the tray on a nearby table and was about to give them the ale.

Her father stopped her. "Come here, my dear. I have a question to ask you. Hank, here, tells me he is desirous of making you his wife. I don't know if you are acquainted with his ability to support you." He paused and waited for her to answer.

She flashed them both her lovely smile. "I haven't the faintest idea of

Hank's financial situation and it doesn't matter to me at all. I'm sure we can manage. The thing is"—she hesitated for a moment, her eyes downcast modestly—"I love him." She was a little embarrassed at her boldness but she wanted the two men, who were the most important in the world to her, to know how she felt. She didn't want any misunderstandings.

Hank was entranced and as he glanced at Dr. Douglas he encountered a knowing smile. Of course, he should have known himself. Marianne wasn't a girl who would demand a wealthy husband—however, she was about to get one. "Darling!" Hank called joyfully. "We have your father's consent. Will you have me? Just as I am?"

Marianne nodded shyly, thinking this was a most unusual proposal. She always thought of being wooed in some romantic spot but her feelings were so strong about Hank it didn't really matter.

"Then, darling, let me confess. I'm Hank Salsbury, but I'm also the Earl of Helmcrest." He chuckled to himself, very pleased at the outcome. She loved him for himself just as he had hoped she would.

Marianne's eyes widened in disbelief. "I don't think I can be a countess." She couldn't imagine herself fulfilling the many duties required of persons of the peerage. "I've not the background to succeed. I would disgrace you."

"Marianne, remember you promised you would have me just as I am!" Hank retorted firmly. "We'll worry about the details at a later time, but I know you could never disgrace me. We'll learn together."

Hank took her hand and raised it to his lips, his eyes telling her what she wanted to know. "I must leave you for now. I intend to stay at the inn tonight in order to hear what comes of the Entwhistle incident." If there was any trouble he wanted to be here and take full responsibility. He was positive the greengrocer would keep his mouth shut because he had frightened the man half to death.

Dr. Douglas understood what was in Hank's mind and he nodded his agreement. The boy had a head on his shoulders. The doctor was very grateful and he felt at peace with the world. He could forget the insistent pains in his chest with the way things were working out. He was sure that Hank would take special care of his daughter and that she would have her every wish granted. What a splendid young man he had for a future son-in-law. He would have the best night's sleep tonight that he had had in a long time.

The next morning Hank rode back to the Douglas cottage. The maid opened the door, her swollen face and tear-stained cheeks alerting Hank to trouble. "Please come in, Mr. Salsbury." She dabbed her eyes with a big white handkerchief. "Marianne will be here in a minute." She turned away and almost ran for the kitchen, sniffing as she went.

Marianne, hearing the door, came running into the room, her face ravaged by the tears that had been running unchecked down her cheeks.

"What has happened?" he asked as he enfolded her in his arms. He patted her soothingly and a suspicion of the problem entered his mind.

"It's Papa. I found him in bed this morning." She tried hard for control but she looked so pathetic Hank's heart went out to her.

"Come, let me see to make sure." Hank spoke commandingly and held her arm comfortingly as they made their way to Dr. Douglas' bedchamber.

The old doctor's head lay on his pillow, a peaceful smile on his face. It was easy to see that his last thoughts had been happy ones. His last mission in life had been fulfilled.

Hank reached down and held his wrist, checking for a pulse, but he knew without this gesture that Dr. Douglas had gone. He picked up the edge of the sheet and gently pulled it over the old man's face.

"I'm very sorry, darling. He must have died in his sleep, a very easy way to go. I believe he has been keeping himself going on sheer determination. He's been so concerned about you that when he knew you were safe and that I would take care of you, he felt he could let go."

"Oh, Hank, I'll miss him so!" She pulled a dainty handkerchief from her pocket and dabbed at her eyes. He had been her confidant and life for so long it was hard to imagine being without him.

Hank took the handkerchief from her and carefully blotted her tears, noting that they sparkled on her lashes. He tightened his grip on her and smoothed her lovely hair away from her face. "You have me. You also will have my sister and I know you'll love her."

That gave her thoughts another direction. "If you're the Earl of Helmcrest, who is your sister? I thought she was a doctor—unless you have another sister?" She tilted her head on one side to catch his answer but didn't offer to stir from the welcome circle of his arms.

That caused Hank to smile. He knew the old doctor would appreciate this. He hadn't had the opportunity to tell him, but somewhere he was probably listening.

"I have only one sister. She's the Duchess of Belfort." He was greatly amused at the widening of her eyes as she heard this news.

"But she's a doctor," she protested.

"That's part of the story but it will keep. First, we must take care of your father. Are you content to leave matters in my hands?"

She nodded her agreement. She was happy to have him take charge. It was such a feeling of comfort to have him to rely on.

"I'll go to the village and make arrangements. I suggest we have the services tomorrow. I don't want you alone here longer than necessary." He was thinking of the gossip that would attend the doctor's demise. Speculation about Marianne's future would be the primary source of talk.

Just as he had thought, someone had found Entwhistle and reported him being shot by footpads. Most seemed to think he had gotten just what he deserved, so Hank was relieved of that worry.

"I can get our daily maid, Anne, to stay overnight for once. She offered to do anything to help."

"As I remember, you have no relatives closer than Scotland who might be willing to have you?" He thought of the doctor's sister.

"There's no one there who truly cares about me." She was thinking of all the times Papa had mentioned taking her to London for a season and getting his sister to sponsor her. Aunt had never confirmed that she was willing, but rather had excuses why she couldn't do it this year. Marianne didn't, for one minute, believe the story of illness in the family. It seemed to happen only if Papa made a request, and her uncle's excuses were even weaker.

The way she said this indicated to Hank that she was very lonesome. The sooner he could marry her, the better. If he had his way it would be right now, but with her father not even buried yet, it would be too hard on her.

"Well, I care, more than you know. You won't be alone any longer." He tilted her chin up with a loving gesture. "Let's sit down and make some plans." He led her into the small drawing room.

Marianne sat with folded hands, her eyes on Hank. She was still so shaken she could hardly think, but she knew that he would take care of everything.

"I'll go to the village and engage the undertaker. Then I'll see your minister and arrange for services tomorrow, if possible. I shall announce that we are being married at Helmcrest in a very quiet ceremony, under the circumstances. Does that meet with your approval?"

It seemed to be rushing things but she had no better alternative to suggest. Not trusting herself to speak, she nodded. She was grateful for his presence. She couldn't imagine how she would have dealt with this without him.

"After the service tomorrow we'll drive to Helmcrest. To satisfy your scandal-loving neighbors, we'll take Anne along. I'll see that she is driven home by one of my people. I suggest you select the things you'd like to take with you and I'll hire a wagon to take them over to Helmcrest." As he paused he thought that he had done more talking since he came to England than he'd done in all the previous years of his life. "Am I correct in assuming you rent this cottage from the Entwhistle estate?"

At her assent he nodded grimly. Entwhistle wouldn't be collecting the rent anymore. It was probable that the entire village and estate would benefit by his action. He wasn't trying to justify himself that way. It was just a small benefit. He had shot the man in self-defense, and from the way some were talking in the pub, Entwhistle might already have sent men to put him out of the way. It was something Hank wouldn't have put past that lecher. He was glad they were leaving the area tomorrow. If Entwhistle had hired someone, that person would soon have the news that his lordship was gone and could not pay him. Just the same Hank would be on the lookout until they left the village.

He took her hands in his, pressing them lightly, letting his eyes tell her how much she was cherished. There would be plenty of time later to show her how much she meant to him.

Marianne watched him go regretfully. It was surprising how much he had come to mean to her in so few months. Resolutely she turned to the problems at hand and started to make a mental list of the few pieces of furniture she wanted to take with her. Naturally, her father's instruments and books would go.

The service was over and they had said their farewell to the doctor. She sat in the post chaise that Hank had sent for, from the larger village up the road. She was very conscious of Hank's presence beside her and felt her heart swelling with pride as she peeked out from under her long lashes to view him. In a matter of days her entire existence had been changed. Her father was gone and instead she had Hank. She had left her home behind and was embarking on a new adventure. It was at this point in the fairy tales that the story ended—"and they rode off in the sunset and lived happily ever after." She knew of Hank's love for her and she was sure of hers for him, but she wondered if she would fit as easily as he said into his way of life. She rested against the velvet squabs and enjoyed the luxury.

Hank, studying her, said nothing but was content to watch her face and let her have a little time to herself. He knew that without proper chaperonage he couldn't stay at Helmcrest with her until they were married, but he had already solved that problem in his mind. He would introduce her to the staff, put her under his housekeeper's wing, and take the train to London to hunt up his sister. Samantha had been gone for weeks now and he was sure that she would come home to help him. She could chaperon Marianne and help her select a wardrobe and whatever she would need. Personally he didn't care if she were married in a sack but he knew these things meant a lot to a girl and he wanted her to have her heart's desire.

Marianne, getting her first glimpse of Helmcrest, couldn't help a cry of delight. The embellished gate, the tall ash trees, the light sparkling on the windows, and the cream-colored stone of the huge building all helped to make the picture enchanting, just like her favorite fairy tale. The hall was much bigger than she had believed possible. She knew she would get lost in such a place. She turned to Hank for his comfort.

Hank had a warm feeling of possession as he saw the familiar surroundings and the hall. His father had been right when he told him of his fierce pride in the hall and that if Hank ever saw it he would be just as proud. It gave one a sense of belonging, a fortress against the forces of the world.

Marianne turned to him and in a breathless voice asked, "Does all this belong to you?"

The childlike way she asked made him smile. He took one of her hands in his. "No, darling, it belongs to both of us."

He couldn't have said anything that was more touching to her. She looked down at her faded blue dress, styled as those of years ago. There was nothing in her meager wardrobe that could compete with the magnificence of this ancestral home. She shook her head as if to wake up from a dream, none of which had been so heavily laden with grandeur. It was beyond her wildest expectations. She shyly looked at Hank and found him smiling at her. She was glad he approved her father's wishes in regards to mourning. The doctor didn't believe in the wearing of black and giving up all activities for a period of time. He had always said he was going to a better place where he knew he would find happiness and be reunited with his wife. He could see no reason to mourn that.

As the chaise rolled to a stop before the portico, the huge oak doors were opened by the stately butler, Meadows, who bowed them in regally. Mrs. Clarke was standing in the background, having been alerted by the underfootman that his lordship was home and bringing a female guest. She came forward to be presented, having surmised from the servant's hall gossip that his lordship was in love and that this must be the young lady in question.

Servants seemed to have the most complete information system anywhere. Invariably they knew what was happening almost before their employers. From the repeated trips to Whistlehurst they had gathered that someone special resided there. The glowing look on his lordship's face was enough to tell all that the young girl must be a lady.

Hank performed the necessary introductions. "I'll not be staying the night. I'm off for London and if I hurry I can catch the evening train. Mrs. Clarke, I'm putting you in charge of Miss Douglas and ask that you take special care of my bride-to-be." Hank let his gaze wander tenderly over Marianne.

Mrs. Clarke curtsied with a broad smile on her face, while Marianne blushed very becomingly. The housekeeper loved a romance.

"Marianne, if you need anything, ask Mrs. Clarke or Mr. Clifford, my manager. They'll take care of you until I can return." He was loath to leave, but the sooner he left the sooner he could be back.

Marianne clutched his arm, not wanting him to go without her. This was an enormous place full of strangers and she felt at a loss to deal with it. She understood that conventions must be observed and said nothing, only hoping that he would be home soon.

CHAPTER 14

When the countess heard what was in store the following day, she gladly lent Samantha her carriage and her coachman. She declined to accompany Samantha although the prospect was inviting. She felt that it would be enough of a shock to have one lady show up at a horse auction where only men would be expected. She reflected that life had become extremely amusing since Samantha had come to stay.

Samantha paid particular attention to her dress. A walking dress of two pieces in dark blue contrasted with a white chip hat accented with a flowing gauze veil floating out behind. The top was tailored with matching buttons down the front, revealing a frothy white blouse. There were yards of material in the simple skirt and soft polished black leather boots completed the serviceable yet enchanting ensemble, showing off her lovely curves to perfection.

William coachman knew where the Ingrams resided and expertly made his way. They lived out on Old Marylebone Road, named such after the borough of St. Marylebone's church, St. Mary on the Bourne. They passed the great marble triumphal arch erected in honor of the Duke of Wellington, including a statue of him at its top. Samantha was fascinated listening to William's descriptions and comments on the places they encountered on the way.

The Ingram house was a large imposing structure and it made Samantha wonder how the owner of such an enormous residence could find himself in a position where he had to sell off his horses.

William drove the carriage around to the mews, which were spacious, with an exercise yard, several carriage stalls, and a large tack room. Several men were standing around talking to one another while others had gone into the stable area to inspect the horses coming up for bid. When they saw Samantha as she was descending from her carriage, conversation stood still and expressions of shock and disbelief ran riot among them. The spell was broken as Samantha approached the group, pausing only to notice that her coachman was following her orders to see the horses stabled and then to join her. At a raised eyebrow, William hurried to do her bidding.

He didn't like to leave her until he was sure that things would be all right.

Lord Edgeworth, recognizing her, came forward and admonished her gently. "My dear Marquesa, as I told you last evening, there is no animal here that is fit to carry a lady." He spoke patronizingly and patted her arm as she smiled.

"Thank you, my lord, but I felt I wanted to come to see what was on the market." She flashed him her dazzling smile and he immediately forgave her for her rashness in attending the auction.

A number of young bucks gathered around in an effort to be introduced and more streamed toward the group from the stables in order to catch a glimpse of this most unprecedented event. Some spoke frankly and others withheld their pronouncement on such behavior until they could see how this madcap young miss conducted herself. A few said that it was a refreshing change but disapproval could be read in several pairs of eyes.

At that particular moment a groom brought out a young chestnut gelding, announcing that this was item number one, and all eyes turned to him. He walked the horse up and down so that the viewers could see his action. Then the handler jumped lightly into the saddle and trotted, cantered, and walked him around a small circle. He finished his demonstration by stopping the horse and then backing him. The gelding responded easily. When the handler dismounted and held the horse next to the auction block the auctioneer began the bidding.

Samantha stood quietly watching, finding an English auction greatly resembled an American one. She was careful not to move a finger or blink an eye, for she knew if she did she might become the owner of a horse she didn't want.

There were several bids, the horse finally being sold to a stout middle-aged man who took a deal of chaffing from his friends. Samantha stood by while several other horses were auctioned off. There was some excellent blooded stock, but none tempted her. She was waiting for the last item, the black she had heard Lord Edgeworth speak about.

There was a stir as the final horse was announced. All eyes turned to the stables as two men tried to lead the great black stallion into the exercise yard, one on each side holding him by halter ropes. The horse tried to rear, shaking his head as if to get rid of his persecutors, but the grooms succeeded in bringing him down. The black stallion was a magnificent animal, with a small, well-placed head, fine legs, a silken smooth coat, and a tail that waved valiantly. Samantha came to the conclusion that the horse was frightened, not mean, and a little high-spirited. He looked like some of the horses Hank had bred and sold, having an Arabian background.

She was an excellent judge of horseflesh and she knew that this horse was the finest she had ever seen. She wanted him and she set herself to bid for him.

She grasped her reticule firmly, for it contained a bank draft that she had exchanged for the one the duke had left for her as an emergency measure. Simmons, the Belfort butler, had delivered it to her in a sealed envelope the morning the duke departed. It contained a cursory note about being called away, and this was for an emergency. She had put it away, thinking never to use it, but had brought it to London with her just in case. She was glad she had. It had been so easy, that first week in London, for her to have the countess cash the huge draft and have a new one made without the duke's name on it. As the marquesa she didn't have access to the Duchess of Belfort's accounts, but who would question the large amount of money when it was his aunt who cashed it? Samantha smiled at the simplicity of her plan.

The bidding started low. "What, only a hundred pounds for this animal?" cried the auctioneer. "That's stealing! Come now." He raised his voice and started to chant.

Samantha caught the auctioneer's eye and drooped an eyelid. He appeared startled and looked away as if he were surveying the crowd. His eye came back to her and she nodded slightly, hoping no one else noticed she was bidding on this horse.

Lord Edgeworth raised his hand a fraction, putting in a bid, and the auctioneer praised him as a man who knew a horse when he saw one. Others began to bid in earnest. The pace quickened, the auctioneer's voice making pointed stops each time a bid was made. Most of the bidders had their eyes on the horse but Samantha's never left the auctioneer. She hoped that the antics of the horse would keep the crowd from remarking that she was a most determined bidder. She felt that she would escape detection, for who would expect a lady to bid on a horse like this one.

The price became exceedingly high and most bidders fell out of the running. Just two were left, Samantha and Lord Edgeworth. Finally, there came a point when Lord Edgeworth gave up. "Now that's too much for that horse! He'll need some training to make him a good saddler," he complained.

Samantha was pleased with herself. She unobtrusively gave her bank draft to William with instructions to pay for the stallion and make arrangements for him to be led to the countess' stables. She stood patiently while this transaction took place and couldn't help the hint of a smile when she heard one gentleman ask who had bought the black. Apparently no one recognized the countess' coachman, servants usually being beyond notice, and as Samantha had requested he was not wearing livery today.

William had gotten the carriage harnessed and ready to depart before the bidding started on the black. Seeing a couple of determined young dandies making their way toward her, Samantha turned toward her carriage and covered the distance in march time, seating herself so that as William coachman hurriedly climbed into the driver's seat she was ready to depart. She gave the inquisitive young men standing there a friendly smile as the carriage pulled out.

On the drive back to the countess' house she spent time considering the horse she had bought. She was positive she could ride him but wondered how he would act in the park. Well, if he became too difficult she would get him back to the countess' somehow. She might even need to ask Belfort for help. That idea made her wrinkle her nose. That was the last thing she wanted to do. It was her purpose to gain his utmost respect for her prowess on a horse. She wanted to display her talents. First off, she would send someone to purchase a saddle for her. She wanted none of the regular ladies' saddles, she wanted a man's, for she intended to ride this horse astride. She had had a couple of elegant divided skirts made with this very idea in mind. Besides, this horse would never tolerate a sidesaddle.

Samantha was ushered in by the countess' butler, that worthy bowing low as he felt due her position. She gave him a smile, and hearing that the countess was in the morning room, made her way to her. She drew off her gloves and cast her charming bonnet on a chair as she crossed the room to sit beside her aunt by marriage.

The countess' eyes were alight with anticipation. "Tell me, how did it go?" she demanded.

Samantha laughed joyously. "The men were aghast. You should have seen the look on some of their faces. A woman had dared to enter their sacred portal. The only thing that saved me from a rigorous questioning was the auctioneer, who kept a very fast pace, and anyone wanting to purchase a horse had no time to investigate me. I arrived at the last minute, and I departed speedily before anyone noticed who purchased the horse."

"Well, tell me, did you buy that black you were talking about?"

"Lord Edgeworth was most persistent but I outbid him, much to his disgust. He felt that the price had gone beyond reason but after seeing the animal, I knew I had to have him." She sat for a moment contemplating her strong hands. She was sure she was capable of gentling the black. "Mr. Ingram's grooms are bringing him over shortly. I didn't think you would mind as you have room in your stable." There was a questioning note in her voice.

"Of course, my dear. I wouldn't have it any other way. I should miss this excitement? Oh no! You are making me feel younger every day." Her eyes rested fondly on Samantha. She hoped this prank of hers would work, for she wanted dearly to claim her as her niece. She knew Belfort and could tell he was smitten but was it merely a passing fancy or could it possibly be leading to real love?

"Shall I ring for tea while we're waiting for this horse to make its appearance?" The countess definitely had a twinkle in her eye.

"Give me a few minutes to change into a riding skirt and I'll join you." Samantha dropped a kiss on the old cheek and then hurried for the stairs. She was impatient for the black to arrive as she wanted to go over him herself.

They were having a comfortable prose over the teacups when Samantha remembered to tell the countess she had sent one of her people with a note of authorization to a local saddlery for a saddle for her horse. Correctly interpreting a look that the countess gave her, she grinned. "It took the entire amount of the bank draft to buy the horse, so I charged the saddle in the name of the Marquesa de Cienfuegos to the Earl of Helmcrest's account!"

"You what?" The countess was shocked, not about the large amount for the horse, but charging the saddle to Helmcrest. "You should have charged it to Belfort." She sat up straighter. After all, he was her husband and responsible for her bills.

"I didn't dare take the chance. If he found out right away what I had done he'd either guess who I am or expect something more of me than I am willing to give right now."

The slight frown on the countess' face cleared as if by magic. She should have thought of that herself. She looked with admiration at the composed young woman sitting opposite her. Her eyes were sparkling with mischief and it was easy to see she was thoroughly enjoying herself. Oh, to be young again! The countess uttered a deep sigh. At least she was getting to enjoy life over again vicariously.

The butler entered the room and announced with an impassive face that the horse had arrived. It was plain to see he didn't approve of what he had heard or seen.

"Would you like to come with me to see him?" Samantha had jumped up in her excitement.

The countess sat where she was and slowly shook her head. This was too much for her. She would wait and hear about it secondhand. She had a word of caution for Samantha. "Remember, you are Spanish and supposedly indolent, not much interested in violent forms of exercise."

"Yes, ma'am!" She slowly swept a curtsy and, drawing herself up primly, sedately left the room, causing the countess to chuckle in delight. This girl never failed to amuse her. How she had become a doctor she couldn't understand, for there was nothing about her personality that hinted of either masculinity or the bluestocking.

Samantha made her way to the stables, a flush of excitement on her face. As she entered the stable yard she told the first groom she saw that she intended to make friends with her new horse and would like everyone to stay away while she did so.

"But, yer ladyship," the man protested, "'e be an awful 'andful. I don't think it's safe fer ye." He was very much in earnest.

"If I find I need you, I'll call," she retorted firmly as she walked back to the loose box that housed her new horse.

She approached slowly and started talking to him in a low musical voice. He raised his head and his ears came forward but he stood where he was. She placed a lump of sugar on the flat of her hand and extended it to him, calling him softly. That intelligent animal shook his head and pawed the ground. He was having no part of her coaxing. She examined him closely as he stood there and, seeing the warm brown eyes, made up her mind and carefully opened the gate, stopping just inside. She called again to him and again extended her hand with the sugar. He pranced a little and then gracefully stretched his neck and gently lipped the sugar from her hand, immediately trotting away from her.

"You beauty! I know why your owner called you Joker! You're not in the least what you make yourself out to be. I believe I've got a treasure in you." She turned to one of the grooms, who was standing just out of sight of the horse. "Please bring me his saddle."

When the man deposited the saddle by the gate, she took one look and started to laugh. The shop owner and the servant she had sent must have gotten together for the saddle was an ornate black one with silver trimming. She was going to make an impressive appearance in the park in the morning.

"Tell me," she asked, "do you know how I happened to acquire this particular saddle?"

"Ned, the footman who went to the shop, says as 'ow 'e described the 'orse and the saddler says 'e 'as just the thing. 'E says if ye don't like it, 'e'll take it back."

"No, no I couldn't have done better myself. Tell him I'm grateful." She reached down to pick up the saddle and the groom was shocked.

"That's much too . . . 'eavy fer ye," he protested. Besides this was his work.

Samantha, rightly understanding the complaint, gave in. She wished he could know of the hundreds of times she'd slung a saddle over a horse's back. She might not look it, but her muscles were well developed from the rigorous life she had lived. Furthermore, American saddles were much heavier and bulkier than the English version.

"Very well, let me walk in ahead of you and you move very quietly." She advanced toward the stallion and this time he let her pat his nose. While she was thus engaged, the groom quickly threw the saddle blanket on and followed it with the saddle.

Joker was evidently used to being saddled, for he stood tractably, although both Samantha and the groom were waiting for him to balk. She exchanged the halter for a bridle.

Samantha fed him another lump of sugar and then, taking the reins, started to lead him from his box. The groom stood by tensely, expecting to have to jump at his head when he reared, but to his surprise the horse followed Samantha into the courtyard as amenably as an old workhorse.

When she was in the open she lightly put a foot in the stirrup and swung herself easily into the saddle. By this time all work in the stables had come to a halt. This was quite a show. No one had seen anything like this. It was unbelievable that the marquesa could mount so easily by herself and that she was actually going to attempt to ride the horse. They had seen the animal when he had come in. It had taken three of them to get him in the box.

As soon as her weight hit the saddle the horse began to sidle and prance about but the steady firm hands on the reins and the strength of her knees told him that he had someone here who could ride him. Consequently, after a few playful hops he settled down.

Samantha was transported with him. The thought of taking him out into the park was so powerful she could hardly contain herself until tomorrow. She wondered what Belfort's reaction would be. She neck-reined him a few times in the limited space and was positive that she had found an exceptional horse. It would require concentration to keep him in line, but she could handle it.

The following morning Samantha met the countess at the breakfast table. The latter surveyed her with keen eyes. "You look as fine as fivepence!" she exclaimed. "That is quite some riding habit," she added dryly.

Samantha laughed easily. She pirouetted to show off her skirt. "No one seeing it would guess it's divided, but I am certain that it will cause some comment before the day is out." There was a flash of amusement in her large eyes as she walked over to the sideboard and helped herself from the large variety spread before her. She knew, according to the countess' counsel, that what wouldn't be tolerated in a mere Miss Nobody, would be accepted with complaisance in the fabulously rich marquesa as a sign of high spirits. She would treat it as an everyday occurrence, which at home in Arizona it was.

The countess was toying with a piece of toast and sipping a hot cup of tea. "I had to make an effort to get down this morning as I wanted to see you off. In fact, I'm tempted to have William coachman get out my carriage and drive me in the park just so I can have a first-eye view of what you're up to."

"By all means, madame, I would enjoy having you see Joker perform."

The countess regarded her thoughtfully for a moment and then seemed to make up her mind. "Very well. This sounds like something I don't care to miss." She picked up a bell and rang it sharply.

Her butler answered promptly, a questioning look on his face.

"Lawson, will you send word to the stables that I desire my carriage this morning?" she asked, giving him a pleasant smile.

He nodded his understanding of the request and trod sedately away on his errand.

"I'll see you in Hyde Park shortly," said the countess roguishly. "I hope I don't find you in trouble!"

Samantha was enjoying a substantial breakfast. "I won't have any problem with the horse but I won't guarantee not to have any difficulty with any two-legged animal," she flashed, a militant sparkle in her eye.

"Samantha! A lady doesn't speak like that!" admonished the countess, but her eyes held a hint of laughter. There was no doubt that she was enjoying herself immensely.

Samantha had just finished her breakfast when Lawson reentered the room. "If you please, my lady, the groom has brought your horse around." There was something in his tone that told her Joker must be prancing about and he had his reservations about a lady trying to ride him.

"Thank you. I'll be right there." She picked up her riding crop, placed her tall hat at a rakish angle on her black curls, its gauze veil floating down her back, and pulled on her gloves. She was ready.

"I shall look to see you later," she said to the countess, who was giving her a critical stare as she languidly strolled from the room. It had taken all her will power not to race out to her horse, but knowing the part she must play, felt she should start now. She kept reminding herself that it was the marquesa who was to ride the horse, not Samantha. Margarita had been her mother's name. The Marquesa de Cienfuegos was her grandmother's title and as far as Samantha knew it had died out when her grandmother and grandfather had passed away. She patterned herself after the wonderful woman who had been her grandmother, languorous in her attitudes until something sparked her, then she could be quite energetic until the event had passed. She was a very restful person to be around and she had had a great deal of love for Hank and Samantha.

A groom was walking Joker up and down the street in front of the house and it was easy to see the horse was restive. He kept flinging up his head and dancing on springy legs. The groom was having a trying time to lead him. The horse would sidestep right beside him when a horse trolley bell sounded or something caught his eye.

Samantha walked up to him, talking again in a soft voice, hoping he would start to learn her voice. Then she took the reins and pulled herself gracefully into the saddle. The poor groom was greatly relieved when Samantha took the horse from him and a foolish look crossed his face when he saw how competently she handled the spirited horse. He had been prepared to go to her assistance.

Her skirt was very full and hung in graceful folds, covering part of her high-top riding boots. Her feet were free from impediment to mount. It was quite unexceptional aside from the fact that she was actually riding astride.

The groom felt she should have had an escort and volunteered his services, but with a little smile Samantha refused his offer. He went back around the house mumbling to himself about the ways of the Quality these days.

She started the horse walking down the road the short distance to the park, giving him a pat on the neck, telling him what a fine animal he was. But for the fact that she could feel his strength through the reins and knew he wanted to run, he acted like a well-trained hack.

Samantha passed a few gentlemen on horseback who took a second look, one young buck almost falling off his horse in his effort to keep her in sight. She paid no attention as she had her mind fully occupied with controlling her mount. She had suspected that she would receive a deal of notice on her tour of the park this morning and steeled herself against unseemly comment. The countess had prepared her for this, counseling that if she treated this like an everyday occurrence and displayed no sign of embarrassment then the *ton* would probably grant her indulgence. She lifted her chin higher and entered the park at the east gate.

There were many intersecting paths and a number of riders and carriages were out on this bright spring morning. She hadn't been following her chosen path long when she saw Belfort coming toward her. She continued her trot as she took particular notice of his mount. It was a showy sorrel gelding with good action and well up to his bit. She felt that he was quite worthy of Belfort and wished she could see Belfort put him through his paces.

The duke trotted easily, an imposing figure in his black riding coat, vest, and shining boots. His carriage was erect, showing his confidence, and he exuded masculinity and virility. He had a kind smile for those he passed until he observed Samantha and his eyes held hers. He touched his mount in the flank and cantered to meet her, his smile concentrating on her. With a gasp he recognized the horse she was riding as Ingram's stallion, and wondered how she dared take him out. He took in the tilt of her regal head and her graceful figure. By God, she was riding him astride! As he reached her he swung his horse around beside her, making his horse slow his pace to hers.

His fear for her and his temper merged and he demanded in a cold tone, "What the devil do you mean by trying to ride that horse? If he isn't Ingram's Joker, you may have my leave to call me a blockhead!"

She looked at him, giving him a saucy glance. "Trying to ride, Your Grace? I suppose you are an excellent judge of both horseflesh and horsemanship." She waited only for his assent.

Belfort, who was indeed well known for these abilities, merely bowed in acknowledgment. He hadn't meant to get off to this kind of a start with her, but she had tried him too high.

"Well, then, you must judge!" she exclaimed as she dug her heels into Joker's sides. That horse, who had been pulling on his reins ever since she had mounted him, needed no further urging. One second he was trotting sedately, the next he had started like a bolt of lightning and was tearing up the path. Clumps of dirt flew from his heels as the steady staccato hoofbeats were heard on the ground. The wind seized Samantha's veil and it streamed straight out behind her and made her catch her breath in sheer ecstasy. This was a humdinger! She hadn't had so much fun since she had left Arizona. She rode the flying horse perfectly, her motions completely synchronized with his, in absolute command all the way.

Belfort, for one second, had watched her, frightened, fascinated, and angry, all at the same time. He gave his horse a sharp dig with his boots and his mount leaped forward after hers. He couldn't help but admire her seat and the way she handled the huge horse. He had never seen another woman to compare to her. No Spanish lady he'd ever heard of had so much strength and ability.

By letting his horse go all out and pushing him to the ends of his ability, he managed to pull alongside. "You'd better pull him in! Riding *ventre à terre* isn't done in the park," he added grimly, with a glint in his eye.

Seeing it, she had to laugh and, obediently, she started to pull Joker in.

For a moment Belfort toyed with the idea of reaching across and adding his strong arm on the reins, but seeing Joker come under control, quelled his desire and thus earned her gratitude.

Luckily there was only one man riding on this portion of the path, which was secluded from most of the park by some tall shrubs. By the time they had come out of the cloistered section their horses were only at a light canter, which was slowing to a trot. They continued their tour around the park, Samantha's face flushed and her eyes sparkling with pleasure.

Belfort thought he'd never seen such an entrancing woman. If only— He stopped there. He was married and the girl he'd married had done so in good faith. She had helped him when he had needed it and how had he repaid her? Absolutely deserted her! He might have had some excuse but as soon as he could finish this business with Lord Palmerston on the queen's behalf he would go home and see how the poor unfortunate soul was faring. It was strange that his comptroller or agent hadn't written on her condition. It could only mean that she was alive and death not imminent. Then the words of the fortune-teller came into his mind. Bury her? If she were that ill, it behooved him to get himself home. In the meantime there was this fascinating woman who seemed not unwilling to have his attentions.

"I must apologize," he grinned at her. "You have taken the wind out of my sails. I salute you! I've never seen a better rider but I still wonder if that horse is a safe one for you. He has been known to rear and generally act up." He felt he must add this word of warning.

Samantha smiled her thanks on his compliments and thought he was possibly quite the best horseman she had ever seen herself. The only exception she could think of was her brother, Hank, who had almost been born on a horse.

They rode on in companionable silence for a few minutes each enjoying the lovely green of the spacious park. Flowers were poking their heads up through the soil heralding spring. More people were entering the park and soon horses and carriages were everywhere. The many bright colors of ladies' carriage dresses and habits lent a festive atmosphere to the park.

Down the way they saw the countess' carriage coming toward them and they pulled in to stop to speak with her.

"Ah, Belfort!" cried the countess. "How do you like the marquesa's horse?" There was an innocent look in her eye but Belfort, knowing his old aunt, ignored it.

"How do you happen to be out this early, ma'am? Surely this is a new start for you?" he enquired, his face impassive, but a small muscle was jumping at the corner of his mouth. The old rascal! He knew she'd come out especially to see how he'd react when he saw the marquesa riding Joker.

"How do you like my horse?" asked Samantha, turning her attention to the countess.

The old eyes took her in, noting how easily she seemed to control her horse. "I must say, my dear, you are a constant surprise to me." The look she gave Samantha spoke volumes. "I trust her to your care," she added to Belfort enigmatically, as she gave her coachman the signal to move on.

"I have the feeling that I'm missing something," Belfort stated pensively as they walked their horses. His face was a study and he seemed preoccupied for a short time.

Samantha caught her breath. This husband of hers was very perceptive; he didn't miss the turn of a card. She wondered what he would say if she announced she was his wife. The very idea brought a curve to her lips. Not yet! She must play this out for a while longer. She didn't want an interlude; she wanted love, a lasting attachment.

An interesting thought struck Belfort. After such an exhibition he would love to see the marquesa hunt. This wasn't the right season, but they could still take the dogs out and go for a run if she didn't mind the mud. It would be something to see if she took fences the way she rode.

"Tell me," he began, "do you hunt?"

She was at a loss. She had never hunted in her life, but the kind of riding she had done in the States must be, at the very least, equivalent. She had never hunted animals but she had been the quarry as she had raced over rough ground to flee renegade Indians. She made up her mind and matter-of-factly answered yes.

"I have a hunting lodge a few miles outside of London and maintain a decent stable there. I'm planning a hunting party next week and I would like to have your company." As she started to speak he interrupted her. "I can mount you. It would be a pleasure." He gave her a warm look.

It brought a flush to her cheeks. She asked in a provocative way, "Not some slug that would be last in because he couldn't take a fence?" Her face was serious and nothing in her demeanor suggested otherwise.

Belfort was looking into her telltale eyes and laughed. "After your exhibition I shall give you the liveliest horse in the stables."

She still hesitated and Belfort, correctly guessing why, added that there would be several young couples and he had planned to ask his aunt, seeing she was acting as sort of chaperon to Samantha.

Samantha's face cleared and she accepted the invitation. She had no intention of finding herself alone in a hunting lodge with the duke. She would love the opportunity to join a hunt. If all that was required was merely the ability to ride over rough ground, cross creeks, and jump fences, given a good horse, she would undertake to keep up with anyone.

How Hank would have relished this opportunity. She wondered how he was coming with Marianne. It had been some weeks now since she had seen him. When she returned she would ride over and see Marianne and her father. She'd like to make arrangements to go over occasionally and take care of some of the surgery for him.

"As soon as the details are completed, I'll call on you to let you know." There was a special way that he looked at her that made her breathe faster and caused a fluttering sensation inside her. She tried to analyze just what it was—the look in his eyes, his slight smile, his erect carriage, or his quick mind. Deciding that it was a dab of each, she turned her thoughts to the future. With a few days at the hunting lodge they would be thrown in close company and who knew what might develop.

Belfort accompanied her through the streets to the countess' mews. He explained as she protested, he wanted to be sure that Joker didn't take exception to a stray dog or a tradesman's cart.

The grooms were surprised to see the marquesa returning, apparently having had no trouble with the stallion. There was no doubt she had impressed them.

She jumped down and gave the reins to one of them and stood talking to Belfort for a moment. She felt her morning had been successful as she was certain she had gained his respect. That hunting party had materialized mighty suddenly after he had seen her ability to ride.

The duke wondered at what the *ton* would say if he told them that he was assembling a hunting party, for hunting season was generally during the late fall and winter. He wouldn't label this a hunting party but a small get-together. He thought that he and the marquesa and possibly one or two others would be all that would brave the muddy fields and such. With his usual precision he set about making plans for the marquesa's entertainment.

CHAPTER 15

The countess remarked to Samantha that since her arrival the knocker had never been still. There were a series of morning callers, a predominance of elegant young men who, most certainly, had called to see Samantha. There was a sprinkling of mothers of sons who were looking for a suitable bride. Family position was important but a wealthy wife was not to be despised.

The butler, Lawson, had just seen Sir William Allan out when Belfort arrived. He gave his hat and gloves into that worthy's keeping and, hearing the ladies were in the Blue Salon, made his way there.

"Belfort! How nice of you to call. This is indeed an unexpected pleasure," the countess greeted him. Before Samantha came she was lucky if she saw him once in a twelvemonth.

Belfort pulled his eyebrows together for a moment as he digested that barb and then seeing the amused look on Samantha's countenance smiled ruefully. "You have such added attractions, dear Aunt," he murmured as he bowed.

That tickled the old lady and she gave him her approval. It was hard to get ahead of him. He was as smart as he could stare. She invited him to sit and he chose a chair that put him near Samantha.

Looking at the countess, he said, "I came purposefully to ask if you'd like to help me make up a party at my hunting lodge this coming week. The marquesa feels your presence is necessary."

The countess cocked an eyebrow at Samantha. She knew when hunting season was, but apparently Samantha didn't. She wouldn't enlighten her. "I'd be in the way and you know I'm long past riding."

"Ah, but you'll enjoy my chef and the wines I've laid down. Besides," he coaxed, "I've need of someone to play Mrs. Grundy."

That brought a laugh from both ladies. They had to admit his openness was entertaining. He sat easily cajoling them and it reminded his aunt of the times when he was a schoolboy and wanted her to do something for him.

The countess decided she might be old but her brain still functioned quite well. She weighed her presence at the lodge against what difference it would make if someone else would act as chaperon. She came to the conclusion that matters might progress much better if she were not present at the party.

"I'm sorry, but I have made engagements in London that I don't feel I can break." She noted the disappointment on Samantha's lovely face but she could see Belfort was made of sterner stuff. If she knew him, and she thought she did, he would find a way around this yet.

He was revolving several ideas about in his mind when the countess came to his rescue. "Have you thought of asking Lord and Lady Leicester? They enjoy the hunt and are good company. Besides," she hesitated, "Margarita has already met them." She reflected she would have to watch her tongue. She had almost called her Samantha and would have put the cat among the pigeons.

That brought a smile to Belfort's face. "Jolly good," he answered cordially. "The very people—however, I suppose that I must ask Miss Leicester also." His mind was busy on couples. He certainly didn't want any competition down there. It would defeat his purpose.

"That would be charming. I'd enjoy her company." This time it was Samantha who had a solution to the problem. "Would you care to invite Mr. Randolph? He seemed much interested in her at dinner the other evening."

The duke looked approvingly at her. He didn't think he would have any competition from Randolph and so he would make the perfect gentleman to round out the numbers. He wondered when she suggested him if she realized that her choice would probably assure her being mostly in his own company.

"I'm sorry you can't find it feasible to join us. We would have loved to have you. Your quick tongue is an addition to any party."

The countess gave him a sharp look but his face was exceedingly bland. They understood each other. "Touché," his aunt saluted him.

"I must go and call on the Leicesters. As soon as all arrangements are made I'll do myself the honor of calling upon you."

He turned to leave but at that moment the salon doors opened and Lawson announced the Earl of Helmcrest.

Conflicting emotions were to be seen on the occupants of the room. Samantha wondered how Hank had found her and if he would expose her masquerade. Belfort's first thought was that something had happened to his wife, for why else would his brother-in-law be here? The countess saw the drama unfolding with many subplots being thrown in for good measure and, after her first startled moment, settled back in her chair and prepared to enjoy the proceedings.

Hank strode into the room looking even more handsome than ever, having had time to be outfitted by a first class tailor. His gaze lighted on Samantha and widened in surprise. He turned away from her pleading eyes while he greeted his hostess and spoke to the duke. He tried to interpret Samantha's look and casually strolled over to her. He took her hands and murmured, "You are more beautiful than ever."

At this the countess broke in. "Oh, do you know the Marquesa de Cienfuegos? I was about to introduce you."

These words hit Hank like a plunge in cold water. The minx, she was masquerading as their grandmother. He stole a look at Belfort. It seemed he had taken her at face value. Hank wouldn't put a spoke in her wheel and so joined the farce with vigor. "I'm an old acquaintance of the marquesa's. We stand on no ceremony with each other." He gave her an engaging grin.

Samantha's heart resumed its normal beat and she looked to the duke to see how he would react to that statement.

Belfort was listening acutely, deciding he didn't think he liked the implications. Drat the fellow! He could hardly complain as the fellow was his brother-in-law and was free to send out lures to any female he desired. In the meantime he would like to know why he had shown up in London.

"Do you bring me any news from Belfort?" he enquired. He was afraid to think what the answer might be. If anything had gone wrong, he would never cease to blame himself.

"Nothing of importance. My sister decided to come to Helmcrest and keep me company for a few weeks. You will be pleased to know that I think she is improving remarkably." He gave Samantha a stealthy look and, catching her eye, winked at her. "I have just run up on a few days' business with my solicitor, some estate matters. I was wondering where to find you and thought of your charming aunt d'Avigny, who might know of your direction." This last improvisation surprised himself. He didn't know he had it in him.

Belfort felt himself giving a sigh of relief. He knew he should be thinking of the poor woman who was his wife but somehow the marquesa had worked her way into his mind so that he found himself thinking of her constantly. If all were well at home then he could feel easier about staying in London for a while longer. Any day now the queen would take a stand on England's neutrality concerning the problems of the United States and the Confederacy and there would be no valid reason for him to stay away from Belfort.

One thing, he was not leaving the field open to Helmcrest in his absence. He had said he had come looking for him and so, by God, he'd have him. He found it hard to understand why no one had thought to direct him to his house in Grosvenor Square. It was only on the other side of the square from his aunt's.

"I will be happy to put you up. I have an excellent chef here and can promise you a capital dinner." His tone was easy and inviting, assurance of an acceptance radiating from him.

Hank grinned at him. "I appreciate your hospitality but I find I have other matters to attend to. I'm sure you'll excuse me if I'll cry off. I am glad to bring you the news of Samantha's improved health." As he spoke he looked directly at his sister.

She managed to suppress a giggle only by dint of great effort. This was better than Samantha had hoped for. Seeing the dark look on Belfort's face she wondered if he were regarding Hank as a possible rival. It struck her as intensely humorous. She caught a glance from the countess and, by the sparkle in those old eyes, knew she was enjoying the situation.

With a shock, Belfort found it hard to believe the fellow was actually refusing him. It was unprecedented. He ground his teeth inaudibly. There was nothing to excuse his lingering as he had already started to leave when Helmcrest arrived and short of actually dragging the fellow with him he could think of no other way to get him out of there. He had, however, considerable address and successfully concealed his feelings as he politely bid them good-bye, reminding the marquesa he would call on her to see if his final arrangements were satisfactory to her.

After he strode from the room and the front door had clicked shut, the three of them broke into peals of laughter. The countess produced a tiny lace handkerchief and wiped away a tear that threatened to run down her old cheek. "Oh, my dears, you have certainly brightened my existence! Now sit down, Helmcrest, and tell us what brought you here."

At her command he dropped lazily into the nearest chair. He noticed the luxurious furnishings, the Queen Anne chairs and sofa, the rich draperies, and the gilt mirror and paintings on the walls. "I hadn't seen or heard of my sister in weeks so I decided to come to London and see if anything was amiss." He broke off for a moment while he regarded her. "You're a featherbrain! Going off and telling your staff you were coming to me and neglecting to tell me about it personally. With such a scarity of details I had problems making arrangements with my staff. Knowing your penchant for mischief, I decided to see what kind of a rig you were running. The only person I could think of who might know where you were was the countess, hence my first call, and I struck gold. If your aunt d'Avigny hadn't given me her address, I wouldn't have known where to start. I've had to tell my people that if anyone enquires from Belfort as to your health they are to say you are indisposed and cannot see anyone at present. Smythe, my valet, knows better. He is a very discerning man and I am sure of his loyalty. I gave him your aunt's address so that in case of emergency he would know where to find me." He reflected it had been a good day's work when he brought Smythe out of retirement. He had been able to steer him through several social pitfalls. Thanks to him he was now dressed in the finest of fashion and he had attained a quiet elegance.

Smythe had taken a few of the old servants into his confidence and they had closed Samantha's old room, giving it out that she was ill. Mary, her maid, had been summoned from Belfort to attend her.

Hank had been waiting patiently for his opportunity to tell her about Marianne and his decision to marry her as soon as possible. He planned to confide in her about Entwhistle but decided that could wait until they could be private.

Hank's words stung Samantha. "I thought you would be so busy with Marianne and her father that you would never think of me for such a short time. I didn't expect to be here for more than a few weeks at the most." She gave him a saucy look. "Now that you have seen me tell me what do you think?"

"No fishing, my girl. You know what I and every male that sees you thinks. It's apparent that poor Belfort is not only full of admiration for you but was immediately jealous of me. Seems like you have quite a situation going."

That was putting it mildly, thought the countess. She wondered how Samantha planned to end this comedy.

At this point Samantha wasn't sure herself how this was going to turn out. "I've accepted an invitation to Belfort's hunting lodge for a few days." Noticing Hank's raised eyebrows she added, "There is a small party going and Lord and Lady Leicester are to act as chaperons."

Hank thought this over for a few seconds and then nodded. "This will throw you in Belfort's company and you should see enough of him to know what you want to do."

Samantha already knew what she wanted but this was going to be her attempt to have him declare himself in love with her, and ultimately admit that it was impossible because he was married. She couldn't quite see how she was going to reveal who she was, but, she hoped fervently, time would help her find a way. It was possible that no man would go that far in admissions of love. Well, she would wait to see what the party would bring. Maybe all he wanted was a new exciting mistress. "That's enough about me. How is Marianne? Is our patient doing well?" She knew that in this length of time he should be completely well.

Hank hesitated and cast a look at the countess.

The old lady, catching it, rightly interpreted the look as meaning he had something private he wanted to say to his sister. "If you'll excuse me, I have some things I must attend to."

She started to rise but Samantha gave Hank a beseeching look. She knew they could trust the countess with any confidences and besides the old lady loved being in the thick of things. "The countess has been my confidante throughout this time, Hank." She gave the countess a special smile, saying, "I have come to love her dearly, and I'm positive that you will too."

Hank liked and respected the old lady and didn't hesitate. If Sam thought it was all right, then it was. "I have quite a story to tell you about Marianne and her father. First, your patient is up and about doing well."

Samantha flushed with pleasure. She had been sure the operation would prove to be successful.

"However, this week Dr. Douglas died in his sleep, leaving Marianne with no one to go to," he continued.

At this Samantha cried out instantly, "She must come to me. I would love to have her."

Hank smiled warmly at his sister. He knew she'd say that but he had other plans. "The night before the doctor died I asked for Marianne's hand in marriage and he gladly gave it. I told him confidentially of my circumstances and he was so happy I could see moisture in his eyes. I think the relief caused him to let go of his grasp on life. I didn't tell Marianne who I was until after she accepted me as plain Hank Salsbury."

"What a lovely romance!" The countess was enchanted with Hank's story.

Samantha gave Hank a searching look. She knew her brother better than anyone else and could feel when he was skirting details. She was positive that there was more to this story than he was telling.

Picking his words carefully, Hank continued. "There was some difficulty. Before Dr. Douglas died, Marianne was kidnapped by some local lord."

Samantha's eyes flew wide open. Entwhistle! She bit her lip and waited for him to continue.

"I happened to come along at the right time and rescued her." He told the story matter-of-factly.

Samantha couldn't wait to hear the full details of this tale, knowing there was much more to tell than Hank let on with his few sparse words.

"What happened to the abductor?" She was careful not to mention any names or seem too cognizant of the story.

A martial light came into Hank's eyes. "I heard it on good authority that some highwayman came across him, robbed and killed him. His empty pistol was beside him so I imagine he tried to defend himself." There was a note of satisfaction in his voice.

"My! What a story!" The countess accepted it at face value.

Not so with Samantha; she knew her brother was telling her plainly that he had killed Entwhistle but that he had covered his tracks. Well, the man deserved to die. She couldn't feel the slightest bit sorry that he was gone, in fact, reflecting on the matter, the village would probably be better off at his passing.

"Where did you leave Marianne?" Samantha thought of the poor girl all alone somewhere.

"I saw to her father's funeral and then took her to Helmcrest and put her in charge of my housekeeper. I've told her I'll return as quickly as possible and that we'll be married when I return. What I came specifically for was to take you back with me to help her and so make it conventional for me to be in the house. Now I find you setting out on a hunting party and probably not until next week. Hang the thing! I need you."

He was very much in earnest and Samantha could understand his haste. He was deeply in love and concerned about his darling.

"Hank, give me the time I need to attend this hunting party with Belfort. It is only to last for three days and if I can get him to set the date for two or three days from now, I could be available to you in less than a week. Regardless of the outcome I promise I'll come right to Helmcrest and help Marianne." She was hoping mightily that the outcome she envisioned would come to pass.

Hank managed to restrain his impatience. After all, Samantha deserved her chance at happiness too. Less than a week. He hoped that they could make it in five days. He would send word to Marianne when to expect him and that Samantha would be there to support her. That would make her feel better. "Now, Sam, I want you to promise that this won't take any longer. You won't stay on, regardless?"

"I promise, regardless of what happens, I'll come to Helmcrest to help both of you." She thought for a moment about the time she would be gone. "But where will you stay?"

Hank was about to reply that he had been put up for membership at White's and could go there but the countess intervened.

"There can be no question about that. I should be most happy to have you stay here." She raised a delicate hand as Hank started to protest.

"Nonsense. Feel free to come and go as you please. I shall enjoy having a man in the house."

"Thank you, ma'am." Hank had no choice but to accept and reflected it would make it easy to return with Samantha. He'd know immediately when she returned. "Under the circumstances I'll stay at White's until Samantha leaves for the lodge. If Belfort finds me installed here I hate to think of what might go on in his mind. If ever I saw a jealous man . . ." His eyes rolled back in his head and a comical expression appeared on his face.

Samantha's eyes sparkled. "You actually think he was jealous?" Perhaps this was going to work out after all. She let her mind wander to the letter she must compose to Belfort.

Hank ignored her question. "When do you think this hunting party will take place? If it isn't for a week, or even a little less, you're shot down!"

Samantha had been contemplating that very thing. "I shall send Belfort word that owing to some previous engagement I must be back in town on Monday, six days from now." She thought about it for a few seconds and turned to the countess. "Do you suppose that he can put that party together so quickly?" There was doubt in her voice.

"Most assuredly! When Belfort wants something he gets it. I've never known anyone to refuse one of his invitations. They are prized." The countess sounded very sure of herself.

This gave Samantha another light on Belfort and she thought about it as she moved over to a small French desk and took out a piece of paper and a pen. Quickly she dashed off a few lines. As she reread them it sounded like she was chasing Belfort but under the circumstances she couldn't help it. Was he such an excellent host? Why was he so popular? He must have been surprised when Hank turned down his invitation. She smiled at the thought.

Hank broke in on her musings. "If you ladies will excuse me, there are some things that I must attend to. I will get in touch with you later and see when and if you are going to Belfort's lodge." Bowing with grace, he left them.

"It looks as if my stay in London is coming to an end. I have loved it so much that I almost hate to leave." There was a little droop to her lips. She loved the theater, the opera, the balls, and the parties, but most of all she minded leaving Belfort. She had a dull ache inside her every time she thought about losing him. She had never had him actually, being a wife in name only. She wanted to confess to him that she was his wife, but she couldn't seem to find the right words or time.

"You'll be back. Now don't feel bad. I haven't the gift of second sight but I feel very strongly that you are going to solve all your problems." The countess was very much in earnest.

Samantha ran over to her and threw her arms around the tiny body. "Bless you! You do pick my spirits up. Now, if I'm to go to the duke's party within the next two or three days I'd better accomplish the few things I've wanted to do, but haven't yet found the time." She left the room with the countess' words floating after her.

"Now don't get into any mischief."

When the duke left the countess' he made up his mind to get his party organized as quickly as possible, and so started to run down Lord Leicester. He found him at Brooke's, an exclusive men's club to which he also belonged. Lord Palmerston was a member there.

Leicester was sitting in the lounge perusing the London *Gazette* when Belfort spied him. "Leicester! Just the man I want to see," greeted Belfort.

Leicester raised his head slowly, reluctant to put down the paper. There was a frown on his face, which disappeared when he saw who it was that had disturbed him. "Ah, Belfort, what's new with you?"

"I need to speak to you for a moment. Can we go into the cardroom where we won't disturb anyone?"

Already there were several dark looks being sent their way. This was, by general agreement, to be a quiet room.

Leicester rose to his feet, folded his paper, tucking it under an arm, and followed Belfort to the next room. They pulled out chairs at an empty table and Belfort lost no time in inviting him, Lady Leicester, and his daughter, Lady Elizabeth, for three days' riding at his lodge. Lord Leicester was flattered that he had been singled out and stated he would undertake to answer for his family. They would be ecstatic. He knew the superb horseflesh that was in the stables and Belfort's chef was highly renowned. They could disregard the mud. It would be a delightful holiday. "What date are you planning on?" he asked. It really didn't matter, for if it proved to interfere with another engagement, that one would be sent a note of apology.

Belfort was about to set a date for the following week when a porter handed him a note. The countess' lackey had caught up with him and had sent in the message. Excusing himself, he read it through hastily. "I find that the marquesa has other engagements she can't put off and she wonders if we can get together by the day after tomorrow."

Leicester raised his bushy eyebrows. "Ah, the lovely marquesa is to be one of the party?"

Belfort smiled a little self-consciously. There was something in the way Leicester said that, that made him uncomfortable.

Leicester eyed him closely. He harrumphed a time or two and then asked, "Are you inviting Helmcrest?"

"Helmcrest?" Belfort was puzzled. Why should Leicester think he would invite Helmcrest? "No," he answered coolly, "I've invited Randolph to escort Lady Elizabeth and make the party even." His curiosity got the better of him. "Why do you ask?"

Leicester scratched his head thoughtfully. Now he wished he had said nothing. "It's just that Amanda Farnsworth is a very close friend of Lady Leicester's and she told her, in strictest confidence, that she had heard it on good authority that the marquesa charged a very expensive saddle to Helmcrest." He paused as he saw thunderclouds building up on Belfort's face. "Of course," he added hurriedly, "it was probably wrong and didn't mean anything."

Belfort managed to choke down his rage. The marquesa, the mistress of Helmcrest? This was impossible. But remembering how intimate they seemed at the countess', he found himself giving credence to the tale. Well, if that was true there was nothing to prevent him from annexing her himself. He couldn't very easily say something to Helmcrest as, unfortunately, he was his brother-in-law, not married, and free to have all the mistresses he wanted. But why did he need to select Margarita? He admitted to himself that he was more than taken with her. She had completely bewitched him. The party at the hunting lodge should prove to be extremely interesting.

He calmed himself enough to discuss transportation down to Belle Maison, his hunting lodge, Leicester deciding to take the daily train and be met at the station by Belfort's people. Belfort had himself under control by this time and discussed sporting events for a few minutes before he bid Leicester a good day.

Back outside, he surveyed the street, looking for his curricle, which was being driven by his groom. As he sauntered down St. James he greeted acquaintances and friends. This street was famous for all the gentlemen's clubs. There was an array of white stone fronts, bay windows, cast-iron railings, and several unique doors. Many gentlemen were parading down the street chatting as they went. Belfort beckoned his groom as he swung around the corner and jumped in with ease.

Belfort let his mind wander, but it always seemed to revert to the marquesa. He was determined he would drive her down to Belle Maison. It would give him some time alone with her. Could he find out about her relationship with Helmcrest? What the devil did she see in that American? He admitted to himself, upon reflection, that he was personable and he was a man in every sense of the word. He couldn't seem to unscramble his feelings, or abide the thought of the marquesa being someone else's mistress. But what could he offer her but that? Nothing better, for there was his wife. He groaned. Was ever a man so plagued? He would send Margarita word in the morning about when he would pick her up. He didn't think it would take long to catch up with Randolph and he would be very surprised if he refused the invitation. The Rosses and Somersets had accepted, he needed only to give them the date.

The next morning Samantha was up early. She had ordered the carriage and planned to be driven to one of the poorer sections of the city. Someone had told her about a place between St. Katherine's docks and Rosemary Lane. She wanted to see firsthand how these poor people were faring for medical help. She felt if she could see the neighborhood and the people living there she would have a good idea of what was needed. She didn't mention her destination to the countess for she knew that lady and would earn her disapproval. It was much simpler to go and be sorry afterward.

She was dressed in her plainest outfit as she did not want to call attention to herself. She had selected a large reticule and had carefully put in a few of her precious instruments, just in case. It would be very gratifying if she could come across someone who needed a cut sutured or a boil opened.

The coachman assisted her into the carriage and as he did so she gave him her destination. He gaped at her, thinking he hadn't heard right. The butler's eyebrows almost disappeared into his hairline as he shut the door shaking his head.

Very politely but firmly she reiterated her orders. The coachman shrugged his shoulders. He had never understood the Quality. Why did she want to drive down those old streets? Resignedly, he climbed up on the box, grabbed his reins, and clucked to his team. They moved forward slowly down the street.

They had been driving for some time, passing familiar sights, when the coach started down a narrow street. Samantha watched unbelieving as the houses became more cramped. The coach twisted and turned down several more narrow dirty streets before Samantha finally called to the driver.

"Stop!" She was leaning out the window.

The bewildered coachman pulled up.

She was looking at an alley with broken-down houses leaning on each other. Shutters were falling off and a new coat of paint hadn't been seen in years. "I'm going to walk down this alley. Please walk the horses up and down until I return. If I am not back within fifteen minutes find someone to watch the horses and come for me." She knew he was to be trusted and would not leave her. She jumped down easily, leaving an indignant coachman behind.

She advanced slowly, taking in the squalid conditions, hanging laundry still grimy, garbage strewn about, and stench reeking everywhere. It looked as if a good wind would blow the place down. An old woman was sweeping off her front step and as she saw Samantha she stopped and gawked at her. Though Samantha was wearing her plainest dress, the woman looked her up and down thinking she had never seen anything so fine. She leaned on her broom, chewing a hunk of tobacco, giving Samantha a baneful look.

"What are ye doin' 'ere?" she demanded in a strident voice. She was incensed that the Quality was walking down her road. What right had they to flaunt their riches over them?

Samantha stopped in front of the old woman, giving her look for look. She answered in her politest tone, "I am here to see if anyone needs any medical help. I am prepared to do what I can."

"Ha!" the woman snorted. "Medical 'elp! That's a good un. Us get no 'elp at all. 'Sides, us wouldn't trust one of them doctors anyway. They'd probably kill us off." She used her broom to punctuate her words and ended with a hand around her neck showing a possible choking. Her face contorted and Samantha stared, fascinated.

Samantha was appalled by the woman's answer. She never dreamed there was no help at all for these poor people or that their attitude was so sour. She would like to set up a clinic one day a week in this area, but would they accept help?

"What do you do if someone is ill or has a bad cut?"

The woman continued to stare at her as if she was some kind of unusual bug. "What do us do?" She spat on the ground, narrowly missing Samantha. "We manage on our own, that's what." With that she turned on her heel clutching her broom and disappeared into her miserable-looking house.

Samantha stood there staring at the closed door for a moment. This was worse than she had dreamed. With all the money at her disposal she ought to be able to engage a doctor to give a day to these people. She could make it well worth his while. She would talk to Hank about it and see what he suggested. He would know how to communicate with them. She wished she were free to speak to Belfort and get his reaction, but that would have to wait. Perhaps something might come of the hunting party.

Her mind busy with her problems, she walked on. Two disreputable-looking ruffians approached her with greedy eyes. One of them smacked his unsavory lips and the other rubbed his hands together in anticipation. They walked straight up to her, blocking her way. Only then did she get her head out of the clouds and realize she was facing trouble with the presence of one large and tall man and one short and thin man.

"'Ere's a nice prize fer us," gloated the larger of the two, as he leered at her.

Samantha drew a deep breath, lifting her chin, and stood still. She felt she had faced worse dangers in her life and if she kept her head she would get out of this. "What do you want?" she asked in a steady voice.

"Hoity, toity. Us 'as caught a fine bird. First off, 'and over yer purse," demanded the second man.

Samantha, looking at him, decided he was the more dangerous of the two. He might be smaller, but he seemed to be the more deadly. The easiest thing to do would be to give him her reticule, but it contained her precious instruments. She wouldn't part with them without a fight, but what could she do against two bullies?

"I have nothing of value," she answered. "I'll give you what money I have but there are some things I cannot easily replace." She kept her tone calm, all the time looking for some means of escape. There wasn't a soul on the lane and she doubted even if there were that anyone would come to her rescue. If she could delay them, her coachman would be coming to look for her, for she was sure that her fifteen minutes were up.

The smaller of the two laughed, a raucous sound. "Something you can't replace. That sounds like something Ned and me could use. Give it over or we'll take it and it'll be the worse fer ye."

"Me friend is speakin' plain, missus. Ye'd better do as 'e tells ye. 'Eaven 'elp ye if ye get 'is temper up." The large man was very earnest and gave the impression he wasn't all in favor of molesting her.

Listening to them she decided to gamble on the larger of the two not attacking her. If she could get a head start she could run, and knowing her ability on these lines, felt sure she could outrun them to the main street where she could get help. The conditions were not a great deal better but there were vehicles of sorts traveling up and down.

Grasping the strings of her reticule, she waited until the smaller of the two men turned aside to say something to the other. She firmly swung it with all her force at the head of the smaller man. Not expecting such an attack, he failed to dodge and it caught him on the side of his face jerking his head back and almost spinning him off his feet. He let out a cry, clutching his cheek, stunned for a moment.

That was all Samantha needed. Picking up her skirt in one hand, she spun on her heel and started to race down the alley. The larger of the two men stood there dumbfounded. He didn't offer to chase after her, but the smaller man, after catching his breath, started in pursuit, pouring maledictions on her.

Samantha was gasping for breath, her vision blurring for a moment, and she ran headlong into a tall figure who promptly caught her in his arms. She looked up at him in astonishment.

Belfort put her on one side and stepped forward to meet the would-be robber. With one swift punch he knocked the man down, stretching his length on the cobblestones. He grabbed Samantha around the waist and propelled her toward the main street.

"How did you come to be here?" she panted.

He ignored the question and proceeded to rake her over the coals. "What in the name of God are you doing in this neighborhood?" There was cold rage in his voice. He had been frightened for her and his relief in her safety found itself in his anger. "I can't see how a delicately brought up Spanish lady can have so much strength and run so fast." He had been fortunate enough to see Samantha's blow to the man's head. It was an enigma to him how she could have so many facets. There were some pieces to this puzzle that didn't quite fit, but for the life of him, he couldn't figure out why.

His words hit Samantha with stunning force. She was forgetting her role; that would never do. "Oh dear, I feel so weak I think I'm going to faint." She fluttered her eyelashes, managing to peek beneath them to see how Belfort took this. She was gratified with the result. He picked her up as if she were a piece of fine china and effortlessly strode toward the carriage.

She could feel the strength of his arms around her and found herself putting her arms around his neck. She placed her head against his protective shoulder and uttered a little sigh. It was one of pure happiness but he thought it was of distress.

"Don't be alarmed. We'll have you at the carriage in a moment." His face was inscrutable as he surveyed her.

She opened her eyes and looked up at him, trying to read his face, but not being able to gain anything from it. How did he happen to come across her? The fact of his seeking her out augured well. She gloried in the fact he was concerned for her, his anger she could cheerfully ignore.

The countess' coach approached and Belfort put her on her feet and assisted her in. She noticed he had already tied his horse on behind, so she knew he had planned to ride back with her even before rescuing her.

Samantha sank back against the seat and daintily dabbed at her face with her handkerchief. She had no need to wipe away tears but rather to cover her small smile, which wouldn't be repressed. She determined to play out her part and composed her face before Belfort settled himself in the seat next to her. She felt good to think she had gotten the best of the ruffians.

"I rode over to the countess' to tell you we had our plans all set for tomorrow to go to Belle Maison. The butler told me you had gone out in the carriage and gave me your direction. Praise the Lord, he overheard your instructions to the coachman. It was only luck that I recognized the countess' carriage driving up and down here and stopped the coachman. He told me of your mad idea to walk down that alley." His voice was stern. "Perhaps after what you have been through you won't be able to stand the trip to my lodge." He was irritated and could see his carefully laid plans dissolving in the mist.

Nothing was going to interfere with that pleasure for Samantha and she lost no time in disabusing him of that thought. "I am very grateful you came along when you did. I don't know what I would have done. My mind seems to be a blank." She fluttered her eyelashes again. "All I seem to remember is those awful men threatening me and my running away." She peeked at his profile to see how he took this. He still looked very stern. "I shall rest today and I'm certain I'll have no problem. After all, driving down with you will be very restful."

That calmed his fears but still didn't explain what she was doing in this locality. "Why did you walk down that street?" He waited for an explanation while studying her face.

Samantha's mind was spinning. She had known he was going to ask that question, but no satisfactory answer seemed to come. After some hesitation she answered with as much of the truth as she could tell him without confessing. That would spoil everything. "I have plenty of money that I can use for the poor. I wanted to see firsthand just how they lived and what they needed."

Belfort was charmed; such a thoughtful woman, such compassion. He had never been associated with a lady before who had any consideration for others, much less the unfortunate poor. The more he saw of this woman the more attracted he became. The fact that she had been married for a short time and had lost her husband didn't bother him but why did she choose to be a mistress, and Helmcrest's at that? There could be no other answer to the fact that she felt she could charge a saddle to his account. How then did she claim to have so much money she could give it to the poor? Did that come from Helmcrest also? He didn't like the thought at all. If she was wealthy in her own right, why choose this style of life? Why not wait for someone to offer marriage? He was positive that there were scores of men who would jump at the chance. Did she hope to become Helmcrest's wife? That thought haunted him, but he determined to get some answers while they were at Belle Maison.

CHAPTER 16

Early the next morning there was quite a bustle in front of the countess' house. Belfort's luggage chaise, with his groom driving and his valet inside, had pulled up and was waiting for Felicia, the marquesa's maid, and the luggage. Several footmen were carrying miscellaneous items out while Felicia supervised the lot, making sure that they had forgotten nothing. Belfort had pulled his curricle behind and had tossed the reins to a waiting lackey.

He strode purposefully to the door and was ushered in with great ceremony. Belfort was shown into the library where, with the double doors standing open, he would have an excellent view of the stairs. Glancing at his watch, as he was impatient to be gone, he was certain that he would be kept kicking his heels here for some time before the marquesa was ready. Much to his surprise in rather less than five minutes he heard skirts rustling at the top of the stairs.

He came forward to gain an even better view as the marquesa floated down the stairs, a vision of loveliness in a leaf-green carriage dress. The tight waist showed off her figure to perfection and the full skirt brushed the steps behind her as she came down, a welcoming smile on her face. She carried a matching pelisse over her arm of the same green velvet.

"The weather is a little brisk," he greeted her. "Are you sure you want to ride in an open carriage?"

"Most assuredly." She wouldn't miss this for anything. "I'll enjoy the lovely English countryside much more this way. I've dressed warmly and I don't anticipate being the least uncomfortable." She handed him her sable-lined pelisse and smiled to herself as he attentively helped her into it. If his hands lingered longer on her shoulders than strictly proper, she didn't mind the least little bit.

He looked keenly at her, seeking for signs that yesterday's experience had been too much for her sensitive feelings, but saw only a very sparkling countenance. She looked to be in a mood of great expectancy and he meant to fulfill her every desire.

The countess had made a special effort to arise in time to see the party off and gave Samantha a bespeaking look as she wished them both a happy time. She waved as they walked out to the curricle.

The luggage chaise with their servants had lumbered out of sight sometime previously. It would arrive shortly before Belfort. It was not in his plans to hurry the drive down.

Belfort assisted Samantha into the curricle. Samantha watched with interest as he skillfully tooled his horses through the crowded streets of London. On a crowded street he passed between two carriages going in different directions without a check to his speed. Samantha felt she was a good judge and Belfort's driving was exceptional. He was quiet as he threaded his way through the traffic heading for the pike road. Once there he turned to her and enquired if she had been concerned about the demanding driving through the busy streets.

Samantha answered truthfully. "I have great confidence in your driving, Your Grace." There was a warm note in her voice that made him look at her sharply. Did she mean something by that? He fervently hoped so. He was not one to rush his fences so he turned the conversation to the blossoming countryside.

Flowers were just as beautiful here as they were at Belfort last fall. Granted, Belfort gardens were probably the most spectacular she had ever had the privilege to see. She had taken a deal of pleasure in working in the gardens helping to decide which flowers from the hot house to plant where. This was so different from the desert country she knew. In the spring when the cacti came into bloom it was a gorgeous sight but that didn't last long. This country seemed green and alive most of the time.

When Belfort judged his horses had had time to have worked some of their liveliness out of them he turned to her and asked, "How would you like to learn to drive a team?" This was an unprecedented offer as he never let anyone drive his horses. He had been so impressed with her horsemanship he wanted to see what she could do driving; besides, it would give him an excellent opportunity to hold her hands. He knew he could keep perfect control over his horses even if her hands were on the reins. He smiled at her encouragingly.

She nodded her assent and looked at him sharply. Her learn to drive a team? It almost made her chuckle. She'd been driving a team ever since she was knee-high to a pistol. Then remembering her role, she gave him a pert smile and said she would love to if he thought she could.

He pulled the horses to a stop and while they stood restively he put the reins in her hands, showing her how to thread them through her fingers. She had to exercise great care not to gather them up easily and expertly. The feel of his strong fingers on hers as he arranged the reins to his satis-

faction sent a shiver of pleasure through her. She found she wasn't changing her mind about this husband of hers. The six months had been over
in March and she found that she loved him more each time they were together. Could she walk away from him if this didn't work out? She
pushed such thoughts from her mind and determined to put forth every
effort to make him return her love. Her heart beat a little faster as she
thought that this trip might win him for her.

Finally, the reins suited him, and holding his hands near hers, he
showed her how to start them off into an easy trot. This was a pleasure
she hadn't had since she had left Arizona and she was going to savor it to
the hilt.

The breeze blew lightly against her face and the sun was gentle over-
head. Birds were singing to their mates and happiness permeated the air.

Belfort, keeping close watch on her, thought she was the most be-
witching woman he had ever met. Why couldn't he have met her before
he'd married Helmcrest's sister? That had been a disaster and one he was
going to have to face. After all, she was his wife and there was nothing to
be done about that. She might have even improved drastically since he
had seen her last. It had been about eight months now. That wasn't the
question at hand. If the marquesa was living under the protection of a
gentleman there was no reason why he couldn't cut Helmcrest out. He
would receive a vast amount of satisfaction if he could do it. That thought
brought a wicked glint in his eye. He couldn't wait to get to Belle Maison
where for all intents and purposes he could have her to himself.

The horses had been trotting easily for a few miles, Samantha relishing
every minute. Belfort had been so pleased with his pupil that he had let
her take the reins by herself. She was a natural. After watching her
closely for some time, he decided that he could take his attention from the
road for a moment to bend down and reach into the picnic basket beneath
their feet. The drive would only be a couple of hours but he'd had his
chef prepare a few snacks anyway. If he found the opportunity, they
could stop. It was at this moment, with Belfort's head down to the picnic
basket, that disaster struck.

A fox raced across the road almost under the horses' hooves. This startled the lead pair and they began to rear and plunge. Belfort, perched pre-
cariously, was knocked forward as the curricle came to a stop. By the time
he had jumped up to grab the reins, he found that Samantha was already
steadying the team expertly and they were again moving easily. His face
was a study as he reached over and took the reins from her.

Samantha flashed him a brilliant smile. "What, not satisfied with my
driving, Your Grace?" She knew she had blown it, for her driving was

anything but that of a beginner, however she found she was receiving a great deal of satisfaction from the look on Belfort's face.

"You wretched girl!" he replied. "How dare you pretend you didn't know how to drive! That exhibition of yours was first rate. Now, we'll have some explanations if you please."

There was no doubt he meant business, and catching a look at his profile, she decided she must come up with a plausible explanation. It seemed to her that every time they met she had to come up with an explanation for something. It was always easiest to tell what portion of the truth she could. She sat primly, her hands folded in her lap. "Well, I haven't driven for a while and not in this country." That was true enough, she thought. "I didn't know how well I'd do as far as your standards are concerned and I was certain that you would be an excellent teacher." She felt that would cover the matter.

Belfort handled his team easily, the picnic forgotten, as he retorted, "Now that won't do. You haven't explained how you learned to drive!" He was determined to have a complete answer.

"My family had a large estate and my father thought it was necessary that I be able to handle a team and to ride well. He said I never would know when it might prove to be necessary." She was bound she wouldn't tell all. That was the truth, but if he took it for an estate in Spain and learning in that country, that was up to him.

The answer satisfied him, as it was logical. "You know you are the most interesting girl. I'd like you to tell me more about yourself." He waited with anticipation.

"What would you like to know?" She tipped her head saucily. She was afraid that she must come up with some answers that were entirely fictitious and hoped she could keep her story straight. If she could judge by his expression the kind of questions he had in mind, she would need to keep her wits about her.

"First off, tell me something about your husband. How did you happen to select him?"

"I didn't select him." That was true enough. "He was sort of forced on me. My family persuaded me into the marriage." Hank had offered many arguments in the cause of this marriage. "He was older than I and—well—something happened and he was gone. We never lived together as man and wife." Couldn't he hear her heart in her mouth? If anyone ever tried to tell the truth but make it sound quite like something else, it was her. This wasn't going as she had planned. She wanted desperately to confess the whole of it to him, but resolutely rejected the idea. She had promised herself that she would not tell him until he told her that he loved her. Her pulse was erratic and she could feel a flush creep up her face.

Belfort picked it up immediately. "He died before your marriage was consummated? What an awful shock for you." Belfort was thinking that this was most unusual, but things like that did happen. Still, that didn't explain her relationship with Helmcrest. He wanted painfully to believe that there was some other explanation but no matter how hard he thought, he couldn't come up with a plausible reason. Was she so lonely that Helmcrest had gotten around her? He couldn't ask that. One thing was certain and that was he wanted this woman as he had never wanted anything in his life. She was an obsession with him. He would have her one way or another. Divorce was rare but it could be done. The only thing was that it wasn't fair to the poor creature who had come so far to help him out of a fix. He felt that his mind was going in circles, first one idea and then another chasing themselves around in his brain. Did he want a duchess who had been someone else's mistress? She should be above reproach. He clung to the thought that the gypsy had given him.

> Money you wanted, money you got.
> A wife you wed and have her not.
> Bury the first and seek anew
> A glorious life is waiting for you.

He felt if he could solve the riddle, he would solve the enigma of the marquesa. He didn't usually believe in fortune-telling but in this case it was the only hope he had.

Samantha was also lost in reflections. Her mind took her through many things that had happened to her and the things that had passed between her and the duke since she had met him. The gypsy's singsong verse came back to her and she wondered if there was any truth in it.

> You have lost your husband. I see the tears.
> Now is the time to part with fears.
> The love of your life is drawing near,
> But I can see no marriage here.

Was the reason the gypsy woman could see no marriage because it had already taken place? Or was the reason that it was never to be? She couldn't, wouldn't, believe that. There was a simple answer to this coil somewhere and she would find it.

Before they knew it the horses were turning in at the drive. Belfort flipped the reins to a groom who came running up and turned to assist Samantha. That young lady was gazing about in delight. Belle Maison was built in the Tudor style with many roof lines and shuttered windows. It stood in a clearing with woods around it. A large stable could be seen off to the left and a smaller building, possibly to house servants, to the right.

A footman flung open the door and as they entered the house he murmured to the duke, "Mr. Randolph and Lord Leicester's party are here."

"Thank you." Belfort was always very courteous to his servants. It cost him very little effort and was handsomely rewarded with faithful service.

An older woman, dressed in black silk with the keys of her office tied about her waist, entered the hall.

"Ah, Mrs. Evans, would you please escort the Marquesa de Cienfuegos to her room?" The woman bobbed a curtsy as the duke turned to Samantha. "This is Mrs. Evans, my housekeeper. She will see you have everything you need." A sudden thought struck him. "Did my baggage coach arrive?"

"Yes, Your Grace. The marquesa's maid is upstairs now unpacking." With that the housekeeper led the way, Samantha following in her wake. She gave Belfort a happy smile as she left.

She looked so innocent and lovely it made him draw a deep breath. The picture of Helmcrest rose before him and he found himself gritting his teeth. Somehow, he would get things straightened out. He turned to enter his library where he found a cozy party drawn up before the brightly burning fireplace. They gave him a warm welcome as he greeted each one. He noted that the other two couples had not as yet arrived but he expected them to come together as they were close friends.

"Our lunch will be ready in about an hour and I can assure you that Raoul, my chef, has outdone himself. In the meantime, as soon as the marquesa joins us, how would you like to go over to the stables and select yourselves a mount for tomorrow?"

There was no question of the answer as they all turned eager faces to him. Each one was an avid hunter and had looked forward to riding the duke's superlative horses. This might not be an actual meet, but they would enjoy themselves just the same. They sat chatting about the forthcoming ride. Samantha had freshened up in a very short space of time and had sat down next to Lady Elizabeth to converse. She was a sweet girl and Samantha had found her easy to talk to.

The duke was gathering up his party when the sound of wheels was heard. "That will be the Rosses and the Somersets. Shall we wait for a few minutes and we'll all go together?" Everyone was agreeable.

The door opened and in swept Cynthia Ross, closely followed by her husband and the Somersets. They were both young couples, well known

to everyone in the party except the marquesa. Belfort introduced the
marquesa to the Rosses and Somersets. They stood on no ceremony and
had such pleasant manners. Both parties were so interested in seeing the
horses they postponed freshening up until they returned from the stables.

Belfort, a perfect host, had moved to escort Lady Leicester while Lord
Leicester was walking with the marquesa. They had only a short walk before the stables loomed before them.

There were stalls on each side spanning most of the length of the building. At the far end were two rooms, one on each side of the wide alley.
The one on the left contained the various items of tack used on the horses.
The other room was larger and opened on the far side, housing carriages
and the like.

Belfort halted them as they entered the stables. "Now, ladies and gentlemen, you may have your pick of any horse. The last four on the left are
riding hacks but all the rest are hunters. I can guarantee every one as giving you an excellent ride."

They streamed forward, each going to a different stall. Samantha, spy-
ing a pure black with a white blaze, moved over to him. She was taking in
his points and had decided there could be no better in the stable when
Belfort came up behind her.

"How do you like him?" he asked, watching the way she patted his
neck.

"He looks perfect and without looking further, I would like to ride
him." She gave him a little-girl look as if she were asking for a special
treat.

Belfort laughed so heartily that several others turned to see what was so
amusing. "You are an expert judge of a horse. That's Caesar, my own favorite. He's a handful but he's an excellent jumper. I don't believe he has
an equal."

"I wouldn't presume to ride your favorite, but which is your second
choice? You see, I think you unsurpassed in your selection of horseflesh."
She was pleased to find him so knowledgeable.

"That bay in the next stall. He'll give you a great ride." He smiled
warmly down at her, a soft light coming into his eyes.

Samantha felt a lump in her throat as she noticed his appraisal. She interpreted the look correctly and found her face getting warm. She moved
over to the stall where the bay was standing to remove herself from his
perception. He always had that effect on her. Her knees were getting
weak and she could feel her heart swelling as she felt his regard.

Belfort excused himself to see how the others were faring.

She spoke to the horse, pulling on his ears, when she felt someone behind her. She whirled around, startled by a sense of annoyance. Mr. Randolph stood there with a pleasant smile on his face.

"Did I frighten you? I must apologize. I merely wanted to see which horse you had selected."

There was nothing in his tone to upset her but the feeling of disquiet persisted. She felt the hair on the back of her neck standing straight up and knew a sense of foreboding.

He looked quickly about to see if anyone was in earshot. No one seeming to pay any attention to them, he lowered his voice. "I have uncovered your impersonation. I want you to meet me after lunch and we'll take a turn in the garden. I have something to discuss with you." His voice was as easy as if he was speaking about the weather. It made it all the more deadly.

Samantha turned white. She couldn't see how he could have found out what she was doing. It would spoil everything if the truth came out now. She must be the one to tell Belfort when the time came. With difficulty she found her voice. "And if I don't come?" Her tone was casual.

He looked at her with appreciation. This woman had a good deal of courage. "You'll give me no alternative. I will go to Belfort."

That was the last thing she wanted. Better listen to what he had to say. It was evident he had blackmail in mind. She wondered how large a sum he was planning to ask. She took a deep breath. "All right. I will speak with you after lunch." She tried to sound confident and in control of the situation.

"You're as wise as you are beautiful. Until later." He lightly saluted her and went sauntering down the line of stalls ostensibly to select something for himself.

Samantha found her heart racing. She was in the devil's own fix. She had never, as she recollected, seen him until the countess' dinner and, to her knowledge, there had been no place for him to have seen her before she arrived at Helmcrest. Could she have met him in the States, New York possibly? She thought not, for wasn't he from the South? She would think on it. Before long she would have her answer one way or another.

The guests trooped back to the house, talking animatedly about the morrow's ride. Each declared he or she had the best horse in the stables. It was a gay party that sat down to the elegant lunch Raoul had prepared.

Samantha found she had no appetite. Her mind was on the forthcoming interview. She wondered just how Randolph would be able to cut Belfort out, for she was certain the duke would not let Randolph monopolize her. She dabbed at her food visualizing Randolph's sinister face.

Belfort kept the conversation moving and his guests were in great spirits. He glanced frequently at Samantha, wondering why she was so quiet. Did she have something on her mind? As they were finishing their lunch, he addressed his guests. "If you gentlemen would like a game of cards we can adjourn to the cardroom. Perhaps the ladies would like to rest or take a turn about the gardens. Our topiary work is much admired, I'm told. Please feel free to make yourselves at home."

The ladies rose and stood talking together for a moment. Lady Leicester decided to go to her room for a rest but Cynthia Ross and Martha Somerset stated their intention of going back to the stables for a more comprehensive look at the horses. Listening to them, Elizabeth decided to join them, urging Samantha to come too.

Samantha shook her head. She had to meet Randolph in the garden. "I think I'll take a walk about the garden, then perhaps I'll come down to the stables." She hoped she didn't sound as if she weren't sociable but she had no choice.

The ladies didn't question her but agreed amiably to see her later. Samantha went upstairs to her room to get a wrap as the weather was chilly and then made her way outside, wondering how Randolph would find her. The gardens were much larger than she expected. May was a lovely month for flowers and there were many varieties.

She needn't have worried for Randolph made his excuses to Belfort, saying he had planned to walk in the garden for a few minutes with a lady and then would join him in the cardroom. He had already reconnoitered the garden and discovered the only place to be private with Samantha.

Belfort assumed that he was taking Lady Elizabeth out and was pleased that his guests were so congenial.

Samantha walked aimlessly down a path, pretending to look at the flowers, but her mind was occupied in planning a campaign. Randolph had no trouble locating her and they continued to walk the length of the garden. He led her to a marble bench surrounded by foliage.

"I think this will do us quite well," he said. "This should afford us the privacy we need." He waited politely for her to sit and then sat down beside her.

Samantha raised questioning eyes to his but said nothing. She waited patiently for him to make the first move.

"In my business, I find it necessary to know everything about the people around me." He eyed her speculatively.

"What is your business?" Samantha asked coolly. She had no intention of throwing herself on this man's mercy. She would wait to see what he wanted.

"Under the circumstances, I believe there is no necessity of hiding from you what my mission is. I am working for the Confederate States of America." There was a note of pride in his voice. He fully believed in what he was doing.

"A spy!" Samantha was startled.

An expression of annoyance crossed Randolph's face. "Let us say, I am an agent. There is a difference. I am here to try to get England to sell us several ironclad vessels. They will make it possible for us to break the blockade the North has thrown against us. I believe England would be happy to sell to us if it weren't for Belfort's influence. He keeps insisting on England's neutrality."

Samantha found this information extremely interesting but what it had to do with her, she couldn't imagine.

Seeing the puzzled look in her eyes, he answered her unspoken question. "I have looked into your background." Here Samantha drew a deep breath. "I have had enquiries made in Spain and I found that the Marquesa de Cienfuegos was a much older woman than you. In fact, she went to America nearly thirty years ago and reports say she died there." He looked to see how she took this news and was gratified to note a vivid flush rising in her cheeks while she expelled a deep breath. What he took for fear was, in fact, relief.

She had an overwhelming impulse to laugh but she contrived to choke it down. She kept her gaze on him but refused to speak.

He was satisfied with her reactions. "I know you are after Belfort's money but I have no intention of exposing you. Instead, I am offering you the chance to make ten thousand pounds sterling plus whatever you get out of Belfort." It was the type of proposition that would appeal to an adventurer. He had dealt with many in his time.

"What must I do to make this money?" She couldn't quite grasp what he had in his mind. She schooled her face to polite interest.

"I must dispose of Belfort." Seeing a look of repulsion flit across her face, he hurriedly added, "I mean to put him out of action for a time. I . . . propose to wing him and that would keep him from attending the strategic meetings. I must get him alone in a suitable spot and that's where you come in. You lead him to me and I'll do the rest." He hoped she couldn't detect what was in his mind. When this was over he would leave incriminating evidence, manufactured if necessary, to implicate her, and flee the scene. It was part of his job and he had great confidence in his ability to do it properly.

Samantha's first thought was to tell him what he could do and just where he could go but second thoughts stopped her. If she refused, he might get someone else in another place to work with him and she would be unable to stop it. If she told Belfort what Randolph proposed, he wouldn't believe her unless she confessed to her identity. If she could trap Randolph in the act of shooting Belfort, Randolph would be disposed of and Belfort would be safe. She pressed her lips tightly together to get her composure and then agreed to Randolph's proposal.

"What are your plans?" She must know in advance so she could make some of her own.

"I have given it careful thought. I believe the best time would be when we are coming back from the hunt. I'll make some excuse to break away from the party and head back to the home wood. You'll have to pass down the lane to get to the stables. I will be on the right side fixing my cinch. When you see me step out, drop back, and give me a clear shot." He would throw the gun down beside her and race to the lodge to say that she had shot the duke. Since he gave the alarm, they would assume he, not the marquesa, was telling the truth. He had it worked out perfectly, so he thought.

Samantha dug her fingers into her palms to keep from protesting. A slow anger filled her and her throat felt like it was on fire. She swallowed with difficulty and rasped out the words, "For this I get ten thousand pounds?"

His lips curved in a smile but his eyes were cold. Just as he figured. Women of this type were all alike. All they wanted was money. "I'll see you get it. Remember, you must let the rest of the group get ahead of you. If you fail me, I'll see that Belfort knows you are an adventuress." There was a definite threatening note in his voice. Randolph planned to tell the others anyway, but she needn't know that. It was the part of the plan that would tighten the noose about her neck. He carried papers with him, forged of course, that proved he was a British agent and proved the death of the marquesa thirty years ago. He would turn her over to the local authorities and say his mission was completed and leave the scene without regret. It was a masterful plan.

Listening to him, Samantha felt a shiver run down her spine. This man was evil. He was due for a surprise however, as his investigations hadn't told him exactly who she was and what she was capable of. "You needn't worry. I never fail my obligations." She was pleased her voice was steady. With this statement she felt she had given him warning. She would meet her obligations and they were to Belfort, her husband, even if he had rejected her. She rose and made her way back to the lodge, leaving Randolph standing there looking after her.

The next morning found the stable alive with activity. Grooms were carrying tack to different stalls, others were saddling horses, and still others were leading them out to their riders. Belfort walked over to Samantha, who had already been given her gelding. She was standing beside him, stroking his nose and whispering to him. He admired the picture she made, so at home with a horse, her habit of blue velvet cut in the latest style, a froth of lace at her throat, and a lighter blue veil streaming down from her hat. He told her how enchanting she looked and she demurred engagingly.

She noted his appearance was very fine in his well-cut buckskins. It was a stylish country riding costume. His smile was dazzling as he spoke to her. "It's too bad this isn't the right time of year for a real fox hunt because most of the fields are planted and growing, but there are plenty of paths, trails, and a few fields we can cross to make the day interesting. We'll turn the dogs out and give them a treat. We'll have some interesting country to view and a few good jumps." As he looked down at her the expression in his eyes was caressing and very warm.

Samantha asked herself if it was possible that he was falling in love with her. Her spirits soared and she flashed a brilliant smile in return. She was glad he knew of her ability to ride astride and that he had so ordered for her.

The last horse was brought out and at that everyone mounted up, Belfort placing both hands around Samantha's waist and easily lifting her up. She swung her leg over and flushed with pleasure as she felt the strength of his hands. She had expected him to cup his hands for her to step into but she had to admit to herself she liked his method.

A pack of hounds was brought out, each excited over the prospect of a run. Belfort gave a signal and a groom turned them loose. They milled about the yard for a minute and then one old dog bayed and started down the path through the home wood, the rest trailing after him.

Belfort gave them a start and then called his party to follow him. He would stick to the trails around most of the fields and thereby not damage the crops. It would be easy to follow the dogs and all would understand that these were not hardened winter fields. He was certain of the marquesa's ability to sit her horse but watched her carefully just the same. She was one of the finest riders he had ever seen. Seeing her erect carriage and the confidence with which she handled the gelding, he picked up the pace. The rest of the party streamed out behind them. Belfort led them a hard chase.

When they came out of the home wood there were several paths around the fields and Belfort selected the one to the right as the closest way to the direction the dogs had taken. The path went down the hill, crossed a small stream, and on up the other side. Belfort pushed his horse forward to lead the way to the best crossing. He thundered toward the stream, lifting his reins at its bank to signal the jump and his horse stretched, taking the stream in an easy leap.

Samantha was hard on his heels and sailed over just behind him. She was exhilarated to be riding such a fine animal and she beamed at her companion as they bounded up the far slope.

Belfort was pleased with her expertise. She had taken the jump as if she had had years of practice. As he looked at her profile something seemed familiar about it as if he had seen it before. He couldn't remember where, but it would come to him.

They came to a pole fence surrounding a meadow and Belfort put his horse to it signaling everyone to follow him. They all took the jump in stride, pursuing Belfort. On the other side of the meadow another wood stood with leaves trembling in the breeze. Belfort pulled up.

When the rest of the party surrounded him he explained, "I thought this would be the turning point. We'll start back now. Feel free to go at your own pace. We'll meet at dinner, I hope, with good appetites from our outing. Raoul has planned a superlative dinner for us."

There were smiles and nods of appreciation. Belfort was a magnificent host. He always gave his guests time to do what they wanted to please themselves and saw that the food would excite even the most particular gourmet.

Samantha started to follow the others but Belfort placed a restraining hand on her reins. "Let's let them get ahead a little, shall we?" His eyes seemed to penetrate her defenses.

With a sinking heart she realized he was playing directly into Randolph's hands. However, if he hadn't suggested waiting she would have had to. Her right hand patted her deep pocket. Her Colt revolver was still safely there. She began to have qualms about what lay ahead. Perhaps she was making a mistake in not warning him. His eyes willed her to reveal all. "I'd like that," she answered. She took her courage in both hands and said boldly, "I have a strange feeling that you are not safe—that someone wishes to hurt you." Her expression was very solemn and she waited to see what his reaction would be.

He looked at her in amazement. What had brought this about? "I'm flattered you are thinking of my welfare but I assure you there is no reason to fear for me. I'm well able to take care of myself."

She thought he did indeed look extremely self-sufficient but he didn't know of the danger ahead. "I can't tell you why I have this feeling, but I beg you consider the possibility." She wondered how close Randolph would be to the path.

"You actually think that something might happen to me on my own estate?" The thought was incomprehensible.

Samantha knew it was hopeless to make him understand. She must take care of it by herself. Lifting the reins, she started her horse. They chatted on about inconsequential things as they rode slowly toward Belle Maison. Samantha's eyes scanned the wood when they reached it, intent on finding Randolph. She unobtrusively pulled her pistol from her pocket and held it in the folds of her skirt.

As they came around a bend in the path she saw Randolph. He was standing beside his horse fiddling with the saddle girth. As they rode up to him, he gave Samantha an encouraging look, which she ignored.

"Having trouble?" asked Belfort. "Perhaps I can be of assistance?"

Randolph stepped forward as if to speak to Belfort. One hand was behind his back and his face was determined.

Samantha had planned in advance. She meant to hit him in the deltoid muscle, a thick powerful muscle which covers the shoulder and gives roundness to the upper part of the arm. At the expression of pure hatred on Randolph's face she perceived that he was going to kill Belfort so he could not testify against him. Dead men could not tell tales. As he brought his arm around to aim at Belfort, Samantha raised her gun and unhesitatingly pulled the trigger. Her aim was true and the bullet tore a hole in the muscle that controlled lifting the arm. His shot discharged in the air as he fell.

Belfort's face registered stupefaction, momentarily looking from Randolph to Samantha. The man could have killed him. His heart started to beat again and he jumped down from his horse to get to Randolph, who was struggling to sit up.

Fast as he was, Samantha was faster. She sped toward the man on the ground. Hate flashed in his eyes and he started to curse her. Violent oaths came hurling from his mouth. Samantha paid him no heed but bent beside him, tearing his coat to get at the wound. She was a doctor first, and although she was guilty of shooting him, her instincts were to stop the bleeding and save his life. Blood was running down his arm but a close exam showed it to be only a flesh wound.

Belfort stood over her watching those expert fingers at work. The thought flashed through his mind that she was as skillful as a doctor. He gave her profile a searching look as she bent so purposefully over Randolph's arm. That profile! His mind raced back to that disastrous day. It boggled his mind, this stunning woman was Samantha, his wife! There couldn't be two women doctors in this part of the country. But the change in her! She didn't look like the same woman. Could he possibly be mistaken? He eyed her critically, noting her high cheekbones. There was no doubt in his mind. This woman definitely had medical training. She knew exactly what she was about as she unhesitatingly pulled up her skirt and tore a piece of petticoat off. She made a pad and then applied a pressure bandage over it.

Looking up at Belfort, Samantha commented, "I believe he'll do until we can get him to a doctor." She gazed at him to see how he was accepting the lightning events of the last few minutes.

Belfort wasn't a diplomat for nothing. No sign of recognition crossed his face. The minx! She wanted to play games, did she? Well, he'd deal himself in on this hand. He had an idea that brought a wicked glint to his eye. He reviewed the incident, remembering her warning. She had known that an attempt on his life was planned and had come prepared by carrying that pistol with her. Was there ever such a woman? She'd proved she could shoot and not just at a target. Her western background was most likely responsible. That also explained her competence with a horse. How could he have been so fooled? She had some explaining to do but in the meantime something had to be done about Randolph.

"Why did you feel you must shoot me?" Belfort enquired. He failed to see a good reason and hoped Randolph would shed some light on how Samantha knew about it. He reflected it was easy to think of her as Samantha rather than Margarita, the marquesa.

Randolph was surprised to find himself being given expert medical help. This woman had fooled him. He started to shrug his shoulders but the pain in his arm halted him. "I wanted to stop your influence on Lord Palmerston and the queen. You're the one that's holding up the sale of the ironclad vessels we desperately need."

Now Belfort understood. Well, thanks to Samantha, his attempt failed and it was up to him to see that Randolph left the country. For several reasons he didn't want to press charges against him, the most important being involving Samantha. "Let me assist you up." His strength was such that he easily lifted Randolph to his feet. "Can you ride?"

Randolph nodded mutely. This was one of his accomplishments. He could ride under any conditions. A feeling of despair came over him. He had failed and put Belfort on his guard at the same time. "What do you plan to do with me?" He had difficulty in getting the words out and his eyes were filled with pain. He could be spending a great many years in jail or worse.

Belfort lifted him easily into the saddle and then went back to where

Samantha's gelding was standing beside his own horse. He tossed her into the saddle, saying nothing but giving her such a warm, loving look he felt it must let her know the depth of his feeling.

Samantha's heart started to pound uncontrollably and she felt her cheeks grow pink. She blew hot and cold at the same time wondering why just a look in her direction did this to her. She tried to imagine her reaction if he touched or kissed her.

They fell in on each side of Randolph, Belfort ready to render instant aid if needed. They slowly made their way back to the stables. When they arrived the others had long since gone into the house. The grooms came running.

Belfort lifted his voice. "Ned," he called. "Hitch up a carriage for Mr. Randolph. Tom, run up to the house and tell Mr. Randolph's valet to pack immediately and come down here."

Each rushed to do his bidding, another groom staying to relieve Belfort of the horses. The yard was a flurry of motion.

Belfort had dismounted in the midst of his orders and was walking around to assist Samantha. She sat there quietly, appreciating Belfort's competence. He swung her easily to the ground and turned his attention to Randolph, who was drooping in the saddle. He helped him down and then supported him to a wooden bench beside the stable door. Randolph sank into it with a sigh.

Although no one dared ask, Belfort could see the questions in the groom's eyes. "We must have a poacher near the home wood. He shot Randolph by mistake. When one of you has time I'd like you to ride out and see if anyone's about." He lied deliberately but felt it was for the best, and in doing so, had to send someone out, for it would be unheard of not to investigate a poacher who had endangered a guest's life. He turned to Randolph. "I'll have one of my people drive you to the station. If we've missed the train he can drive you into London as it isn't that far. Either way I give you forty-eight hours to have your arm taken care of and to leave the country. If I hear that you haven't gone, I'll make it my business to call upon you and see that you do." This was spoken in a low tone, only for Randolph's ears, but that man fully recognized the deadly menace in Belfort's voice.

Randolph nodded. He was getting off easily. He was tempted to betray the marquesa, but thinking it over, decided it was a small revenge to extract from Belfort, to have him caught by an adventuress.

Within a few minutes the carriage was brought from the stables ready to travel and Randolph was assisted into it. His valet came hurrying from the house carrying valises and cases under his arms, not understanding what was going on. Seeing his master's ashen face and a bandage on his shoulder, he hurried over to him. "What has happened?" he cried, but Randolph brushed him off. He loaded the bags he carried into the waiting carriage and ran back to the front steps to pick up the rest of the luggage deposited there by a footman. He knew his master didn't feel like making any explanations at this moment.

Samantha watched a groom drive them off with a sigh of relief. She knew she had taken good care of Randolph's arm but she would feel better when another doctor had looked at it and most likely sutured it. She had none on hand and wouldn't have dared use it for fear of discovery. Did Belfort notice how easily she had taken care of the wound? He'd probably not given it a thought. She found out how wrong she was in the next few minutes.

They strolled toward the house, Belfort tucking her arm in his. His touch sent a tingle through her and she had the urge to put her head on his strong shoulder and confess the whole story to him. She was certain that he had some tender feelings for her. If he would only voice his thoughts. She didn't want to return to Arizona but resolved that if Belfort didn't love her the pain would be too great if she stayed. She had come to love this country, its green blanket, its array of flowers, and even the frequent rain. Belfort seemed to have a hand in everything. Tenant cottages at Belfort were much improved, the farms were planted well with the crops being rotated, his speeches were much listened to in Parliament, and the queen had announced British neutrality. Everyone Samantha spoke with had a kind word for Belfort. He was in her every thought and she was proud of his accomplishments.

She stole a peek at him from under her provocative eyelashes to find him regarding her closely. His eyes looked right through her and she felt herself blush profusely. For a second she felt he could read her thoughts. She looked at the lodge to hide her confusion. She asked about the thatched roof to turn the subject and steer the conversation to less dangerous channels.

He told her how the thatcher came and put branches over the rafters, followed by sods, and finally the thatch. The man would start at the bottom and work his way up, tying and cutting bunches as he went. As she ventured to look away from the roof and her eyes moved to Belfort she found him still viewing her with a look of admiration.

She seemed to grow quite confused at that particular look. She hoped he couldn't hear her heart beating, for it was drumming in her ears and it was difficult to breathe.

"And now, my dear, perhaps you'd like to enlighten me as to where you learned to care for a wound." His voice was light but he deliberately wanted to place her in an awkward position. He would find a way to make her confess to this disguise.

Samantha had the desire to throw herself into his arms and tell him who she was, but found she didn't have the courage. He must tell her that he loved her first. He was far more observant than she'd given him credit for. Drat the man! She was struggling with an answer when he came to her rescue.

"I suppose you had to learn to do simple dressings on your huge hacienda," he suggested, a gleam in his eye.

Samantha almost gasped with relief. "Yes, of course," she agreed hastily, avoiding his appraisal. She reflected that she had almost given herself away. She couldn't help it for she'd had to help Randolph. With her emergency treatment he'd manage nicely until he got to a doctor.

Belfort chuckled to himself. He almost had her on the ropes that time. This promised to be amusing. Still, he didn't understand the metamorphosis from a repulsive creature to this dazzling woman.

They entered the house and found Lady Elizabeth looking out one of the huge windows. She looked around as they came into the room. "Have you seen Mr. Randolph?" she asked a little shyly. She was interested in that young man.

Belfort and Samantha exchanged looks and it was the duke who answered. "Mr. Randolph has met with an accident. It seems we have a poacher near the home wood and Randolph was shot by mistake."

Elizabeth's eyes dilated with horror and her hand covered her mouth. "Is he dead?" she asked faintly.

"No, it was only a graze but we've sent him in to a doctor so we'll not be seeing him again this stay." He sounded matter-of-fact.

Lady Elizabeth's fears were allayed. "Poor Mr. Randolph. Papa and Mama will call on him when we get back and see how he fares." The mention of her mama brought back a conversation that she had had with her just before they had come to Belfort's lodge. Lord Wrexham was to call upon them on Wednesday. Her mama had had a funny look in her eye as she mentioned it and had also said something about gypsies being truthful but it didn't make sense. Elizabeth would wait and see what the week brought and take pleasure in the riding in the meantime.

Belfort thought that there would be little chance of visiting the Confederate agent as, for the sake of his skin, he would be long gone. He merely gave Elizabeth an encouraging smile as he recalled Lord Leicester's hints to a titled connection being in the wind for his daughter in the near future.

Samantha excused herself as she needed to have a bath and a change of clothes. Her habit was stained with Randolph's blood and she wanted to shed the memories of the morning's drama. She went slowly up the stairs, her heart full of hope that she was going to succeed and have Belfort claim her as his wife. A dreamy smile crossed her face at the thought.

Watching her go, Belfort felt a surge of desire. She stirred him as no other woman had. He longed to crush her to him and devour her with passionate kisses until her senses were reeling. If anyone had told him that he would fall in love with the repugnant woman who had become his wife, he would have thought he was all about in his head. Now he meant to find the reason she felt it necessary to disguise herself and enter his life in this fashion. He had an idea of how he could force an admission from her. He would wait until tonight. He whistled his way to the library, an unholy glint filling his eyes.

CHAPTER 17

Samantha sat before her dressing table while Felicia brushed her short black hair until it crackled. It was very relaxing and Samantha found her mind reviewing the day's achievements. She had been able to scotch Randolph's plans for Belfort knowing that he meant to kill her husband. She should have guessed it before; Randolph had gotten off easily. Grateful for the experience she'd gained with firearms in Arizona, a feeling of pride filled her as she recalled hitting him exactly where she had planned. Belfort sought her company eagerly and she thought that he was interested in her, more than as a passing fancy.

In two more days she would be back in London, packing to go home with Hank to Helmcrest. She was glad that Hank had found the woman he loved. They would be happy together. She sighed. Her time was running short and she wished she had a definite plan to make Belfort declare himself. She would work on it tomorrow.

Felicia had finished and was busy picking up the room. She was proving to be an excellent maid and Samantha decided she'd have to employ her permanently and give Mary a secondary position. She slipped into the huge bed and sank against the feather pillows. Felicia came over and blew out the bedside lamp. A gentle darkness fell upon the room, the fireplace giving off a soft light while the moon was peeking in at the window.

Felicia went out, closing the door quietly behind her. As she made her way to the next floor where all the servants slept, she could see a light under His Grace's door and could hear him whistling as she passed. He was the most notable man she had ever seen, looking like a Greek god, and she hoped her mistress might somehow find permanent favor with him.

Samantha lay awake for a while, her mind turning first one idea and then another over in her mind. Finally she succumbed to her body's demands for sleep, her eyes closing slowly, her long black lashes curling on her cheek.

Several hours later, the moon having risen in the sky, the doorknob of her room turned quietly. Belfort, dressed in a long red satin dressing gown, his ruffled nightshirt showing at the front, stepped noiselessly into the room. His gaze went directly to Samantha, breathing easily, the rise and fall of her breasts intriguing him. A half smile adorned her face as if she was having a pleasant dream. He moved over to the bed and sat on the edge, his eyes drinking in her loveliness.

Her eyes opened sleepily as she felt the weight on her bed and then with alarm as she saw Belfort sitting there so intimately. She sat up abruptly and clutched the bedclothes. She could feel his warm breath on her cheek. "What are you doing here?" she demanded, her eyes flashing in anger. How dared he! As she took in his attire a feeling of fear washed over her. This wasn't what she wanted. She moved carefully to the far side of the bed. He was thinking of her as a mistress, a plaything, who could be discarded at will. She wanted a husband, one who would love and cherish her.

He didn't answer, just sat there and let his gaze roam over her. He had planned this in fun but seeing her his emotions began to get the better of him. He had an ache in his loins that wouldn't go away until she was his in every way. He was tempted, but curbed the rising tide. They would see this comedy through. He moved to the head of the bed, picking up the covers, and started to slide into bed with her. At his first move she flung herself out of the bed on the far side, not realizing that the glow from the fireplace outlined a figure that even Venus could have envied.

His voice caught in his throat. How could this perfect form have ever been that scrawny bag of bones he'd married. Another thought popped, unbidden, into his mind. No wonder she charged bills to Helmcrest. He was her brother, not her lover. He almost cried aloud in his relief. That put a wide grin on his face, which to Samantha looked diabolical.

She slid behind a small marble-topped table and he came striding purposefully toward her. As he moved around the table she ran across the room to the chair flanking the fireplace, not appreciating the fact that he could have easily caught her if he wished. When she felt him getting too close she streaked across the room to the sofa and stood behind it. Would nothing stop him? She couldn't understand his chasing her like this. He was reported to be such an accomplished lover that women fell into his arms. This didn't make any sense.

Belfort was deriving great pleasure from her flight. It was all he could do to keep from laughing out loud. Did the dear delight imagine that he'd rape a guest in his house? She had some strange ideas about him. She might be a doctor, a brilliant woman, but she had a lot to learn about love and he planned to be the one to teach her. Why didn't she admit she was his wife? He was certain he could scare her into it. He made a lunge across the sofa and almost caught her.

She tore across the room again and around the bed to put more distance between them but soon discovered her mistake. As she stood panting on one side he dove across the bed and caught her about the waist, pulling her down on top of him. She hit his arms trying to break loose, but she was no match for him.

He was startled to find the strength in the blows. This woman of his was strong. Pinning her arms to her sides, he bent his head and touched her lips. Blood pulsed in his veins.

At the gentle pressure, which increased, she felt a warmth flow through her and she stopped her resistance. She knew a yearning to respond, and let herself enjoy the heady sensations that washed over her.

Pleased to find her returning his embrace, he kissed her with fervor, raining his kisses upon her face and neck, and knew that she was his for the taking. Why then didn't she say anything? Not a word from her. He released her abruptly and stood up. If he stayed any longer, he would be unable to leave.

"Now, madame," he said coolly, "I like my women willing. You have obviously been running after me and now you want to play games. I'll give you twenty-four hours to make up your mind. I'm an impatient man so I won't wait longer. We'll settle this tomorrow evening after dinner." With that he left the room, a much shaken Samantha staring after him.

As Belfort made his way to his room he chuckled to himself. What would the little minx do now? She hadn't broken down when he scared her and he admitted that he had done a thorough job. Tomorrow should be an interesting day.

Samantha sat where she was for a time, tears forming in her beautiful sad eyes. He had never once said he loved her and wished he could marry her. All he did was to show by his actions that he was interested in only one thing. She must get out of this place, and for some reason, she knew it must be without his knowledge. He wouldn't let her go without an explanation and she couldn't give it to him. She couldn't face him again without blurting out the entire scheme and she would be humiliated in the process when he saw the love in her eyes. She had had a rough time schooling her features in the past and with what had happened here tonight knew it would be impossible in the future.

She rang the bell for Felicia and shortly the faithful maid scratched at her door, her face showing her concern at being called at this hour. She went over and lighted the hand-painted hurricane lamp on the small piecrust table near the bed. The little clock on the mantel over the fireplace showed it was four o'clock.

"Pack my things as quickly as possible. I want to leave here within the hour." She spoke in Spanish so that there could be no possibility of Felicia misunderstanding her orders.

Felicia had a slight suspicion of why her mistress wanted to leave at this hour but said nothing and obediently started to pack Samantha's wardrobe.

As Samantha flung off her exquisite sheer nightgown and started to dress, it struck her that she would need a carriage to get her back to London as the train passed through only during the afternoon. "Felicia, could you leave that for a few minutes and run down to the stable and order a carriage and a groom for me?" She knew the grooms and stable hands had rooms in the building across the way but there was always someone up during the night to check on the horses. "Can you make yourself understood?" she asked doubtfully. Felicia's command of English was limited to very few words.

Samantha was rewarded with a brilliant smile. Felicia had been able to find her way about Belle Maison. "One of His Grace's grooms comes from Spain. I just happened to meet him." Her eyes were cast down and her tone very demure but her attitude was one of simple pride. She would be able to transmit her mistress' orders.

Felicia had found a friend, Samantha guessed, someone whom she had formed an interest in, judging from the expression in her eyes. That made things much easier. While Felicia quietly made her way to the stable Samantha finished dressing and packed her jewel case in the trunk.

The door opened softly and for one moment Samantha's heart stopped beating. She thought that Belfort had returned, but it proved to be Felicia. She gave a long sigh of relief but felt a tinge of regret and her shoulders sagged. She kept remembering those exciting kisses and hurt inside with the want of more. Was she making a mistake in not telling him outright who she was? She bit her lip as she pondered over it and then shook her head. No, she would wait it out. "Let's see what he does when he finds I'm gone," she murmured to herself.

Between them Samantha and Felicia carried the luggage down the stairs. The cases were heavy and Samantha's arms felt as if they would drop off. It was imperative that they make only one trip past Belfort's door.

Samantha spoke to the Spanish groom as he loaded the cases into the carriage. She was amused to find him the one who would carry them to London. His dark complexion labeled his origin. She addressed him in that tongue, telling him it was an unexpected emergency that made her require his services. He nodded his understanding and flashed her a dark smile, showing off large white teeth. His eyes were all for Felicia. Samantha, watching this little byplay, decided she would either have to hire him to come to Belfort or give up Felicia and have the duke find her work down here. They were showing more than a casual interest in each other, so why shouldn't she help them? If only she could solve her own problem so easily. Her stubborn pride stood in her way and yet she couldn't change, but she hadn't given up yet either, she found to her surprise.

It was still very early in the morning when the carriage pulled up in front of the countess'. There were a few moments to wait until the door was opened by a lackey. He was in his shirt sleeves doing his early morning chores. Considerably flustered when he saw the marquesa on the doorstep, he murmured a disjointed greeting, holding the door open wide.

Samantha took one of the cases held by the Spanish groom while Felicia passed the rest on to the lackey. As the man brought the last to the door she thanked him for his services. "I'm certain His Grace will appreciate what you've done for me. Please take time to get yourself a meal and rest the horses before you start back." She pressed a gold piece into his hand and he rewarded her with his brilliant smile.

He touched his forelock respectfully and as he left, he whispered to Felicia, "I must see you again." This caused Felicia's eyes to sparkle and she gave him an encouraging look.

Samantha's hearing was acute and she caught the few words. She would see that they had a chance to renew their friendship. A feeling of depression came over her as she made her way up the stairs to her room. Would she ever attain her heart's desire? What was it that the gypsy fortune-teller had said? "The love of your life is drawing near," but did that mean that she would win him? What would he do when he found out she'd gone and he didn't know where to look for her? Would this send him back to Belfort? Patience was needed but hers was growing thin.

By the time she had changed her clothes and freshened up she felt she dared go down to breakfast. She only hoped that she hadn't awakened the countess with her early arrival.

She was sitting in the small breakfast room drinking the inevitable cup of tea and pushing some scrambled eggs around her plate when her brother came in.

"Samantha! You're back early." He saw the little droop to her lips and knew that something had gone wrong. He waited for her to tell him.

"It was terrible, Hank! Belfort doesn't love me. All he wants is a new mistress and I won't play that role." There was a tremor in her voice, which Hank heard.

He moved around to her at once, taking both of her hands in his. He pressed them warmly and bent down, kissing her affectionately. "It can't be that bad. What made you think he wants you as his mistress?" He was curious to discover her reasoning. Belfort had seemed jealous of him before the hunting party and he couldn't see just what Samantha expected of him under the circumstances.

"He came into my bedchamber late last night and tried to rape me!" she blurted out, her face turning crimson in the process.

"The devil!" His temper was up and flying for a moment. He tried to rationalize the encounter. Belfort was a gentleman. He would never attack a lady, especially in his own home. Unless he knew the lady was willing and then it wouldn't be an attack. Could it be? Most definitely! He pushed the thought around. "Tell me about it."

Samantha flushed as she recalled what had happened. "He tried to get into bed with me and I slipped out and ran. Then he chased me around and around the furniture, finally diving across the bed and pulling me down." She couldn't tell him of those sweet moments when their lips had met and she had succumbed willingly to his embrace. "Then he let me go and told me I had twenty-four hours to come to him willingly as he was an impatient man and wouldn't wait longer for me." There was a martial look in her eye as she remembered his words.

This didn't sound the least like Belfort. Chase her all around the room? The man was as agile as a cat and if he had wanted, he could have pounced on Samantha in seconds. He must have been playing some sort of game. A little smile hovered around Hank's mouth. Belfort was up to something and it looked as if he were trying to scare Samantha, which he had. Hank put himself in the duke's position and tried to think what he would do. Yes, his first instinct was right. He would try to make her confess too. "I'm sorry, Sam, but perhaps he does love you."

The sound of her pet name made her feel better. After all, she had a wonderful brother who loved her and she was soon to have a new sister whom she felt she would love also. She ignored his remark. "Let's go home, Hank."

That suited Hank for he had been kicking his heels waiting for her return. He wanted to get back to his Marianne. The bishop of London had granted him a special license. He had no intention of waiting three weeks for the banns to be read.

The countess entered the breakfast room just in time to hear Samantha's plea.

"When my maid told me you were here I found it incredible. Something has happened. Tell me, did you not enjoy yourself? Why did you return so early?" The old lady was autocratic with her questions as she sank into the chair Hank had pulled out for her. "Well?" she demanded.

She was very fond of this girl and wanted to see her marriage succeed. Whatever could have happened?

Samantha had no intention of telling Belfort's aunt of his conduct. "I found out that he really doesn't love me so I decided to go home."

The countess' eyes narrowed thoughtfully. The saucy child! She wasn't telling the real reason. She would find a way to discover what went on. There was always the servants' gossip, not, of course, that she ever listened to it.

"I'm going to Helmcrest to help Marianne with the wedding." She paused for a moment. "If Belfort comes here looking for me, I am trusting you not to tell him where I am. If he should decide to go home to his poor wife that could be a step forward for me."

The countess pursed her lips as she mulled that over. Yes, that might do the trick. "Very well, my dear, I'll be mum as can be." This was a delightful comedy and she almost hated to see it end but it would be good to see Belfort settled down. After all it was high time he was setting up his nursery. Her arms ached to hold his son. Those two young people were made for each other and she was certain that Belfort wouldn't let her go.

Hank left Samantha at the foot of the stairs to complete her packing while he made a quick trip to the library. He pulled out a crisp sheet of writing paper and dashed off a note. Sealing it with a wafer, he handed it to a footman with orders to see that it was delivered personally. He shoved his hands in his pockets and hummed to himself as he climbed the stairs.

CHAPTER 18

It was with mixed emotions that Samantha rode up the long ash-lined drive at Helmcrest. She had come to love this estate but somehow Belfort had become home to her. After Hank was married she'd return and wait to see if Belfort came back.

The carriage rolled to a stop opposite the great doors and, at the sound of the wheels, a lackey flung them open. Hank assisted her to alight and they entered the hall. Every time Hank entered the great hall he had a feeling of pride. The frescoes on the ceilings were magnificent and the chandelier threw sparkles around the room. Hank had just taken off his hat and gloves and handed them to the lackey when the sound of running footsteps greeted him.

Marianne, having heard Hank's voice, came hurling down the stairs as if she couldn't wait for the treat that she was expecting. Hank opened his arms and she ran into them.

By this time Meadows had arrived on the scene, dismissing his subordinate and eying the proceedings with august approval. He was happy for his lordship.

Marianne disengaged herself, flushing as she did so. "Please excuse me, Your Grace," she said to Samantha. "I don't usually act so immodestly."

Samantha hugged her and kissed her cheek with real affection. "Don't apologize. You are going to fit right into our family."

Hank showed his approval by catching a hand of each girl and squeezing them. "Well, my love," he addressed Marianne, "are you ready for our wedding?"

Marianne's color rose again and Hank, looking at her, thought he'd never seen a lovelier girl.

"Yes, Mrs. Clarke has been very helpful and I have a number of gowns. If Your Grace would stand up with me I would be most grateful."

"I would be honored," Samantha responded, "but only if you'll stop calling me Your Grace. We are to be sisters so please call me Samantha or Sam as Hank does."

Marianne's eyes were shining as she nodded. How fortunate she was to have found the man she loved and to have so charming a new sister.

"Well, now we have that settled shall we get ourselves freshened up and ready for lunch? Then we can talk over any things that we need to attend to."

They had just started up the stairs when a thought struck Samantha. "Tell me, Hank, who are you having for a best man?" After all, they would be paired together and it would be nice if he happened to be someone she knew.

An enigmatic expression crossed Hank's face. "Oh, I'll have to attend to that," he answered.

Samantha gave him a sharp stare. He was evading the question, but why? He always had a good reason for whatever he did so she'd wait and get him alone. "When are you having the wedding? Tonight?"

Now there was no doubt Hank was flustered. "I thought three days from now. That will give Marianne and I a little time to get to know each other better." He knew it was a flimsy excuse but one that Samantha wouldn't question.

Samantha raised her eyebrows at that answer. Impatient Hank waiting three days when he kicked up such a fuss about waiting three days for her to go to Belle Maison? There was something in the wind but she couldn't quite figure it out.

Marianne found no fault with the program, smiling her approval worshipfully. It was plain that anything Hank said was going to be gospel in that household.

Samantha crinkled her forehead at Marianne's acquiescence. They were certainly different. She had her own ideas and opinions as her husband would find out—if he ever claimed her as his wife. She was lonely without him, cherishing the time that they had had together, in the park, at dinner, riding, and even at the lodge. It was not going to be easy taking part in this wedding. To see Hank and Marianne lost in their own little paradise, having eyes only for each other, made her heart ache. She didn't envy them their happiness but wished she could find her own.

Three days later all preparations had been made. The staff had outdone themselves. Every piece of furniture had a silken sheen to it. The house was filled with the scent of carnations, red and white in color. The chef had planned a superlative wedding dinner. The candlelight ceremony was set for seven o'clock in the Helmcrest chapel.

Samantha thought of the similarities of this marriage and hers. Remembering the fiasco her wedding dinner turned out to be, she fervently hoped that nothing would happen to interfere with Hank's evening. She was doomed to be disappointed.

Hank had refused to say anything more about a best man, annoying Samantha no end. She wondered if he wasn't planning on having one. They were to meet in the chapel, Hank going ahead. When Samantha finally pressed the issue of Hank's best man, he told her that if he hadn't shown up by the time they were ready, they would go on without him. Had he asked one of his neighbors and he was away for a couple of days? Did he not want to let her know that there wasn't one? Her thoughts whirled round and round wondering why Hank must be so secretive. She had never known him to be thus. It was a puzzlement.

Marianne looked ethereal in the white gauze and lace wedding gown she'd had made up. Delicate layers of the material floated out behind her as she walked. Samantha had chosen a celestial blue silk gown, deceptively simple with lace peeking out at the hem. The tight waist showed her admirable figure to perfection and the color contrasted with her radiant light complexion.

Meadows walked importantly before them, leading the way to the chapel, making certain that his subordinates opened doors at the proper time. The ladies made their stroll side by side, Samantha giving Marianne an encouraging smile.

The stately butler nodded and the chapel doors flew open, revealing the beautiful vaulted ceiling, stained glass windows, and carved pews. Marianne stopped, awestruck with its magnificence. In front of the altar a kindly appearing elderly man wearing a sparkling white surplice stood. On his right side stood Hank in stunning black. He wore the traditional black coat and tails, form-fitting black pants and a black bow tie with his white tailored shirt. Next to him was a tall handsome man dressed in dark blue, his ensemble cut after the same style.

Samantha could see the broad expanse of his back and the commanding air of his posture. She didn't need to see his face; it was Belfort. Her eyes devoured the figure, wishing that this were her marriage instead of Marianne's. What the devil did Hank mean by this? Did Belfort know her as Samantha or was she still the marquesa? She gritted her teeth, her hands cold and her face burning hot. It would be as much as her countenance would stand to get through this ceremony but she couldn't spoil Marianne's wedding. What would Belfort say when he saw her? Could she tell if he knew who she was? Had Hank told him who she was? Hank always kept his word and had promised not to tell. No wonder he refused to name the best man. Waiting three days to get to know Marianne better, ha! It was to give Belfort time to get here after his party at Belle Maison was over.

Marianne was so enthralled with the chapel and the sight of Hank that she never noticed Samantha's agitation. Her heart was full as she looked about the room.

As the opening strains of the wedding march were heard, Samantha recalled herself and started down the aisle. With the advent of the music both men, who had been speaking quietly to the chaplain, turned to face the ladies as they stepped gracefully up the aisle. Samantha found she couldn't keep her eyes from Belfort and he returned her regard. She thought she would be consumed by the scorching stare he was sending in her direction. It sent waves of emotion through her. She couldn't decide if he was angry or admiring or both. When they reached the chaplain Hank stepped forward and stood beside Marianne, Belfort and Samantha taking their places on either side of them.

The wedding was short and very moving, the sight of Hank's and Marianne's faces bringing tears to Samantha's eyes. The service impressed upon her the sacredness of the vows she had taken almost nine months before. There would never be another man in her life. The six-month trial was long since up, but she'd never been one to give up without a fight.

With the service over, the chaplain produced a book for the bride and groom to sign. While they were doing so Samantha couldn't keep silent any longer. "What are you doing here?"

Belfort retorted, "Why did you run out on me the way you did? Did you think I'd let you go like that?" There was a savage note in his voice and she knew she had aroused his anger.

It sent a delicious chill through her and she tingled with anticipation as she waited to see what else he had to say.

There was no time to answer as Hank was reaching for her to kiss her and Marianne was expecting Belfort to do the same for her. Afterward Belfort and Samantha signed the register as witnesses, the silence charged between them.

As the music resumed and they marched down the aisle Belfort had Samantha's arm tucked securely in his. She was afraid to look at him, fearing what she might see.

Belfort bided his time and as they came to the Blue Salon he addressed Hank in a casual tone. "Would you excuse us for a few minutes? We find we have something we must speak about."

Hank had a twinkle in his eye as he just as casually answered, "Of course, you two are old friends. We'll expect you shortly."

During this interchange Samantha kept herself quiet with great effort.

The curtain was about to come down. In a way she welcomed it. She was tired of her role as the marquesa.

Belfort ushered her into a small salon down the hall. He carefully shut the door behind them and turned to Samantha. Never had she looked more beautiful to him. Her eyes seemed larger than ever and her hair was like a siren of the sea's, begging to be touched. With great discipline, he kept his voice stern. "Why did you run away? Didn't you know that I love you?"

Those were magic words and hearing them tears came into her eyes. "But then why did you treat me like a . . . mistress?" At the questioning look in his eyes she tried to explain. "You chased me all over that bedroom and almost raped me!"

"Now, sweetheart, if I'd wanted to catch you I could have. What an opinion you have of my honor. You see I discovered your disguise when you attended to Randolph's wound. There couldn't be two women doctors in this part of England and it was very easily seen that a skilled person was at work. Then I studied your profile and confirmed my guess. I tried to scare you into admitting the fact that you are Samantha, my wife!" His voice was resonant as he proclaimed her his wife and deep emotion gave it a special quality.

"Oh, Brooke, I was such a fright! I wanted to wait until I'd had a chance to get my hair back and fill out some before we married." Tipping her head enchantingly to one side, she continued, "It was your own fault. You insisted on an immediate marriage!"

With that he reached for her and pulled her into his arms. "*Ma coquine*," he addressed her in French, meaning a cross between naughty girl and pert rascal. "I see I am going to have my hands full with you. I suppose I must share you with that clinic I built on the estate but I warn you, I won't let it take all of your time. I need you. *Je t'adore, chérie.*"

"*Mon coeur!*" she returned, letting her love radiate from her bursting heart.

He held her tightly, kissing her neck and showering her with his caresses. She spoke French. She constantly surprised him.

She found herself raising her lips to his and he welcomed the invitation. His mouth covered hers first tenderly, then seeking its sweetness. His passion deepened and his hands touched the velvet softness of her hair, passed on down her neck and caressed her shoulders. When he finally released her she felt light-headed. The world had dimmed in the distance and all that she could see was her husband, tall, strong, masculine, and very virile.

She opened her thoughts to him and they spilled forth. "I loved you the first time I saw you when you were in New York at a race meeting. I've never changed my mind, only to love you more." She looked at him frankly and courageously.

This was no prissy girl he had married, but a woman of spirit. Her confession so pleased him he reached out for her again besieging her with kisses, punctuating them with such loverlike words as wretched girl, abominable woman.

She responded to his terms of endearment with ardor. Her senses reeled under the onslaught and she wished that he would never stop.

He raised his head and sighed, remembering where they were. "We must make our excuses to Hank and his new countess."

"Excuses? What do you mean?" After all they should be in the dining room as the bridal couple would be waiting for them.

"Do you think for one moment I'm going to sit through an interminable wedding feast watching the two of them radiant in their love, while we could be at Belfort and have our own honeymoon?"

As the import of these words permeated her, an attractive flush rose in her cheeks. She didn't pretend to misunderstand.

"Give me time to change into my riding habit and I'll be ready to go with you, anywhere."

There was a soft light in her eyes that made him want to enfold her in his arms again but wisely, he let it pass. What a woman she was. "Why a riding habit? Wouldn't you prefer to be driven in a carriage?"

"I'd rather ride across country. It will take me longer to change than you so I shall leave it to you to present our excuses to Hank and Marianne. At that, I'll bet I beat you there!" She wrinkled up her nose at him and looked so mischievous he started to reach for her again.

This time she eluded him. "Patience, my love," she called provocatively and she bounded out of the room.

Without another word Belfort strode from the room heading for the dining room and the bridal couple to make their excuses. He reflected that wedding feasts were not too successful in this family and the thought brought a wicked grin to his countenance.

Samantha almost ran up the stairs. She burst into her bedchamber, finding Felicia working with her wardrobe. "Quick, I must change to a riding habit," she rattled off in Spanish. She was pulling off her shoes as she spoke. Giving Felicia the order in her own language made sure the maid knew exactly what her mistress wanted.

Felicia didn't question the order but swiftly unbuttoned Samantha's lovely gown with expert fingers. As she stepped out of it, Felicia was already at the armoire pulling out a deep blue riding habit, which the maid tossed over Samantha's head.

In a surprisingly short time Samantha was prepared for the ride, her high crowned hat sitting firmly on her curly black hair and her riding crop in her hand. Giving Felicia a hug and telling her she would see her at Belfort later, she dashed down the stairs.

Meadows, who was standing in the hall arranging a large bouquet of flowers in a tall Ming vase, looked up in pained astonishment. Whatever was Her Grace up to now? She should be sitting down for the wedding festivities. He moved austerely over to the door and opened it for her. She flashed him a pert smile and darted on her way to the stables.

Peters, seeing her coming, felt there must be some great emergency to send her out in such haste. Normally, she would have sent a servant. He was not long in doubt about what she required.

"Peters, saddle Diablo for me at once. I must get to Belfort quickly." She was breathing deeply from hurrying but she was radiantly lovely.

Peters called to one of the grooms, "Get Diablo's tack. I'll saddle him." Peters knew how difficult Diablo was to handle, but knowing Her Grace wouldn't have ordered him unless she was certain she could, he didn't protest.

Samantha smiled as Peters threw the blanket and saddle over Diablo. Hank would be surprised but he had other things to do for the next day or two which probably didn't include riding Diablo. She'd see that the horse got back.

As she put the toe of her boot into the stirrup and whistled to Diablo she looked back toward the house for a sign of Belfort. She must get there ahead of him if her scheme was to work.

The stable hands had never seen a flying mount, much less one by a lady. They stood gaping as she swung her leg over the saddle, catching the stirrup and racing down the path. Within yards she had Diablo into a hand gallop and within a few more a full gallop. She was exultant. Now let Belfort try to catch up with her! She knew there wasn't a horse in the stable that could outdo Diablo.

Belfort hurriedly presented Samantha's and his own excuses and received a very knowing look from his brother-in-law. That astute young man winked solemnly at him. Marianne was at a loss to understand the situation but seeing that she was to have Hank to herself she couldn't complain. Besides, she was sure he would explain everything to her when they were alone.

With a graceful bow, Belfort hastened from the room and vaulted the stairs to his bedchamber, calling for his valet. That important person was offended at the way Belfort was flinging his clothes about. He was responsible for seeing that His Grace's dress was perfection itself. He protested volubly at the way Belfort shrugged himself into his buckskin riding jacket but found himself brushed off. Seizing his hat and gloves, he raced down the stairs two at a time.

Meadows, still working in the hall and hearing the footsteps on the marble stair, looked up. He stood rigidly as he saw His Grace tearing down the steps. His eyebrows disappeared into his hairline, and in his surprise, he forgot to move to the door. Never in all his days had he seen the like.

Belfort wasn't standing on ceremony; he merely flung open the door himself and sprinted down the path to the stables.

Peters was just turning back into the stables when Belfort rushed up. He stopped at the unusual sight of the duke running into the stable yard at a spanking pace. Something was up and Peters was mightily curious. He pushed back his cap and scratched his head thoughtfully.

"Saddle me the fastest horse in the stables," Belfort commanded. He gazed about but saw no sign of Samantha. Had he beaten her here?

Peters soon set him straight. "Yer pardon, Yer Grace, but Her Grace 'as taken Diablo, 'is lordship's 'orse and 'e be the fastest."

So she was ahead of him, was she? The nerve of her taking Hank's pet horse. "All right, saddle me the next best and please be quick about it." Although he was polite as usual, to servants there was a note in his voice that demanded instant obedience.

Helmcrest had a notable stable and Peters had long been in charge. There should be a fine horse brought out for him. Belfort wasn't disappointed as a long-legged bay was led up to him. Giving the animal a quick perusal he decided that Peters had made an excellent choice for him.

Catching up the reins he leaped into the saddle and was off clattering down the cobblestones to the path. Now he'd see what knowledge of the ground and horsemanship could do. He knew every fence, brook, and jump between here and Belfort. He had seen Samantha ride at his lodge and knew she was a skilled horsewoman, but this was something else again. He wondered if she would see that she could go around the pole fence by Rocky Creek? He didn't want her hurt. With luck he would catch up to her. He urged the horse to a greater effort and set himself firmly, his back ramrod straight, looking as if he grew there. His eyes raked the country ahead and narrowing them he saw her in the distance, about three fields ahead of him. One thing that bothered him was that the light was failing fast. While he knew the country what about Samantha? Could she see well enough to make her way? He rode superbly, guiding his horse over every bit of the country. He was gaining on her but from the way she rode he began to have his doubts about catching her. He had never seen the like of her, the way she handled that brute of a horse.

They would have some excellent rides together and he would glory in her ability. Now he wanted to be at Belfort to welcome her formally and carry her across the threshold. Why did she feel she must get there ahead of him? He was beginning to know her; she must be up to some prank. A smile crossed his lips. Life wasn't going to be dull with this wife of his. She was going to lead him a merry chase and damned if he wasn't going to enjoy every bit of it. He urged his mount over a fence as he anticipated what he had in mind.

Peering intensely, he could make her out sailing over the last difficult jump before Belfort Castle. Drat the girl! He figured how long it would take him to cover the distance and he calculated she'd beaten him by about four minutes.

Samantha raced into the stable yard and pulled Diablo up sharply. That well-trained horse slid his hooves and stopped so quickly that one of the grooms working nearby opened his eyes in wonder.

She was out of the saddle in seconds, calling the lad to cool Diablo out. After all his exercise he should lead without trouble. Not bothering to worry whether he did or not, she raced to the side door, grateful for her Arizona divided skirt that gave her so much freedom of movement.

Simmons was stunned as the sound of the door slamming spun him on his heel. He walked down the hall and he was unable to find his voice as he watched Her Grace rush up the back stairs, dropping her hat, riding crop, and gloves in her wake. He shook his head at these antics as he went forward to retrieve her belongings. Whatever would His Grace have to say to such behavior?

Samantha reached the bridal chamber, which had been assigned to her when she was married. Her breath was coming in gasps as she ripped off her jacket but she was triumphant. She had beaten him! She closed the door and moved over to her dressing table. Seating herself, she pulled off her boots and wiggled her toes. She'd manage better in stocking feet. She took a moment to brush out her hair and dab some perfume behind her ears, on her wrists, and, with an impish smile, a generous amount in her cleavage. She caught a sound in the hall and she stood up at once, watching the door.

Belfort hit the front door and took the stairs several at a time while Simmons called upon heaven to witness he had never seen such behavior in the Quality before.

As Samantha saw the knob turn she ran to the table by the window and stepped behind it.

Belfort was also out of breath and viewed her running to the table. "What the devil do you think you are doing?" he demanded, standing staring at her.

He got a saucy look for his answer. Then as he moved toward her she said, "You claim to have known I was your wife when you chased me around the bedchamber at Belle Maison. You even said you could have caught me if you wished. Well, I'm giving you a chance to prove your words. If you like to play games, I'll not be the one to deny you." Her eyes were brimful of mischief. That she was enjoying herself immensely was plain as a pikestaff.

So she doubted him, did she? And she wanted to play? He pulled off his jacket as she watched and tossed his neckcloth to one side, looking at her with naked desire as he did so. With a wicked glint in his eye he started for her, making for the side of the table.

She watched him coolly and waited until he reached one side of the ample table before she turned and raced for the other side of the room. Belfort was hot on her heels. She squealed as he made a grab for her and took refuge behind one of the Queen Anne armchairs. Her face was flushed and her lips curved in a delicious smile.

Belfort paused in front of the chair, resting both hands on its arms, allowing her to catch her breath. Then as he made a motion to go she slid to one side but Belfort was only feinting and moved with her. His long arm reached across the chair and his strong fingers caught the top of her blouse. It tore in his hands, leaving the blouse in shreds, gaping open at the front. A view of rounded firm breasts straining beneath a thin chemise gave him an enormous amount of satisfaction.

Seeing the appreciative look on his face and the state of her favorite blouse she raged at him. "How dare you?" The smile was replaced by a stormy look, which delighted the duke.

Now she'd see the game was in earnest. He inched his way around the chair, leaving the way open past the bed and on to the window.

Samantha, glancing about the room, made an instant decision to put more space between them. She remembered the last episode, taking time to go around the bed and the disastrous results. She didn't intend to make that mistake again. She raced to the huge bed, leaping on it to gain the other side, but found she had underestimated her husband.

He vaulted the table next to the chair and sprang to the end of the bed, catching her as she flew. Seizing her in his arms he dropped her into its depths.

There was a startled moment when she knew it had taken no effort for him to catch her. She raised her face to view him and looked at him through adoring eyes.

He pushed the hair back from her face, stroking it affectionately. His shirt was open and she touched the rippling muscles and mat of dark hair on his chest. It was a thrilling experience as she watched the flame of desire kindle in his eyes.

He groaned and pulled her closer to him, murmuring sweet terms of endearment in her ear. *"Mia preciosa, mi amorcita,"* he whispered, nibbling on her lobe.

"Tu hablo Español?" she queried in wonderment, her eyes growing large.

"Certainly, I speak Spanish. It made my questioning of your maid easy." His fingers traced a line up and down her neck, sending shivers through her.

"She told you where I was going?" She had trusted Felicia. The only time he could have quizzed her was when Felicia had gone out to order the carriage. Then he couldn't sleep either.

"Naturally, with my great charm," he stated with a debonair manner, his eyes giving off a roguish look, "and a note from your brother."

He was stopped as she reached up and pulled his hair. They laughed easily taking great pleasure in each other's company. They shared tender words of love bound in a mutual embrace.

Desire flamed deliciously hot in the duke's eyes and he covered her mouth with his, exploring its sweetness until he possessed it. His head came up for a few seconds as if to assure himself that this was indeed his very own wife. "You're a vixen but I love you dearly," he confided affectionately, a light of adoration showing in his eyes.

Samantha responded to his renewed embrace feeling giddy and deliriously happy. The room dimmed and she knew only the warmth of his love enveloping her. She yielded to his ardor, finding herself ascending the stairway to heaven.

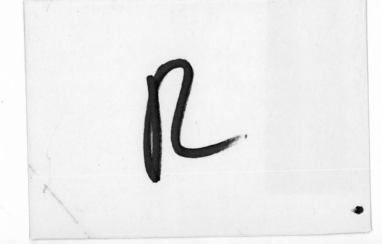